*Lynn*

# TROUBLE IN TRINIDAD

*All the best.*

*Will myf*

*6-1-01*

# Trouble In Trinidad

## by William Manchee

Top Publications, Ltd. Co.
Dallas, Texas

To my son, Jeffrey

Top Publications Paperback

Trouble In Trinidad

This edition published by Top Publications
3100 Independence Parkway, Suite 311 PMB 349
Plano, Texas 75075

ISBN#: 0-966366-7-8
Prepublication Edition
Not For Sale

# Prelude

**April, 2003, Ventura, California**

**Offices of Dr. Stephen Small, M.D.**

"It's Kevin I'm worried about, doctor," Pat Wells said firmly. "He hasn't taken her death well at all. He's just not the same kid he used to be."

"He'll never be the same kid," Dr. Small said in a somber tone. "You've got to realize that, and accept it."

"If he hadn't seen the body. . . . Oh, God! Why did *he* have to see the body?" Pat wiped the tears from her eyes with the back of her hand. Dr. Small handed her a box of tissues. "I shouldn't have gone out of town. This is all my fault."

Dr. Small leaned over and lifted Pat's chin with his finger. He smiled warmly. "It isn't your fault. These things happen. It's a symptom of our society today. Kids experiment with drugs, they drink, they'd just as soon have sex as play a video game. It's not like when we were kids."

"I know, I keep telling myself that. . . . But what about Kevin? He comes home from school and goes straight to his room. He won't talk to anybody, he won't eat. He's losing weight, and God knows he doesn't need to lose any more weight," she sobbed.

"It will take some time. The grieving process affects people differently. He'll get over it eventually and get on with his life."

"But doctor, there are so many teenagers today, who . . . you know, who–" Pat struggled to keep her composure.

"Who *what*?"

"You know, who get depressed and–"

"Oh, you're worried suicide?"

"Well, I don't think he would, but–"

"Listen, Kevin is a smart, well adjusted kid. Sure, he's experienced a tremendous loss. He loved his sister and it's only natural that seeing her the way he did has traumatized him. But he will get over it, you've got to believe that. And when he does get over it, I think the only long term effect will be his level of maturity."

"What do you mean?"

"He's going to realize now that life isn't all fun and games. He's seen the harsh reality of our human existence. . . . The bottom line is, he'll be a much more mature, serious child."

"Well, that's okay, isn't it?"

"It is, except he may have trouble relating to his peers."

"Why?"

"Because many of his peers haven't experienced what he has. Particularly in an affluent society, most children have been sheltered. The evil they've seen has been on TV or at the movies. It isn't real to them. To Kevin, however, it will be all too real. He'll worry about the consequences of his actions, whereas few teenagers today give that much thought."

"So, what can I do help him fit in?"

"Nothing. This is something he'll have to learn to deal with. Just give him a lot of love and understanding. . . . And don't blame yourself for what happened. That will only make things worse, for both of you."

"That may not be so easy, doctor."

He smiled and looked deeply into her sad eyes. "I know. It never is."

# Chapter 1

Five Years Later

Kevin Wells stared at the blackboard, barely cognizant of his surroundings. His mind was on fast forward, racing over the previous evening's confrontation with Paula. He liked her. He liked her a lot. She was every high school boy's wet dream–smart, sexy and sophisticated. And she all but dragged him to her bedroom door. That's when the argument started. He was tempted, oh *was he* tempted. But he just couldn't do it. Paula was popular–*too* popular. Just in the short time he had known her, she had been in several relationships. Each seemed inviolate, yet each crumbled like a doublewide in the path of a tornado. He wondered how he would face his friends at lunch. They wouldn't understand. Nobody understood. They would ridicule him.

Sergeant Walters saw that Kevin wasn't listening. He picked up an eraser and tossed it at him. Kevin never saw it coming and jumped when the erasure hit him in the chest. There was laughter from Kevin's classmates.

"You see," Sergeant Walters said, picking up the erasure that had fallen to the floor, "Kevin wasn't alert. He wasn't concentrating on the task at hand. He let his mind wonder and, consequently, he was taken completely by surprise when this eraser unexpectedly came his way. Had he been alert he could have dealt with the situation quite easily. "*Had you* been alert, Mr. Wells, what could you have done when you saw the eraser coming at you."

"Ah, I could have caught it, deflected it or dodged it, Sergeant," Kevin said.

"Right—or you could have done nothing like you did and just let it bounce off you."

Kevin didn't respond.

"What I'm getting at is—you must not only see potential danger but you must immediately execute an appropriate response. Let's say that was a live grenade I tossed at Mr. Wells. If he hadn't been daydreaming he would have seen it coming and would have a split second to immediately execute an appropriate response—*Which* would be, Mr. Wells?"

"Ah, . . . I suppose to catch it and through it as far away as possible and then duck for cover."

"Good. And that decision would have to be made without hesitation. . . . Now in a combat situation the failure to be alert or the failure to immediately execute an appropriate response to a situation could be disastrous. Opportunities might be lost because of such failure, missions compromised and possibly even soldiers wounded or killed.

"When you are on duty as an officer of the United States Navy, it is imperative that you are always alert–looking, watching and waiting for any hint of trouble. Only if you are totally aware of everything that is happening around you can you immediately effectuate an appropriate response. There is no room for the undisciplined mind in the United States Navy. . . . You got that, Mr. Wells?" Sergeant Walters said.

"Yes, Sergeant," Kevin replied.

Sergeant Walters closed his textbook in conclusion of his lecture to third period ROTC. The classroom erupted in conversation in anticipation of the final bell. Kevin got up and grabbed his windbreaker. Embarrassed by being caught daydreaming, he avoided eye contact with his classmates. Despite what had happened, his thoughts were still on Paula and how she would react to him when she saw him. As much as he tried to stay focused on school work, he couldn't do it. Most of the debate team ate together and Paula was sure to be there. As Kevin picked up his books, Sergeant Walters made a few announcements.

"Now that we've completed our martial arts instruction, on Monday we'll be starting on pugle sticks. I'll expect everyone to have read the instruction manual so we can get a fast start. Also, don't forget, your tactics papers are due Friday. . . . Oh, one more thing, we've been asked to provide a color guard on Thursday for the Caribbean Trade Conference. I'm going to need six volunteers. You'll get to miss all three morning periods."

A dozen cadets raised eager hands. Sergeant Walters smiled at all his enthusiastic volunteers.

"Okay. Stuart, Smalley, Peterson, Becker, Wells and Porter."

Kevin raised his fist and exclaimed, "All right!" then gave a high five to one of the other cadets who had been selected.

The lunch bell rang and everyone left the classroom. Kevin stepped into the flow of traffic heading for the door and plunged into the hot August afternoon. He cringed at the Texas heat as he walked briskly toward the Plano High School Cafeteria. He paused a moment before going in, reluctant to face the humiliation that surely awaited him. Finally he slipped inside, hesitating again, watching his friends from a distance. *Oh shit. I can't do this. I'm gonna just skip lunch today. . . . No, that won't help. Eventually I'll have to face them in debate class. Damn it! I might as well get it over with.*

Taking a deep breath, he walked toward their table. When they saw him approaching, they quit talking.

Kevin smiled and said, "Hey, I can't believe it. I finally

got lucky in ROTC class."

Brent glanced over at him coolly and said, "How's that?"

"I finally got picked for a color guard. I never get picked. It's a miracle."

"A color guard? You call that exciting?" Brent questioned.

"Yeah, you better believe it," he laughed. "I get out of class all morning. No Biology, no French."

Brent nodded. "Nice. So, what's the occasion?"

"Some trade conference downtown."

"A trade conference? . . . That sounds pretty boring."

"Not nearly as boring as French."

"True, but it'll be a pain catching up. You know what a bitch it is if you miss one frickin' day in that class."

Kevin smiled. "I'll borrow Paula's notes."

Brent laughed. "Oh, really. After last night I doubt she'd call 911 if you were bleeding to death."

Brent's comments stung Kevin. It was apparent he was not the only one with a fixation on the events of the previous night.

"What? That was nothing. Just a little difference in philosophy."

Brent snickered, "A difference in philosophy? Oh, I see—like communism vs. capitalism?"

Kevin rolled his eyes. "No, like promiscuity vs. abstinence."

"Abstinence? God, you *are* sick."

Kevin looked away. *I can't win this debate. Give it up.* He stood up and said, "Man, I'm starving. I hope they're having something decent today."

"That would be a first," Brent replied.

Kevin got up and walked across the room to the snack bar. Glancing back he noticed Paula and Alice were joining Brent and the others. He was sure they were talking about him and wished he were a fly on the wall so he could overhear the conversation. He grabbed a sandwich, some chips and a can of Coke® and headed back to the group. They were laughing as he approached the table.

"Speak of the devil," Brent whispered. "Here he comes." They all quit talking.

Kevin looked anxiously at Paula. Her eyes were as cold as a Montana blizzard. She shook her head and looked away.

"Here comes the Virgin Harry," Alice said.

They all laughed.

Kevin gave them a quick artificial smile. "Thanks guys. I really appreciate the ridicule."

"Sorry," Alice said. "I couldn't resist."

"Right," Kevin said shaking his head. "Hey, are we going to have practice tonight after school?"

"No. Tomorrow night," Brent noted.

"Good. I've got a paper due Friday. I'm going to be up all night."

"What's it on?" Paula asked matter-of-factly.

"Desert Warfare, from Rommel to Schwarzkopf," he responded.

"Oh, how fun," Paula said dryly.

Relief flooded over Kevin. Paula didn't seem half as pissed as he had expected. He smiled. "It's fascinating actually."

"I bet. So I suppose you'll be in the library tonight?"

"I'm afraid so. . . . Are you going to be there?"

"I don't know."

"Hmm. . . . So, did your mother have a cow last night when she came home and saw the mess?" Kevin asked.

"No. I cleaned it up before she got home. Luckily, she didn't saunter in until after two. "

"Where was she?"

"She's got a new boyfriend. He's kind of cool. He works for EDS, some kind of computer genius or something. I think they went to Billy Bob's in Fort Worth."

"Well at least he'll keep your mother busy so she won't

be bugging you all the time," Alice interjected.

"That's true," Paula said.

"My parents are always on my case," Alice said. "I really envy you."

Kevin listened intently to Paula and Alice's conversation but didn't jump in. *I have good parents. It wasn't their fault. They've never—"*

"What about your parents, Kevin?" Alice said looking him in the eye. "Do they give you a lot of shit?"

"No," he laughed. "Not really."

"You're lucky. If my real dad was home that would be great, but he lives in Tulsa. I don't see him unless he happens to be driving through Dallas. My stepfather is an asshole. He takes great pleasure in humiliating me whenever possible."

"I guess I *am* lucky. My parents are cool."

"You're damn lucky," Paula said. "I guess that's where you got your strong moral conscience."

Kevin shook his head. *Oh, Jesus. It's never going to end.* "Hey, I'm not saying my philosophy is necessarily better than yours. It's just what I want for me, okay? I just hope you all can respect that."

"Hey, it's a free country," Brent said. "If you want to die a virgin, that's your business. Personally, I'm going to hop as many chicks as I can while I'm young and robust. Life is too short to be wasting a lot of time chasing a fantasy."

"A fantasy?" Kevin said.

"Yeah, Kevin. I hate to break the news to you, old bud, but there aren't any virgins out there. At least none that I'd be caught dead with."

Kevin stared at Brent not knowing how to reply. Paula raised her eyebrows and started to laugh. Luckily the bell rang, giving everyone an excuse to end the awkward encounter.

After school, Kevin went to the library to work on his paper. As he was passing the periodical section of the library, he noticed the daily newspaper. Now that he was going to be a participant, the headline about the Caribbean Trade Conference suddenly interested him. He picked up the paper and began to read the article.

## STAGE IS SET FOR CARIBBEAN
## TRADE CONFERENCE

Rapidly rising gasoline prices will provide added pressure for delegates to reach some kind of a free trade agreement at next week's Caribbean Trade Conference. At their last semi-annual meeting, OPEC members agreed on reduced production quotas sending gasoline prices sharply upward. The American Automobile Association predicts prices this summer will reach three dollars a gallon in some parts of the country.

Last fall's discovery of vast oil reserves near Trinidad-Tobago, spurred the US to propose a Caribbean Free Trade Association. Experts say the Cocos Bay reserves, as it has been named, contain more than five billion barrels of oil. Commerce Secretary William T. Sawyer will host the conference and the keynote speaker will be Ahmad Shah, the newly elected Prime Minister of Trinidad-Tobago, a small Caribbean island-nation, about the size of New Hampshire, located just north of Venezuela.

Commerce Secretary, William T. Sawyer, held a news conference on Monday and outlined the agenda for Thursday's Conference. He noted it was time for the nations of the Caribbean to eliminate all barriers to free trade. He cited the tremendous success of NAFTA and expressed his belief that a similar treaty for the Caribbean would be most advantageous. When asked about the strong opposition of the Cayman Islands to the proposed treaty, Secretary Sawyer indicated he had personally talked to the Cayman ambassador and was assured that they would come to the conference with an open mind.

The keynote speaker, Prime Minister Ahmad Shah of Trinidad-Tobago, in an interview in Port of Spain, predicted an historic accord would be reached at the conference.


Kevin put down the paper. He was about to leave when a pretty young girl stopped him. He didn't know her personally, but he did recognize her as a cheerleader.

"You're Kevin, right?"

"Yes."

"Hi, I'm Stacy Cox."

"Oh. . . . Hi."

"How's your paper coming?" Stacy asked.

"Slow, it's going to be a long night, I'm afraid." He frowned. "So, how did you know I was working on a paper?"

"Well, it's pretty obvious, isn't it? You've been poring through books and taking lots of notes all evening."

Kevin nodded. "Right."

She flashed a smile. Her eyes sparkled. "You're on the swim team, aren't you?"

Adrenalin flooded Kevin's body. Stacy was a knockout and he was about to get KO'd. "Uh huh, and you're a cheerleader."

"How did you know that?"

"I've seen you perform," Kevin said brimming. "You'd be a hard person to forget."

"If that's a compliment, thank you."

"Just an observation. . . . Hey, didn't I see you at the last swim meet?"

"Yes, I watched you dive. You're very good."

"Thanks."

"Listen, Kevin. I heard through the grapevine that you were a virgin."

Kevin's heart plummeted. "What?"

"I just wanted you to know, it's okay. I'm a virgin too."

Kevin looked around suspiciously and smiled. *Give me a break.* Shaking his head, he said, "Okay, who told you I was a virgin?"

"It doesn't matter. We've found each other. The only two virgins in North Texas."

Kevin started to laugh, "Okay, is someone videotaping this?"

"I'm serious," Stacy said. "I was told you honestly believe in chastity before marriage."

"I do, but I think, . . . well actually, I know you're pulling my leg."

"Why is that?" she said indignantly, "You think you're the only moral human being at this school?"

"No, of course not, but—"

"Let's get to know each other, okay? Maybe something might happen between us. You know? The soul-mate thingy."

Kevin could barely contain his disgust, "Right, . . . sure."

Just then, there was laughter from the corner of the library. Kevin looked over and saw Brent, Alice and Paula laughing hysterically. He shook his head and looked back at Stacy who now too was laughing.

"You guys won't let up, will you?" Kevin said. "I don't have time for games tonight, okay? I've got a damn paper to do. Nice meeting you, Stacy. You'll make a fine actress someday."

Kevin gathered his stuff and left to a chorus of laughter. He didn't look back. *I wish I could tell them. Then they wouldn't laugh. Damn it! I wish I could tell them.* Kevin felt a knot in his stomach. He stopped a moment to ponder its cause. Then it hit him. He was worried about what Brent had said. What if he couldn't find his soul mate? What if she didn't exist? . . . Was his search a futile endeavor? Was he crazy to even dream that in this day and age there could be a relationship built on love instead of sex, where a man and woman could be intoxicated with each other's company without the need for booze or marijuana?

When Kevin reached his car, he opened the door and dropped into the driver's seat. Taking a deep breath, he let his head fall back against the headrest. He felt dizzy so he closed his eyes. . . . In his mind, a door opened, a bright light blinded him. He raised his hand to shield himself from its intensity. There were voices, . . . questions, . . . strangers asking so many questions. He tossed and turned. "Why! Why! . . ." He didn't know how long he dozed, but when he opened his eyes, tears were streaming down his cheeks. Wiping them away, he started the car and drove away.

# Chapter 2

Sunlight had just begun to creep into Kevin's bedroom when the alarm went off at six. He hit the snooze button with one quick swipe and then turned over. Nine minutes later the alarm sounded again and Kevin unconsciously repeated the maneuver. Before he could fall back asleep, the door opened and his mother, Pat, stood in the doorway. She turned on the light.

"Kevin, it's time to get up. You're going to be late for your field trip."

Kevin pulled the pillow over his head to protect himself from the glare. He was a night person. Getting up in the morning was pure torture.

"Kevin!" his mother yelled.

Kevin turned over and looked up at her. "Okay. I'm getting up," he said and then turned over and pulled the blanket back over his head.

"Kevin! You said you had to meet Sergeant Walters at seven. If you get up right now, you'll barely have time to eat breakfast."

"All right, shut the door. I'm getting up."

Through eyes squinted against the glare, he saw his Mom frown, shake her head and finally close the door. Kevin kicked off the blankets and jumped out of bed. He went into his adjoining bathroom and turned on the shower. Then he inspected the uniform that he had laid out the night before. After he had showered and shaved, he got dressed and went downstairs for breakfast. His mother had already filled his plate. She handed it to him as he went by.

"Thanks, Mom," Kevin said.

He put the plate on the kitchen table. Before sitting down to eat, he turned around and stood in front of his mother.

"How do I look?"

She smiled approvingly. "Oh, you look handsome!"

"Thanks. Do you think my boots look shiny enough?"

"Well, they look pretty good to me."

"They better be okay, I spent an hour on them. You know how the sergeant has a cow if your boots aren't perfect."

"They look fine, honey. Don't worry. How are you getting to the convention center?"

"Sergeant Walters is driving us in his pickup."

"How long will you be down there?"

"The sergeant said we'd probably stay through Prime Minister Shah's keynote address and then leave. I would imagine we'll probably be there for a couple hours at least."

"Well, I hope you have a good time."

"I'm sure I will. Anything's better than French."

Kevin got up, wiped his mouth, gave his mother a quick kiss and walked to the door leading to the garage. Suddenly he turned around and looked intensely at her.

"No matter what anybody says, you and Dad have always been good parents. I should know, I'm your son. Nobody knows better than me."

She looked back at him sadly, forced a smile and whispered, "Thank you, honey. I love you."

Kevin winked and said, "I love you too. Bye."

Sergeant Walters was waiting in the parking lot, in his Ford pickup, when Kevin arrived. Two cadets were already seated in the extended cab. When the other three cadets showed up, the group left for the Dallas Convention Center. Traffic was heavy on Central Expressway, as usual, so it was nearly an hour before they arrived. When they got there, Sergeant Walters checked in with security and was directed to park in the underground parking garage. Once they had secured their vehicle, a security officer escorted them to a room behind the main stage. Then he addressed the group.

"All right. You'll need to wait here until the ceremonies begin," he said. "You can begin your march to the podium when you hear them introduce you. Secretary Sawyer and Prime Minister Shah will be on the stage along with the mayor and several other diplomats. After you've posted the colors and the invocation has been given, you'll take a seat along the right side of the stage. You'll remain there until Prime Minister Shah concludes his remarks. Then you'll exit out the east side of the convention floor. Do you have any questions?"

"Yes," Sergeant Walters said. "Will the kids be able to meet Secretary Sawyer?"

"He and Prime Minister Shah will stop by and say hello, if there's time before the program begins."

"Excellent," Walters said.

"All right then," the security guard said. "I'll see you on the stage."

Kevin went over to the large double doors that led to the stage. He peered out into the spacious room filled with theater-type seats. There were four main sections in front of the stage. Two directly in front, one to the left and another to the right. Access to the dressing rooms and stage facilities was through a door to the left of the stage. The audience entered the auditorium from four entrances, one on each side of the auditorium and two more in the back of the center sections. The room had a high ceiling, with a bank of spotlights midway between stage and the back door. A thin catwalk provided access to the spotlights from a small door on the left wall of the auditorium.

There were hundreds of people milling around, looking

for their seats. Kevin wondered if the place was going to fill up. As he glanced around the room, he noticed a group of band members setting up in the pit area in front of the stage. One of them got up, looked around nervously and then ducked out a side door carrying his instrument. *Where is he going? He just got here. That's weird. Wrong gig, I guess?*

"Okay, cadets. I want you all to look sharp out there today," Sergeant Walters said. "People all over the world will be watching you. Let's make your parents proud, okay?"

"Is this going to be on television?" Kevin asked.

"I believe so. You'll probably see yourself on the news tonight."

"Cool," Kevin said, wondering if his friends would see him.

The crowd was growing in size by the minute. Kevin noticed a number of security personnel in yellow jackets and saw several Secret Service agents wandering around, inspecting the podium area. After a few minutes, several dignitaries were escorted to the stage where they took their seats.

A security guard entered the back room where Kevin and the other color guard members were waiting. He said, "Ladies and gentlemen. I'm proud to introduce to you, Secretary Sawyer."

Secretary Sawyer entered the room with his wife and personal aide close by his side. He nodded and began to address the group.

"Hello, Sergeant, . . . cadets. I want to thank each of you for helping us out today. You probably don't realize it, but this may be one of the most important political events of the twenty-first century. It will be something to tell your children and grandchildren about. Something you'll remember with pride."

The secretary went around to everyone and shook their

hands. The door opened again. This time, Prime Minister Shah and his wife entered the room. He was a short man of Indian descent, not more than five foot two, black hair and olive skin. His wife was a bit taller and quite attractive. In fact, Kevin and the other male cadets couldn't keep their eyes off her.

"Good morning. I'm Ahmad Shah, and this is my wife, Anila. How are all of you this morning?"

"Just fine, sir," Sergeant Walters said.

"Where are all of you from?"

"Plano High School," several of the students volunteered.

"Is that far from here?" the Prime Minister asked.

"No, only about twenty miles, sir," Sergeant Walters replied.

"Is it a big school?"

"Yes, sir. We've got over twenty-five hundred students."

"Oh my, that's much larger than any high school in our country. Well, I wish I could stay and chat, but I must attend to my duties, you know."

"Of course," Sgt. Walters said.

"It has been a distinct pleasure meeting all of you. Thanks for helping us out today."

"We're glad we could be of assistance," Sergeant Walters said.

The Prime Minister waved and said, "Goodbye."

Sergeant Walters walked Secretary Sawyer and Prime Minister Shah out of the room.

When he returned he said, "All right, let's get ready to go. They'll be introducing us soon."

The cadets scrambled around, getting set to march onto the stage. It took only a minute and everyone was lined up and ready to go. The mayor of Dallas welcomed all the visitors and then introduced Secretary Sawyer. The Secretary made a few remarks and then introduced the color guard.

"At this time, I'd like to introduce our color guard from the Plano High School ROTC. Cadets! Present colors!"

Sergeant Walters opened the door and the ROTC contingent began making their way to the stage. Two cadets led the way, carrying the American and Texas flags. Two other cadets followed with the flags of the Caribbean Federation and Trinidad-Tobago. Kevin and the last cadet walked behind the others. As the cadets arrived on the stage, they placed their flags behind the speaker's chairs and between the flags of all the other nations involved in the conference. They saluted and took their seats on the left side of the stage.

As the Secretary introduced Prime Minister Shah, Kevin sat back in his chair, excited at being in the forefront of such an important event. He looked out into the vast audience, enjoying the energy and excitement of the delegates. As his glance wandered around the auditorium, he noticed movement on the catwalk leading to the stage lights. Assuming someone was up there to work the lights, he gave it little thought.

Suddenly, the memory of the band member leaving the auditorium flashed through his mind. *Maybe he got sick. I wonder if he had a backup.* He looked down at the band, but the trombone player was not there.

Secretary Sawyer concluded his introduction and Prime Mister Shah stood up. Dozens of photographers snapped pictures of the Prime Minister as he approached the podium. The crowd gave him a cordial round of applause. Kevin suddenly felt uneasy and glanced up at the catwalk again. This time, he focused on the man. He squinted. There was something in his hands. *What is that in his hand?* Then he saw the trombone case leaning up against the rail. *What the hell?* Looking back at the man on the catwalk, Kevin felt a surge of recognition. The man held a rifle in his hand – an M21, Kevin knew it well. During boot camp, he had been issued one and was taught to treat it as his best friend. He could take it apart in his sleep and he was a pretty good marksman.

Kevin squirmed in his seat, unsure of what to do. Adrenaline flooded his system and a tingling sensation shot through his spine to his back and legs. He remembered Sergeant Walters' words—"when a situation arises you must immediately effectuate an appropriate response." Then he saw the laser imprint dancing around the podium. Without another thought, he bolted toward the Prime Minister. A Secret Service agent lunged to stop him, but Kevin was quicker and shot past him. Running all out toward the podium, Kevin waved his hands high above his head and yelled at the Prime Minister to get down. The shot echoed through the auditorium. Kevin felt a sharp pain in his back as the bullet pierced his flesh. He collapsed in the arms of the Prime Minister.

Suddenly, everyone in the audience was on their feet, screaming and yelling. Photographers frantically took photographs as the Secret Service rushed Secretary Sawyer and the Prime Minister from the auditorium. In the midst of the chaos, medics swarmed toward Kevin, who was unconscious and bleeding profusely.

"He's been shot! Get an ambulance up here fast!" the first paramedic to reach him yelled. He examined the large gapping hole in Kevin's back and then applied pressure with a bandage to stop the bleeding.

Panic overcame the crowd as they realized an assassination attempt had taken place. Delegates poured out the exits, looking around frantically to see if the assassin might still be lurking about. The press crowded around Kevin's limp body, trying to ascertain his condition.

"Move back! Give him some air!" the paramedic yelled. "Where's that ambulance?" The intensity in his voice left little doubt as to the seriousness of the situation.

Suddenly, Kevin began to choke and cough. His skin

was pale. He quit breathing. The paramedic launched into crisis mode, giving him mouth to mouth resuscitation until he coughed again and his chest began to expand. The medic looked toward the door anxiously, breathing a sigh of relief when he saw security officers clearing a path for the ambulance drivers who rushed in with a gurney. Kevin was quickly placed on it, given oxygen and carried off to the ambulance.

The fading sound of a siren wailing accompanied the security officers who began sealing off the crime scene as delegates stared in shock at the pool of blood behind the podium.

*****

In the several seconds that it took the Secret Service to assess the situation, Peter Gosne made his escape to the roof of the convention center. He looked north anxiously, expecting security police to emerge from the stairwell at any moment. Suddenly a helicopter ascended from a resting-place at the rear of the convention center. It swept down onto the rooftop. Peter threw his trombone case and backpack into the chopper and quickly climbed in. The helicopter took off to the north, toward downtown Dallas and quickly disappeared amongst the maze of urban skyscrapers. By the time security police made it to the roof, it was deserted.

*****

Kevin's mother was at work when she got a call from Sergeant Walters. She heard what he said, but for some reason, none of it made sense. "Blood? What are you talking about?"

"Ma'am, I know this sounds bizarre, but your son has been shot."

"Oh my God! How? Who would want to shoot him?"

"It looks like it was an assassination attempt. Somehow, Kevin saw it happening and tried to save the Prime

Minister's life."

Mrs. Wells began to cry. "Oh, no! Is he okay?"

"I don't know. You need to get down to Parkland Hospital right away."

Mrs. Wells dropped the phone and nearly collapsed. One of the other secretaries was near enough to stop her from falling.

"My Kevin's been shot. Oh God! What am I going to do?"

*****

Kevin's father, Glen Wells, was the manager at Best Buy. He was working on a sales report when one of his salesmen ran into his office in back of the store and summoned him to a TV. The bewildered manager jumped up and followed the salesman to the television department. On the twenty-one screens displayed before him, a special Channel 4 bulletin was in progress.

"The facts are still sketchy. No one knows who attempted this assassination of Prime Minister Shah. No one had any clue what was happening. How this brave teenager from Plano High School was able to detect the assassination attempt and try to prevent it continues to be a real mystery."

"We're talking live with Donna Price at the Dallas Convention Center, where a young Plano High School student has just foiled an attempt on the life of the Prime Minister of Trinidad, Ahmad Shah. We have learned the identity of the Plano student from other cadets at the scene. His name is Kevin Wells. The condition of  this young Plano High School cadet, who took a bullet in the back, is unknown at this time. Paramedics administered first aid at the scene before the young teenager was rushed to Parkland Hospital."

Glen ran out of the store and jumped into his car. His tires shrieked as he took off across the parking lot and onto the access road to Central Expressway. He hit the express dial on his mobile phone to call his wife. When he was told she had already left, he turned on the radio and flipped to *KNEWS*.

"Dennis, we've just gotten word that Kevin Wells is in emergency surgery at Parkland Hospital as we speak. Reportedly, the bullet struck him in the back, near his right shoulder. It is thought that the bullet may have punctured his lung. We're on our way to Parkland Hospital right now."

Tears streamed down Glen's face. He wiped them away as he exited onto LBJ Freeway.

"Okay, Paul, we'll get back to you when you have more news from the hospital. Meanwhile, we've got Barbara Scott at the Dallas Police department where Police Chief Virgil Harris is about to have a news conference."

"Ladies and gentlemen. As you know, there was an attempt on the life of Prime Minister Shah of Trinidad-Tobago, who was to be the keynote speaker at the Caribbean Trade Conference today. Fortunately for Mr. Shah, a young cadet from Plano High School apparently saw the assassination attempt unfolding and tried to stop it. Kevin Wells was a member of the color guard that had just brought the American Flag to the podium at the start of the conference. As the Prime Minister was about to commence his address, an assassin was taking aim at him.

" We're speculating at this point, but somehow Kevin must have seen the assassin. He jumped up suddenly and ran toward the Prime Minister. Just as he got to the podium, a bullet struck him in the back.

"Kevin Wells is in surgery right now and no one knows his condition. Immediately after the assassination attempt, police officers searched the convention center for the assailant. We believe the attack came from a single individual who had positioned himself on a catwalk leading to the stage lights. It seems the assailant disguised himself as a member of the band that was scheduled to play the national anthem later in the program. Members of the band have been questioned. Reportedly, one of the players is missing. It appears the assailant may have escaped by helicopter. One was seen near the convention center about the time the assassination attempt took place.

"Secretary Sawyer and the Prime Minister were immediately taken away to a safe location. They are both shaken, but physically fine. The FBI is already on the scene. They're working closely with military and security police from Trinidad-Tobago to try to determine who is responsible for the attack. A white Chevrolet Cavalier has been found abandoned in the convention center parking lot. It is thought to be the would-be assassin's vehicle and has been impounded by the FBI.

"That's about all we know right now. I'll be happy to answer any questions at this time." Chief Harris concluded.

"Chief Harris, any word on the missing band member?" a reporter asked.

"No, we've contacted relatives and no one seems to know his whereabouts. He was last seen early this morning by his girlfriend when he left to go to the convention center. According to security records, he checked in, but no one has confirmed that they ever saw him."

"Chief Harris, does the Prime Minister have any idea who might be responsible for this attack?"

"I haven't talked to the Prime Minister, but we've been told by members of his staff that there's a lot of political dissension in Trinidad over the Prime Minister's support of a Caribbean Free Trade Treaty. Perhaps the attack had something to do with that."

*****

Glen barely slowed down as he went through the tollbooth on the Dallas North Tollway. The alarm went off but he paid it no heed. He exited on Wycliff and then went south to Harry Hines to get to Parkland. Pat Wells was already sitting on a sofa in the intensive care waiting room when he arrived. Glen hurried over to her and they embraced.

"Have you heard anything, honey?" Glen asked.

"No, he's still in surgery," she wailed. "How could this have happened? When I sent Kevin off this morning, I had no idea he was in danger. How could they have let this happen? Didn't they have any security?"

Glen helped his wife back to the couch and sat down beside her. His hand shook as he ran it through his thinning hair, struggling to stay calm. "I heard on the radio the assailant disguised himself as a member of the band."

A tall man in a light blue suit entered the waiting room. He looked around and approached Glen and Pat.

"You must be Mr. and Mrs. Wells," he said.

"That's right," Glen replied. "Are you a doctor?"

The man pulled out a badge and flashed it in front of Glen's face. "I'm Agent Simmons with the FBI. I'm sorry about your son. Is he going to be all right?"

"We don't know yet. No one's told us anything."

Agent Simmons sat in a chair facing the couple. "Well I want you to know there's a massive manhunt going on right now to find the terrorist responsible for this outrageous act."

"Any leads yet?" Glen asked.

"Oh yeah, we've got leads, but nothing has materialized yet. Hey, your son, boy he's one brave kid, huh? Takes a lot of courage to jump in front of a bullet like that."

"Kevin's never been an ordinary kid," Glen said. "He's so much more mature than I was at his age. He worries about things that never even occurred to me when I was young."

Agent Simmons nodded as if he understood. "Really? Well maybe he should consider a political career. Kevin Wells will be a household name by tomorrow at this time. We're all hoping he comes through this okay."

Glen clenched his teeth at the thought that Kevin might not pull through. "He'll make it. Kevin's a tenacious fighter.

He never gives up. He'll pull through this thing. I know he will."

"I hope you're right. Without his help we may never know who it was."

Just then a doctor walked into the room.

"Mr. and Mrs. Wells? May I have a word with you?"

"Yes," Glen said as he and Patricia walked toward the doctor with Agent Simmons close behind.

"Your son is out of surgery. His condition is critical, but stable. The bullet pierced through his lung and lodged in one of his ribs. We were able to remove the bullet and there is some lung function at this time. Your son lost a lot of blood on the way to the hospital."

Pat began to sob. Glen put his arm around her and gave her a squeeze to comfort her.

"In fact, he lost so much blood we had to give him three units during surgery."

"Is he going to be all right?" Glen asked.

"It's too early to tell. He stopped breathing a couple of times. We'll have to watch him carefully. There could be brain damage."

"Oh my God!" Pat wailed. Glen pulled Pat up next to him and stroked her head.

"Kevin's going to be all right, honey. I just know he will."

"I wish I had better news for you, but you need to know what we're up against."

"We want you to be honest with us, Doctor," Glen said.

"Of course. Your son is in intensive care. You can visit him now. However, I want to warn you, he's unconscious and he looks pretty bad."

Glen and Pat immediately went to the intensive care unit. Kevin was lying there, limp, with dozens of machines hooked up to his body. A nurse smiled at them as they made their way to the head of the bed. Pat held his left hand as she stroked his forehead. Glen wiped a tear from his eyes as he looked down at Kevin's pale face.

"Do you think he'll be all right? " Pat asked.

"He'll pull through, honey. I know he will," Glen replied.

"Why did this happen? Kevin is the nicest boy in the world. He would never hurt anyone. I don't understand, Glen. I just don't understand why he got shot."

"The bullet wasn't intended for him, honey. He was trying to protect someone, a prime minister from Trinidad, I think."

"Why would he do that? Why did he have to get involved?"

"That's just the way he is, honey. You know how he's always so concerned about doing the right thing. He's so afraid-"

"But he didn't have to get shot, did he?"

Glen tried to console his wife with little success. After fifteen minutes, the nurse told them they must leave. Glen looked at his watch and saw it was nearly noon. The nurse informed them they could come back for another fifteen-minute visit at one-thirty. Glen took Pat's hand and gently led her out of the room.

When Glen and Pat returned to the waiting room, they saw that Agent Simmons had been joined by two Dallas police detectives. Agent Simmons introduced them and the detectives filled them in on the latest developments.

"There's a big crowd gathering outside, curious about your son's condition. All the local and national media have set up camp down the street. The lobby of the hospital is so full, no one can move."

"Really?" Glen said.

"Yeah, your son's a real hero. The whole nation is praying he'll pull through this thing. If you turn on the television, you'll see what I mean."

Glen went over to the TV and pushed the power button. The picture came on and Howard Slocum, the President's news secretary, was in the middle of reading a statement.

"At this moment, we do not understand the motivation

behind this senseless act of violence. Whether political opponents of the Prime Minister or those in opposition to free trade sponsored it, we do not know. But what we do know is that one young man, without the slightest hesitation, put his life in jeopardy to protect someone he didn't even know. For all the critics out there who have constantly complained about the immorality and indifference of our youth today, take heed. There are heroes amongst our young people. Kevin Wells proved that today.

"This administration will not tolerate terrorism. Those responsible for this outrageous act will be brought to justice. If they thought this attack would derail our efforts to bring free trade to the Caribbean, they were dead wrong. The conference will go on. There will be an even greater urgency because of what has happened here today.

"I will be praying, as will all Americans and millions of people around the world, that Kevin Wells will survive and recover fully from today's assault. We all want to meet and get to know this extraordinary young man. I look forward to meeting him personally when he recovers. Thank you, and may God be with you, Kevin Wells."

Glen pushed the power button and the TV screen went blank. Everyone in the room was silent. Glen walked over and sat on the sofa next to his wife. She laid her head on his shoulder and wiped the tears from her eyes. Agent Simmons looked at the two detectives and motioned that they should all leave. The room was quiet as Pat and Glen waited to learn if their son would live or die.

# Chapter 3

Ten days later, Kevin was still in a coma. His overall health had improved considerably. He was breathing on his own and his lungs seemed to be healing satisfactorily. The doctors were quite pleased overall, but still didn't know if there had been any brain damage. Pat and Glen had been by their son's side twenty-four hours a day, ever since he had been moved to a private room. They talked to him, read him books and did everything possible to try to stimulate him to a state of consciousness. However, nothing seemed to be helping.

It was Sunday and Paula, Brent and Alice had come to visit Kevin. Once they arrived, Pat and Glen left to go to mass in the hospital chapel. The threesome wandered around the room looking at the dozens of floral arrangements and stacks and stacks of cards from well-wishers.

"Look at this!" Paula said. "I couldn't have imagined anything so bizarre happening to Kevin."

"I know, I feel so guilty, the way we teased him," Alice added.

Paula walked over and sat on the side of Kevin's bed. She picked up his hand and began to play with it. Brent watched her with much amusement.

Paula continued. "Well, I think Kevin knew we were just giving him a bad time. We were all probably a little jealous, I guess, or feeling guilty that we didn't have his moral resolve."

"Speak for yourself. I still think morality stinks," Brent said.

"Shut up, he might hear you," Paula said.

Brent laughed. "Look at him. He's out to lunch."

"Brent, you don't know. He might be hearing everything you're saying. So be nice."

"Nice? He wasn't so nice to you the other night at the party." Brent said. "What happened anyway? I never heard the whole story."

Paula looked away. "Oh it was no big deal. We were dancing and I could tell he was getting a little excited. So I thought I'd be nice to him and take him up to my bedroom. . . . I thought he *wanted* me, like I *wanted* him."

Brent stared at Paula incredulously. "You were going to bed with him? Holy shit! And he turned that down?"

Paula shrugged. "That's about the size of it. He's looking for his soul mate and whoever she is, she's gotta be a virgin. That kind of ruled me out."

Brent shook his head. "What an arrogant bastard, not to mention being a fool. Why didn't you come and get me?"

Alice kicked Brent in the ass. "Cause you were screwing me at the time you lousy piece of shit."

Brent cracked a smile. "That's alright. We coulda done a threesome."

"In your dreams," Paula said as she leaned down and kissed Kevin on the forehead. Brent shook his head and walked away. She smiled down at him and began caressing his face with her right hand.

Alice smiled at her, sat down and began looking through a magazine. "Look at this. Kevin's picture is on the cover of *Time* magazine."

"You've got to be kidding!" Brent said. He rushed over and pulled the magazine out of Alice's hand. "Can you believe this? 'Kevin Wells, an American hero'," he said, looking at the cover and shaking his head.

"I wonder if he'll ever know how famous he's become,"

Paula said. "God, I hope he wakes up."

"After he humiliated you in front of all your friends, you still have a thing for him," Brent said. "I can't believe it."

"I don't have a thing for him," Paula said glaring at Brent. "He's our friend. I just want to be here for him. Isn't that why you two are here?"

Brent shrugged. "I'm here cause Alice is here. Frankly I can't stomach any of this. All of a sudden this sanctimonious jerk is a hero. It makes me sick. In fact, I'm out of here."

Brent turned and left. Paula gave Alice a concerned look. Alice shook her head and said, "Don't worry. He didn't mean it."

*****

Brent walked down the corridor, past the nurse's station and stopped in front of the elevator where another man was waiting. The man glanced over and smiled. Brent nodded and waited nervously for the elevator. Finally the door opened and they got in. The man kept looking at Brent until he finally said, "Aren't you one of Kevin Wells' friends?"

Brent frowned. "We went to school together. Who are you?"

"I'm a freelance reporter. I heard about what happened and thought I'd come on over and see if I could get the reaction of Kevin's family and friends."

"I don't know any more than you do, actually."

"Maybe so, but you know a lot about Kevin Wells, don't you?"

"Yeah, I suppose."

"Tell me about him."

Brent sighed. "Tell you what? He's a high school student. There's really not much to tell."

"How did you know him?"

"We're on the debate team together. He's my partner."

"Is he a good debater?"

"Yeah, very good."

"Do you spend a lot of time together?"

"Yeah, the debate team is a pretty close knit group. We spend a lot of time together practicing and then going to tournaments. So, you know, we're all pretty close."

"So tell me about Kevin. What kind of guy is he?"

Brent thought for a minute, wondering what he should say. "He's kind of different."

"Different?"

"Yeah, you know, old fashioned, patriotic, not a big drinker, never smokes weed and– "

"And what?"

"And . . . well," Brent snickered. "He's saving himself for his soul mate."

"Seriously?"

"Cross my heart. He's searching for a virgin. . . . Good luck!"

The reporter chuckled. "Okay, so he's a clean-cut guy with old fashioned values. . . . Well, thank you Brent. That was very insightful."

*****

Paula took a deep breath and turned back to Kevin. She looked at him longingly and then lowered her head and rested it on his chest to listen to his heart beating. Suddenly she sat up and looked at his hand. "I felt him squeeze my hand!"

"What?" Alice said. "Are you sure?"

"Yes, he squeezed my hand. I felt it. I really did."

Alice got up and moved to the side of the bed.

"Kevin. Kevin, can you hear me?" Paula said.

Not getting any response, Paula looked up at Alice and frowned. "He really did squeeze my hand. I didn't make it up."

"It's all right, Paula," Alice said. "You want it to happen so bad you probably imagined it."

"No. It was real!"

"It was probably just a reflex."

Paula's eyes lit up. "There it is again! He's squeezing my hand!"

Kevin began to squirm in his bed. "No... no... no! Please God! No," he cried out. "Let it be me, take me!"

"Kevin, wake up! You're dreaming," Paula said.

Kevin's eyes began to move slightly, as if he were trying to open them. Finally, they opened. Kevin looked at Paula and then, looked around the room.

"Kevin! You're awake," Paula said.

"Huh? . . . Paula?"

"Get the nurse! Kevin's awake!" Paula screamed.

Paula leaned over and gave Kevin a passionate kiss. He gave her a confused look and then ran his finger over his lips.

"I'm so happy you're awake! You've been in a coma for ten days."

"Ten days?. . . What happened?"

"You saved the Prime Minister's life. You're a hero."

"A hero? What are you talking about?"

Suddenly, the door flew open and a nurse entered the room. When she saw Kevin wide awake she said, "Okay, we've got a live one in here after all. Hello, Kevin. Do you know where you are?"

"A hospital, obviously," he said.

"Good. Do you recognize the people in the room?"

"Sure, they're my friends."

"You're damn right. They've been sitting in here for hours praying you'd come to."

Paula began to cry. "I'm so happy you're okay, Kevin."

The door flew open again and Kevin's doctor rushed in.

"Well, Mr. Wells, it's so nice to see you awake." The doctor pulled out a small flashlight and began to examine Kevin's eyes. "Your eyes look clear. How do you feel?"

"Okay, I guess. Just kind of tired, a little light headed and—"

The door opened again, and Glen and Pat rushed in.

"Kevin! Oh, Kevin! You're okay," Pat said.

"Yes, Mom. I'm fine, but I wish someone would tell me what happened to me."

"We almost lost you, son," Glen said.

"You scared the hell out of us," Pat sobbed.

"I'm okay, I feel fine, except I'm a little tired and my shoulder hurts like hell."

"It's no wonder. That's where the bullet hit you," Paula said.

"What bullet?"

"The assassin's bullet, silly," Paula replied.

"Didn't you know you'd be shot when you jumped in front of the Prime Minister?"

Kevin squinted at Paula and then replied, "The Prime Minister?"

"Yes, don't you remember the Caribbean Trade Conference?"

"Ohhh. Yeah, right. The color guard.... It's kind of fuzzy, but it's coming back."

"Okay, let's clear the room so I can examine my patient," the doctor said. "You all can come back later."

\*\*\*\*\*

The news of Kevin's recovery spread fast. The President issued another statement, thanking God for saving Kevin Wells and renewing his resolve to find the people responsible for the attack. Hundreds of letters and cards arrived every day. Visitors flocked to the hospital to see him, as he had become an overnight celebrity.

In honor of his contribution to the cause of free trade, the members at the Caribbean Trade Conference hammered out a treaty, which they called the Wells Accord. Kevin Wells was the first teenager in history to have a treaty named after him.

After another week of convalescence, Kevin was ready to go home. It was Sunday afternoon. He was packing up his things when the nurse walked in to advise him he had visitors. The news didn't please him as he was anxious to get home.

"Who is it this time?" he moaned.

"I think you'll want to see this visitor," the nurse said.

"I seriously doubt it, who is it?"

Just then a man in a blue coat walked in and quickly scanned the room. "It's okay, Mr. President."

The President walked in and smiled broadly at Kevin. Kevin froze, not quite sure how to react. He had been told the President wanted to see him but didn't really believe it would actually happen.

"I've been very anxious to meet you, Kevin," the President said.

"Really? . . . Well, I've always wanted to meet you too, sir," Kevin replied.

"You're looking good. How do you feel?"

"I'm feeling fine. I'll feel a lot better when I get home. I'm so tired of being cooped up in a hospital room all day."

"I bet. Well, I guess you know you've really touched the hearts of the American people."

"That's what I've heard, but I really didn't do anything that extraordinary."

The President laughed. "Oh, really? Well, when you decide to do something extraordinary let me know, will you? I want to be there to see it."

Kevin shook his head and smiled. "I can't believe I'm talking to the President of the United States."

"It's me, in the flesh. So, what are you going to do when you get out of this place?"

"Get some decent food."

The President laughed, "Well, I wish I had time to buy you dinner, but I've got to get back to Washington by eight o'clock. Maybe I'll invite you to dinner at the White House. Would you like that?"

Kevin nodded enthusiastically. "Absolutely!"

"Oh, I've brought someone with me who is very anxious to meet you."

"Really, who is it?"

"Bring her in," the President said to his aide.

Kevin looked toward the door, extremely curious to see who the President had brought with him. Much to his delight, a young lady about his age walked in and smiled at him. She had long black hair, exquisite green eyes and an alluring smile. Kevin stared at her, his mouth slightly open.

"Kevin, I'd like you to meet Kiran Shah."

Kiran smiled and extended her hand. Kevin stood up, took it and squeezed it gently. A rush of blood immediately went to his head. He felt faint and nearly collapsed.

"Are you all right?" Kiran asked.

Kevin sat down and Kiran knelt before him.

"Now I am," he said.

"I guess you figured out, Kiran is Prime Minister Shah's daughter," the President said. "She was traveling with the Prime Minister and witnessed what happened. The Prime Minister had to get back to Trinidad to make sure everything was okay there. He felt badly that he couldn't stay to personally thank you for saving his life. I suggested he leave Kiran behind to do that."

Kevin looked into Kiran's eyes and replied, "I'm sure glad he followed your advice."

Kiran laughed and then stood up.

"Mr. Wells, I want to thank you for saving my father's life. What you did was the most courageous thing I have ever seen. I will always be in your debt. On behalf of the people of Trinidad-Tobago, I give you our warmest and most sincere thanks. You will always be honored in our country."

"You're welcome. I'm glad I was there at the right time to save your father. I don't know him, but I understand the people of your country really love him."

Kiran smiled. A tear ran down her cheek as she leaned

over and gave Kevin a gentle kiss. Kevin closed his eyes and savored her sweet lips, but he was not prepared for the jolt of sexual energy that she aroused in him. He stood up and gazed excitedly into her eyes. She backed off slightly surprised by his reaction.

"Well, I must go," Kiran said.

She extended her hand one more time. Kevin quickly seized it and shook it firmly. Kiran smiled one last time and then left.

"I think she likes you," the President said and winked at Kevin

"Really?"

"Uh huh, I believe you're the first man she's ever kissed."

Kevin stared at the empty doorway, wondering if he'd ever see Kiran again. She had come so unexpectedly and left so quickly. Her presence seemed like nothing more than a dream. He took a deep breath, still smelling the sweet scent of her perfume. Then he ran his tongue over his lips, reliving the taste of her tender kiss. He was excited at the thought that he had been blessed with her first kiss. Could that really be true? He wanted to kiss her again and again.

Is this the woman I've been searching for? *She must be. I've never felt this way before.* He had such an intense exhilarating feeling, so erotic, that he could think of nothing but her. *Oh God! Now that I've met you, how can I ever live without you?*

"Well, I've got to go," the President said, jerking him back to the present.

Kevin blinked and then forced a smile. "Thank you, Mr. President. I'm honored that you came to visit me."

"I don't know," he said smiling. "Somehow I think you enjoyed meeting Kiran more than you did me."

Kevin grinned and waved to the President as he left. *What a lucky day! God, what a lucky day!*

# Chapter 4

The last time Kevin was in Los Angeles, he was nine years old on a trip to Disneyland. The Wells family was middle class and therefore forced to live on a budget. Accordingly, they stayed at a Motel Six rather than the Disneyland Hotel. And back then they ate fast food rather than dining in expensive restaurants.

This time it was different. Kevin and his family were picked up by a limousine and taken to the Century Plaza Hotel. They were given a luxury suite and every amenity money could buy. Early in the afternoon, a representative from NBC knocked at their door and informed them it was time to go to the studio. Kevin and his family went downstairs and were taken away by limousine to the NBC studios in Burbank. Kevin was taken back stage and his family was seated in the audience. The show began at four o'clock.

"Ladies and gentlemen, from Burbank, California, it's time for the Tonight Show starring the one and only, Jaaaaaay . . . Leno!"

Jay Leno appeared from behind the curtain and walked out onto the stage. Elegantly casual, he paused long enough to shake hands with several people who had crowded up to the base of the stage. The Tonight Show band played in the background and the crowd yelled wildly. Finally, Jay went back up onto the stage and started his monologue.

"Good evening, ladies and gentlemen. We've got an

excellent show tonight. The sexy Uma Thurman, the music of Crimson Tide and a special treat–America's newest hero, Kevin Wells."

The crowd yelled and screamed in delight. Kevin was back stage watching on a monitor. He was very excited and extremely nervous at the prospect of being on national television. And the thought of sitting next to Uma Thurman did little to calm his nerves. As Jay's interview with Uma moved towards its conclusion, Kevin was moved to a chair directly behind the curtain.

"Well Uma, are you excited about meeting Kevin Wells tonight?" Jay asked.

"Oh God, yes. He was so brave, I could just kiss him," she cooed.

"Uweee...," the crowd roared.

"Oh. Well, now I know what it takes to impress a woman. All you've got to do is take a bullet, guys. Well, now you know."

Uma giggled and the crowd laughed hysterically.

"Okay, we'll be right back after this message from Duracell."

The camera went to a commercial depicting an auditorium full of screaming delegates. Suddenly the Energizer® bunny appears, wearing a cadet's uniform. As it moves down the aisles it is pelted with gunfire. The bunny falls over, but quickly gets up and keeps on moving. It's pelted again with gunfire, and falls over once again. After a second, it's on its feet once more, with several gaping holes through it. Another barrage of gunfire is heard and the bunny goes down one more time. There's a pause and the screen is momentarily blank. Suddenly, the bunny appears and keeps on moving toward the podium. Finally, a message appears; *The Duracell battery keeps on going and going and going.* . . .

The Tonight Show band then struck up some music and Jay Leno beat his pencil on the desk.

"Okay. The moment we've been waiting for has arrived. Ladies and gentlemen, meet America's teenage hero, Kevin Wells!"

Kevin walked out from behind the curtain and waved at the crowd. At the request of NBC, he was dressed in a military dress uniform. As he approached the guest chair, Jay intercepted him and shook his hand. The crowd went wild. Before he could sit down, Uma Thurman grabbed him, put her arms around him and gave him a big hug. Kevin didn't know what to do, other than enjoy the moment. Then, she kissed him passionately and the crowd went ballistic.

"Did you see that?" Jay asked. "Uma never kissed me like that. I'm telling you, see what a bullet in the back will do for you, guys?"

Uma finally let go of Kevin. She returned to her chair, sat down and crossed her legs. Kevin stood in front of Jay's desk, seemingly paralyzed. Jay got up, went over to him and waved his hand in front of his face.

"Okay, Kevin. The kiss is over, you can sit down."

The crowd roared. Kevin smiled and sat down.

"It's all right, Kevin. Uma has that effect on a lot of men. Isn't that right, guys?"

The men in the audience howled in response.

"Speaking of kisses, Kevin. I heard you got a kiss from Prime Minister Shah's daughter."

Kevin raised his eyebrows and said, "Yes, I sure did."

"Well she was obviously glad that you saved her father's life. So I can understand why she wanted to kiss you. She was very grateful, I guess?"

"Yes, she was very grateful," Kevin replied.

"What was a shock to me though," Jay continued, "was that when she kissed you, I understand it was the first time she had ever kissed a man."

Kevin shook his head affirmatively.

"That's what the President said."

Jay turned his head thoughtfully. "So the President told

you that when he visited you? I wonder how he knew. You think the CIA told him? Have they had a spy satellite focused on her?"

Laughter came from the crowd.

"No," Kevin laughed. "She told him on the way over to see me."

"Okay, I'm going to put you on the spot now. You've just received an incredible kiss from Uma Thurman. Now I want you to compare that kiss and the kiss of the Prime Minister's daughter."

Kevin suddenly went numb as he recalled Kiran's tender kiss.

Jay smiled in amusement. "Hello, Kevin?"

He blinked, looked at Jay and returned the smile. "I'm sorry, I was just trying to compare them in my mind."

"Oh, good. Take your time, I know it's going to be a tough call."

Kevin looked a Uma and smiled. "Well, Uma's kiss was incredible and I'll always remember it. I really will." Then he looked back at Jay.    But, there was something about Kiran's kiss. It's hard to describe. It was just so sweet and tender. . . yet, so passionate. . . . I don't know.  To be honest I  could scarcely think of anything else for days."

"Ewww. . .," the crowd yelled.

Uma sat up in her chair pretending to pout then she broke into a smile and laughed. "Can I try again, Kevin? I'll be more tender this time."

"No, you had your chance," Jay said emphatically. "You're too old for Kevin anyway, come on."

"But I like younger men. What can I say?" Uma replied.

"Okay. Seriously. I've been wanting to ask you a bunch of questions about what happened. Tell me, Kevin. What went through your mind when you realized an assassin was about to take out the Prime Minister?"

"Nothing, really. There wasn't time to think."

"But obviously something happened in your mind to

make you react so quickly."

"Yes, I remembered what Sergeant Walters had taught us in ROTC class."

"Oh, really? What was that?"

"'He said when you are confronted with a situation you must immediately effectuate an appropriate response.'"

"I see. So it was your military training that prepared you for this situation."

"Correct," Kevin replied. "Its strange when I think of it now, but I was actually tested a few days before."

"Tested? What do you mean?"

"Well, the Saturday before the assassination attempt I was at a swim meet and the cheerleaders had made a giant sign for us ten feet wide. They had worked hard on it and it really looked great. While I was waiting for my dive a couple of kids started messing around and they knocked one of the supports for the sign loose. I was watching just a few feet away when the sign started to fall."

"Oh, no," Jay said. "So–"

"So, I probably could have caught the sign and kept it from falling, but I couldn't move. I just sat there and watched it fall and rip apart."

"Oh, I get it. You didn't immediately effectuate an appropriate response and the sign was destroyed."

Kevin shrugged, feeling the blush creep up his neck. "Right, I just didn't react quickly enough. It made me so mad."

"Well, it was just a sign," Jay said.

Kevin smiled. "Yeah, but I could have been a hero with all those cheerleaders watching."

The crowd roared with laughter.

"So I vowed the next time something like that happened, I'd be ready."

Jay nodded. "I see, so this time you *were* ready?"

"Right. I guess," he squirmed in his seat, uncomfortable with all the attention. Jay seemed to be expecting more, so he added, "I saw the guy on the catwalk. When I looked back at the Prime Minister and saw the little red dot, it all clicked."

"What's the last thing you remember as you ran up there onto the podium?"

"I remember sidestepping a Secret Service agent who tried to tackle me."

"Yes, I saw that on CNN. The Rams want to see you after the show," Jay laughed.

"It was weird – everything seemed like it was in slow motion. I remember the Prime Minister looked shocked when he saw me coming."

"Did you feel the bullet hit you?"

"Not really. I just vaguely remember a pain in my back. Then, it's a blank, until I woke up ten days later."

"Wow! That's incredible. Okay, so what do you have planned now that you're a celebrity? Politics? Maybe a career in acting?"

"No, I'm just going to go back to Plano and finish high school."

"Well, that's good to hear. Ladies and gentlemen, take a good look at a true American hero, Kevin Wells."

The crowd gave Kevin a standing ovation. He nodded and smiled back appreciatively.

"Kevin, thanks for being our guest and good luck to you in the future," Jay said. Don't take anymore bullets, okay?"

"No. No more bullets."

Kevin shook hands with Jay and then with members of the band. Uma gave him one last hug as the Tonight Show broke for a commercial.

*****

Kevin was high as a kite as he left the studio. He and his family were taken to a posh restaurant for dinner and then to a party hosted by several NBC executives. That night, when Kevin returned to the hotel, he was in a daze. Since he awakened from his coma, everything seemed like a dream. He could hardly sleep that night. Finally, well past midnight, he dropped off into a shallow slumber.

It was dark. He was in the front of his house. Blue and white lights from a squad car were flashing. Cameras were going off in his face. Strangers were asking questions, so many questions. He began to run toward the house. . . . "No! No!" Kevin screamed. "Oh, God! Please. No!"

"Kevin, wake up. You're dreaming," Mrs. Wells said.

Kevin opened his eyes and looked at his mother. He sat up.

"What's wrong?"

"You were moaning and groaning. You must have had a nightmare."

"I don't know how he could be having nightmares after spending the evening kissing Uma Thurman," Mr. Wells commented. "It was probably an erotic dream. You just misinterpreted the moaning and groaning."

"Glen, that's enough. Uma's not good enough for my boy."

Kevin sat up and smiled at his parents.

"Some evening, huh?"

"Yeah, I just hope you're ready to come back to reality, Kevin. This can't last forever. You've got to get back to school. You've missed so much already."

"I know. I'm ready to go back to a normal life. It's been fun, but it's starting to wear me out."

"I can imagine. You're still recuperating from the surgery for godsakes," Mr. Wells said.

"I miss my friends, too."

"Well, we'll be home tomorrow, so you'll have a couple days to rest before you start back to school on Monday.

"Good, wake me up Monday morning."

# Chapter 5

The flight back to Dallas was uneventful until it came time to land. A line of thunderstorms was approaching the Dallas-Fort Worth Airport from the northwest. The pilot advised the passengers that he thought he could beat the storm. Otherwise, they'd have to circle a while. As the American Airlines jet made its approach, the plane was jolted up and down. A few of the passengers verbalized their displeasure at being jostled around. When the wheels finally hit the runway, everyone gave a sigh of relief.

The ride home was slowed by a driving rain. LBJ Freeway was jammed up. It took nearly an hour and a half for the Wells family to get back to Plano. It was still drizzling when they pulled into their driveway. They had barely made it in the door when the phone rang. Pat Wells answered it.

"Hello."

"Hi, Mrs. Wells. Is Kevin there?"

"Sure, hang on."

"Kevin, it's for you."

Kevin went upstairs to his room and picked up the phone.

"Hello."

"Kevin?" Paula asked.

"Oh hi, Paula," Kevin replied.

"I saw you last night on Leno. You were fabulous."

"Oh, thank you."

"I didn't like that slut, Uma Thurman, kissing you though."

"She's not a slut, she's nice. She's one of my favorite actresses."

"Really. Well anyway, forget her. I just wanted to see if you wanted to get together and hang out a while."

"Sure, that would be great. Let me check with my mom, I don't know if she has anything planned. I'll call you tomorrow."

"Okay, I'll be in all morning."

"Okay, bye."

"Bye."

Kevin hung up the phone and was about to go downstairs to help unload the luggage from the car when the phone rang again.

"Hello."

"Kevin, my man."

"Brent, what's going on?"

"Hey, I saw you on Leno last night. Oh God! You kissed Uma Thurman. What was it like?"

"Interesting."

"Interesting? Right, . . . yeah very interesting, I bet. Hey, I've got a *Playboy* layout of her I stole from my big brother. I'll bring it over if you want to see it?"

"No, that's okay. I don't want to spoil the memory."

"You're right. You don't have to fantasize. You've felt her sweet, succulent lips. Oh God, what luck you've had!"

"I know."

"What if Jay would have had Phyllis Diller on?" Brent laughed.

"I wouldn't have let her get near me. If she'd tried to kiss me, I would have puked on national television."

"That would have been cute. Hey, you want to catch a movie tonight?"

"I don't know, I'm kind of tired."

"Come on, I haven't seen you in weeks."

"Okay, I need to get unpacked and have dinner first. We can go to a late show."

"Good, I'll pick you up at nine-thirty."

"Okay, see you then."

Kevin hung up the phone and started to go downstairs again. Before he got to the door, the phone rang again.

"Shit! . . . Hello."

"Kevin?"

"Yes, who's this?"

"Stacy."

Kevin drew a blank. "Stacy?"

"Yes, the library, remember?"

"Oh, right. . . . Stacy. How are you?"

"Fine. Listen, about our last meeting. You know, when Paula had me give you a hard time about the virginity thing? Well, I've really been feeling bad about that. It was mean, I know."

"Forget it. It was all in good fun. Paula's a real tease sometimes."

"What I told you about being a virgin?" Stacy said, "Well, it's not really true. Obviously it's not true. I mean, who is a virgin anymore these days?"

Kevin laughed. "Right."

"But, I'm almost a virgin. I mean I never have sex with two guys at the same time."

"Really?"

"I mean. . . . You know. . . . I just do it with the guy I'm going with. I'm faithful to my guy."

"Well, that's good to hear."

"So, do you want to get together?"

"Us? Well, I'm hanging around with Paula tomorrow. Why don't you come too? Maybe we can find something interesting to do."

"Oh good! I'll call Paula and tell her you invited me to hang with you guys."

"Cool. See you tomorrow."

"Okay, bye."

Kevin started to hang up the phone, but then hesitated a minute. Instead of hanging it up he placed the receiver next to the phone and then went downstairs.

"Who was that on the phone, honey?"

"Paula, Brent, and then, Stacy."

"Oh boy. I'm afraid your life won't be the same for a while."

"It's okay, they're my friends. I don't want to let this thing go to my head. I'm still the same guy I was three months ago. The only thing that's changed is everybody in the world knows I exist now."

"And wherever you go, people will recognize you, because you've been on Leno."

"That could have its advantages," Kevin said.

"That's right, absolutely."

"And its drawbacks."

"Don't worry about it, honey. It will all work out."

That night, Brent and Kevin went to the movies. Afterward, they went to Starbucks for coffee where they ran into a couple of their friends. Kevin told them all about his trip to California, meeting the President and kissing Uma Thurman. When he got home after midnight, he was exhausted. Without even getting undressed, he collapsed on his bed and fell asleep.

In his mind, he traveled back in time to the day he left the hospital. He turned toward the door and saw Kiran stroll into the room. She was so beautiful, the sight of her sent a tingling sensation throughout his body. She smiled as she knelt down in front of him and took his hands in hers. The feel of her warm grasp excited him beyond belief. He pulled her up next to him and looked deep into her eyes. She laughed and pulled away. When she turned her back on him, he put his arms on her shoulders and turned her abruptly around. Without the slightest resistance, she let him pull her close to him. He felt her warmth and radiant energy. His lips were drawn to hers by a force so strong it was futile to resist. In the midst of their passion, the door flew open, rudely interrupting them. Kiran looked up and quickly pulled herself away. She looked back at Kevin, smiled and ran out the door. He followed after her, but beyond the door was a thick fog through which he could see nothing.

"Kiran, come back! Come back!" he yelled. The outcry jolted him from his slumber.

He shook his head, trying to clear his mind. His face was wet and his clothes were saturated. He looked at his clock radio. It was one-thirty. After taking a deep breath and contemplating his dream for a moment, he turned over and went back to sleep.

The following day was Sunday. After mass, Paula called and suggested they go to the mall, have lunch and mess around. Kevin agreed and promised to meet them at the food court. When he arrived, he was in a somber mood. His thoughts had been on Kiran all morning. He wanted to see her again, but he knew that would never happen. She was thousands of miles away—gone forever. When he saw Paula and Stacy, he forced a smile.

"Hi, girls."

"Hi, Kevin," they said cheerfully.

"So what's for lunch?"

"We can't decide. It's between a stuffed potato or a salad."

"How about Arby's?"

"Arby's?" Paula said with a frown. "That kind of food will clog your arteries, won't it Stacy?"

Stacy nodded.

Kevin shrugged. "Maybe so, but it tastes good."

"Okay, whatever."

Kevin led the way to Arby's and the threesome ordered. After getting their food, they sat down at a table overlooking a beautiful fountain.

"I love the mall," Stacy said. "It's always so warm and dry, even if it's raining outside."

"I think that was the plan, Stacy," Kevin laughed.

"I know. The people who built this place were pretty

smart," Stacy said.

Paula stared at Stacy for a moment and then cleared her throat. She said, "So, Kevin, how did it feel to be on Leno?"

"Pretty weird, actually. It was like I was in a dream.    I kept expecting to wake up."

"I can imagine," Paula said.

"How is your back?" Stacy asked. "It must have hurt when that bullet hit you."

"No shit!" Kevin said.

Paula began to laugh, Kevin smiled at her and Stacy gave her a dirty look.

"What's so funny? I bet you wouldn't like it if someone shot you in the back."

"No, I'm sorry," Paula said. "I wouldn't."

"So when is our next tournament, Paula?" Kevin asked.

"Next weekend, at South Garland High School."

"God, I'm so far behind on everything, I don't know if I'll be ready by next weekend."

"I'll help you get ready, don't worry."

"Thanks. Can I get all your notes from class for the last few weeks?"

"Sure."

"Brent offered me his, but somehow I doubt everything Mrs. White lectured on could fit on a single index card."

"No. I've got at least fifty pages of notes."

"Good."

After the trio had finished lunch, they walked around the mall for a while and talked, but Kevin didn't have his mind on his companions. He was off in Trinidad, with his new found love, Kiran.

"So what shall we do now, guys?" Stacy inquired.

"Hey, listen. It's been fun, but I need to get home and start catching up on my homework. I'm probably not going to be such great company right now anyway. My mind can't seem to focus."

"Okay, I understand, Kevin. Do you want me to come with you and help?" Paula said.

"No, I'm so far behind, it's going to take me a while to get organized enough to know what help I need. I'll get with you next week when I know better where I'm at."

"You sure?"

"Yeah, I'll see you girls later."

After Kevin had left, the two girls turned into Dillard's and began looking at blouses.

"Look at this. I'd die to have this," Stacy said.

"It's a little flashy don't you think?"

"Maybe."

"I hope Kevin's going to be all right."

"What do you mean?" Stacy asked.

"He seemed very depressed."

"Huh? I didn't notice that."

"You don't know him as well as I do," Paula noted. "Something is bothering him."

Stacy frowned. "I wonder what it is?"

"Who knows? Maybe he's got a crush on Uma Thurman."

# Chapter 6

South Garland High School was packed with students from all over the state. It was the regional debate championships. In past tournaments, Plano High School had been the team to beat and they were favorites again this year. It was late Saturday afternoon, Paula and Alice were watching Kevin's third round debate. The round wasn't going well for Kevin who was up against a tenacious young lady from Clebourne.

"What's wrong with Kevin, I wonder?" Paula said.

"I don't know. Maybe he's just rusty from being out of school so long," Alice suggested.

"No. I worked with him Thursday night and he knew everything cold."

"Huh. Then why is he letting that little cheese-ball walk all over him?"

"He's not concentrating. Look at him, his mind is off in la la land."

"It's this celibacy thing," Alice said. "The guy needs a good screw."

"No, that's not it. Something has been bothering him ever since he left the hospital."

"Well, if you ask me, if you and I locked him in a room and fucked the shit out of him, he'd be fine."

"Well, he wouldn't let us do that, he'd high tail it." Paula laughed.

"Hell, we'll put burglar bars on the windows and dead

bolts on the door."

Paula shook her head skeptically. "Somehow, I don't think that would work."

When the debate was over, a somber Kevin walked the girls back to Plano's staging area.

"So. I hope you girls did better than I did today."

"We both won our rounds," Paula said.

"Good. How's the team doing?"

"We're in second place," Paula replied.

"We needed you to win, Kevin," Alice said. "How come you let that little Nazi beat you?"

"I don't know. I just can't get psyched up since I've been back."

"Well, don't worry about it." Paula sighed. "I still think we'll win the tournament. Everyone else is doing well."

"I hate to be a drag on the team. I just wish I could forget everything that's happened to me. I can't concentrate anymore. I don't know what's the matter with me."

"Will you come watch my final round? You can give me some moral support, at least," Paula said.

"Sure, I'd love to."

"Good. I'll be in room 232B, at three forty-five."

"I'll be there."

The girls went off to their next event. Kevin walked outside and strolled around the campus. That was one thing Kevin hated about debate tournaments. If you lost, there was nothing to do but twiddle your thumbs the rest of the day. Kevin found a pleasant spot overlooking a pond. He watched two ducks sliding across the water and a kid fishing from the bank. Before long his mind began to wander and he started to daydream.

He was in a magnificent bedroom, ornately decorated in eastern decor. He was wearing only silk pajama bottoms. He went to the mirror and admired his fine muscular body. Hearing a noise, he looked up and saw Kiran walking toward him. She was so beautiful, a surge of joy exploded within him. She wore a long, sheer nightgown, white as snow and clear as a crystal goblet. Kevin tried to breathe, but he couldn't. Finally, she strutted over to him, twirled around so he could see every part of her and then stood directly in front of him.

"Oh, my God! You're more beautiful than I could ever have imagined."

"Are you sure?"

"Of course, I'm sure."

"What about that girl, Uma? Am I more beautiful than Uma?"

Kevin laughed, "Oh yes. Much more beautiful than her. He took her by the hand and gently pulled her towards him. Their eyes locked, then he pushed her gently onto the bed and leaned over to get a good look at her. He gazed at her supple breasts and smooth, flat stomach. She lay motionless, beckoning him to explore every part of her body. He rose to remove his pants. Then, carefully, he pulled her nightgown up over her head and dropped it to the ground. She smiled slyly, waiting patiently as he gazed at her naked body.

"Kevin, wake up!" Alice yelled.

Kevin jumped. "Huh?"

"Wake up! What are you doing out here? You're supposed to be watching Paula's debate. She's going to be pissed if you're not there. Come on. It's about to start."

Kevin jumped, startled by Alice's sudden appearance. He shot her an annoyed look. "Okay. Okay. I'm coming." He wanted to close his eyes again and return to the bed of his lover, but he knew it was no use. *Damn you, Alice!*

After slowly getting up, he followed her to the classroom where Paula was about to start her debate. They took a couple of seats near hers. She shook her head.

"Where have you two been? I thought you deserted me."

"This big lug was outside, sound asleep. It took me thirty

minutes to find him."

Kevin shrugged in response to Paula's disgusted look. The debate began and it wasn't long before it was clear Paula would be victorious. She had the ability to destroy any opponent with subtle sarcasm. Her opponent today was no match for her. Unfortunately, Plano came up two points short and placed second in the tournament. Kevin felt badly. If he had won but one more round, Plano would be the regional champions. The bus ride home was somber and Kevin avoided everyone for the remainder of the weekend.

*****

On Monday, Kevin had an appointment with the FBI. Since he was the only person who had seen the would-be assassin, the FBI wanted him to look through mug sheets and computer photographs of possible suspects. He left at eight-thirty, drove downtown to the FBI headquarters and asked for Agent Simmons. After a minute, Simmons strolled into the waiting room.

"Hey, Kevin. Thanks for coming down today," Agent Simmons said.

"No problem."

"How's the hole in your back?"

"Healing nicely, I believe."

"Good. We've got everything set up for you."

"Okay, I'm ready, I guess. I just hope I can remember what he looked like."

"I'm sure you will. We've got a lot of pictures for you to look at. I hope you planned to be here the whole day."

"Yeah. I told my counselor I'd have to miss all my classes. I'll need a note from you though, so they won't count it as an unexcused absence."

"No problem. Don't let me forget to give it to you before you leave."

Agent Simmons led Kevin through a door and down a long corridor. After a minute, they came to another door, with a security pad on it. Simmons punched in the code and a buzzer sounded. He held the door open so Kevin could enter. Inside the room was a large table with numerous stacks of mug books and a computer terminal.

"Okay, just sit down. I'll turn the computer on and show you how to flip from one photo to the other."

Kevin watched the screen illuminate. Agent Simmons typed some commands on the keyboard and a picture of a black male in his mid-twenties appeared.

"That's not him."

"Well, just hit return when you want to move on to the next picture. There were about two thousand pictures that came up from the parameters we fed the computer."

"Two thousand?"

"Yeah," agent Simmons laughed. "Don't worry though. You'll get through them pretty fast. When you're done with them, we've got eight or nine mug books."

"Jesus! Come get me next week."

"It won't be that bad. I'll check on you in a couple hours. If you happen to find anyone that looks familiar, pick up the telephone and dial two-three-one-four. That's my extension."

"Okay."

Agent Simmons left the room and Kevin began to flip through the computer photographs. It was slow going at first, because Kevin studied each face carefully. As time went on, he began flipping the pictures more and more quickly. After going through the first thousand or so, he got up to stretch his legs. He went to the bathroom, snooped around the room a little, then sat back down and started going through the remainder of the pictures. He was getting pretty bored, so he started flipping the pictures faster and faster. Suddenly, he saw someone who looked familiar. He stopped a moment. Then he flipped back to the last picture he had seen. It was the picture of Ray Mohammed from San Fernando, Trinidad. He had dark skin, a beard and a scar above his left cheek bone. His eyes were brown with a slight greenish tint. Kevin closed his eyes and thought back to when he saw the assassin sitting with the band. He could see the man in his mind's eye, but he wasn't sure about the scar. He hadn't been close enough for it to stick out.

Kevin wrote down the number of the photo and went on. Hundreds of photos later, he ran across another photograph that also looked like his assailant. This photograph was identified as Peter Gosne from Tunapuna, Trinidad. This man didn't have a scar, but looked very similar to the first suspect. Kevin stared at the face on the screen. Again, he closed his eyes to try to determine if this was the man. He opened up his eyes again and looked at the sinister character, who seemed to be staring back at him. Just then the door opened and Agent Simmons walked in.

"How are we doing?"

"I don't know. I've found two photographs and either one could be the man."

"Good, who are they?"

"This guy, Peter Gosne and then, another guy named Ray Mohammed."

"Hmm. Let me print them out. We'll get them out on the wire and see what happens. Nice job."

"I just hope one of them is the guy. It's so hard to be sure. I just saw him for maybe thirty seconds."

"There must have been something about him that got your attention, otherwise you would have no recollection of him at all."

"Well, I was watching the band setting up in the pit in front of the stage when I noticed him just standing there, looking around. He must have felt my stare, because he glanced at me, then picked up his case and slipped away, out a side door. I think it was the fact that he took his instrument that got my attention. I wondered why he would be leaving before the band had performed. It was just kind of strange, I thought."

"Hmm. . . . Well, it's nearly five o'clock. I think you've done enough today. Go on home and I'll keep you posted. Okay?"

"All right. I'll need that note."

"Oh, sure," Agent Simmons said as he pulled an envelope out of his inside pocket. "I've got it right here."

Agent Simmons walked Kevin to the waiting room and thanked him again for coming. Kevin left and headed back home on Central Expressway. It was rush hour, so traffic was slow. As he was sitting in traffic, he thought about Kiran and how much he wanted to see her. He knew that the likelihood of that was next to nil. His depression intensified as he analyzed his desperate predicament. *What if Kiran didn't have as strong of feelings for me as I do for her? I could spurn every woman I met, hoping, praying for the day I'd finally meet her, only to be rejected.*

Suddenly he realized how foolish he had been. He had to forget Kiran. She was just a dream, a figment of his imagination. She wasn't real. When Kevin got back to Plano, he decided to stop by Plano High. He wanted to pick up some books so he could study when he got home. He walked into the main building and headed for his locker. As he was rummaging through his books, deciding what to take home, he felt a hand on his shoulder. He turned around quickly and was surprised to see Stacy smiling at him. She was wearing a halter top and the shortest shorts Kevin had ever seen. Her legs were sleek and deeply tanned. It was a pleasant surprise.

"Oh. Hi, Stacy. You startled me. I didn't hear you walk up."

She smiled, obviously amused at his reaction. "You're here awfully late," she said.

"Yeah, I had to go downtown today and look through mug shots."

"Mug shots?"

"Yeah, the FBI asked me to do it. You know, to see if I could identify the guy who shot me."

Stacy nodded.

"Since I missed some classes, I thought I better get some books so I could study tonight. . . . Although I don't feel much like it, actually."

"How come?"

Kevin closed his locker and shrugged. "I don't know. I've just been kind of down lately. I guess I'm just coming back to earth after all the excitement in my life."

"You feel kind of lost, right? Like you just don't know what to do next?"

"Yeah. . . . Something like that."

"I know what you mean. I feel that way every year when football season is over and there are no more cheerleading practices to go to. It's like—What am I going to do all afternoon everyday?"

"Hmm. . . . So is that why you're here so late today?"

"Right, we have it every day."

"Don't you get tired of practicing everyday?"

"No, I like it and it keeps me in shape."

Kevin gave Stacy's body a once over.

"I can see that."

Stacy's eyes thanked him for the compliment. She said, "Hey my parents are going out tonight. We could study together."

"Study together? Hmm. I don't know. . . . I haven't eaten yet and I should probably get home."

"I'll cook for you," Stacy replied.

Kevin pondered the idea a moment, obviously intrigued. "That's really nice of you, but I wouldn't want to impose."

"It's not any trouble."

"Do you like to cook?"

"Sure, I make great lasagna. We can stop on the way home and get what we need. It would be fun. Come on. Let me cook for you and then we can study."

Kevin shrugged. "All right, if you're sure, but it seems like a lot of trouble."

"I've got to eat anyway. If I were alone, I'd probably have junk food. This will be better. You can tell me all about what happened today."

"It wasn't very exciting. I think I looked through two or three thousand photographs."

"That's sounds pretty exciting to me. You know, helping the FBI and everything," she said taking his hand. "Let's go, you can tell me about it on the way. I'll drive, since I know where we're going.

Kevin laughed at Stacy's enthusiasm. What she was lacking in intellect, she certainly made up in charm and beauty. Stacy led Kevin out to the parking lot to Stacy's Mazda Miata convertible. Kevin stopped a few feet away and gave the car a good look.

He smiled and said, "I love your car. It's definitely you."

"My dad gave it to me when I made the cheerleading squad. He said since I was the prettiest girl at Plano High School, I needed a car that complimented my beauty."

"Well, I think you'd look good in just about any car, Stacy."

"Do you really think so?"

"I wouldn't have said it if I didn't mean it. You're probably the prettiest girl I've ever seen."

"Including Uma Thurman?"

Kevin laughed, then shook his head affirmatively. "Yes, absolutely. She doesn't hold a candle to you."

"Oh, you're so sweet, Kevin. We're going to have so much fun tonight!"

A few minutes later, they were shopping at Tom Thumb. Kevin enjoyed watching Stacy shop. He couldn't believe that any human being could get so much joy out of buying tomato paste and ricotta cheese. Stacy's happiness was becoming intoxicating. Soon, Kevin was laughing and having a great time. Once they finished shopping, Stacy drove them to her house. It was a nice home at the end of a cul-de-sac. Kevin looked around to see if anyone had noticed them drive up. The street was quiet.

"When will your parents be home?"

"Oh, not until after midnight. They're going to dinner with some friends. Then they've got theater tickets. After the show, they usually stop off at a club and have a few drinks. We've got the place to ourselves for at least six hours."

"Huh. You sure live in a nice neighborhood."

"Thank you."

Stacy grabbed Kevin's hand again and led him to the front door. Kevin felt a tinge of excitement feeling Stacy's warm grasp. But when she opened the door and he walked into the spacious house, he suddenly felt awkward. *What am I doing here?*

"Come on in. Let's go back to the kitchen. We can have some wine to drink while I'm cooking."

"I don't know if we should be drinking if we plan to get any studying done."

"Oh, come on. One glass won't hurt you."

Kevin raised his eyebrows but didn't argue the point.

"Nice house," he said.

"Thank you."

"My dad is a dentist. He does pretty well, unless the economy gets sluggish. Daddy says that dentists are the first thing people drop from their budget if cash gets tight. That's why he always saves as much money as he can."

"Your dad's a smart guy."

"He is. He's wonderful."

Stacy began pulling out bowls and ingredients for her lasagna, spreading them out on the counter. Kevin watched her in amazement. He never had imagined her being such a whiz in the kitchen.

"Oh, the wine. It's in the refrigerator, in the bar. Get us some blush, okay?"

Kevin hesitated. He had promised himself he'd never drink again, but he hated to spoil the party. Stacy was having so much fun.

"I don't drink, actually," he finally blurted out.

She smiled and shook her head. "Don't be silly. You may be able to fool your friends, but you can't fool me."

"Excuse me?" Kevin said.

She laughed. "Go, silly. It's in the bar."

Kevin didn't move. Stacy stopped and their eyes locked. They stared at each other for several long seconds before Kevin finally looked away.

"Please Kevin, get the wine. You can't eat Italian without wine."

He threw up his hands. "Okay, okay, I'll get the wine."

Kevin went in the direction Stacy had pointed and spotted a bar in the den. He opened the refrigerator. Sure enough, there were several bottles of blush, as well as an assortment of other wines. If they ran out, he noted there was a full wine rack above the bar filled with at least fifty bottles. Kevin grabbed a bottle of blush and a couple of glasses and went back into the kitchen. He opened the bottle and poured two glasses to the brim.

Stacy smiled at him, grabbed one of the glasses and took a swig.

"Oh, I love this stuff."

Kevin gave it a whiff and then tried it. It had an interesting bite he thought. He took another sip.

"Yeah, not bad," he said.

Before long Stacy had her masterpiece in the oven. She and Kevin sat down at the kitchen table to talk and drink their wine. Since Kevin did not often drink, consuming the wine on an empty stomach began to take its toll. When the first bottle was gone, Stacy got up and got another. When the lasagna was almost done, Stacy set out a salad and hot bread for each of them. Finally, she served her lasagna.

"Oh, this is excellent, Stacy. You amaze me. I didn't know you were such a good cook."

"My dad taught me. He's really good at it."

Hearing so much about Stacy's dad made him curious about her mother.

"What does your mom do?"

"She's a lawyer."

"Really? Wow!"

"I don't see much of her. You know, being a partner and everything, . . . but we have some good quality time together."

"Oh, . . . well. That's good. What do you like to do with her, . . . with her the most?"

"Shopping. I love to go shopping with her."

"Oh. Yeah. . . . Shopping," he nodded approvingly. "That's cool."

"Unfortunately, she doesn't like to shop."

Kevin smiled, then burst out laughing. "Bummer."

At first Stacy frowned but then she began to laugh too.

"It *is* pretty pathetic isn't it?" she said.

"No, no," he said rubbing his temples. "I'm sorry, I know it's not funny. I've just had one too many glasses of wine."

Stacy got up and extended her hand. " It's okay. . . . Come on, let's go to the den."

Once they were seated comfortably on the sofa, she kicked off her shoes and nestled up close to him.

"You want to watch television a little while before we start studying?" Kevin asked.

"No, I just want to talk to you. I never have anyone to talk to. Every day I come home to this empty house. This beautiful, empty house."

"You get lonely, huh?"

"Uh huh. Sometimes I run outside just to see if any of the neighbors are around, so I can talk to them. They never are, though." Stacy shook her head. "So, you know what I do sometimes?"

"What?"

"I go next door to borrow a cup of sugar. Can you believe it? I never need the sugar. We never run out of anything. Mom is super efficient. . . . Do you think I'm nuts?"

"No, not at all." Kevin laughed. "I've made up stories to get what I want before."

"Really?"

"Sure."

Suddenly Stacy sat up and looked Kevin in the eyes. "You know what I want to do? You're going to think it's silly."

"What?"

"I want to kiss you like Uma did."

He frowned. "Really? Why?"

"To get your opinion. You know-how I stack up compared to Uma and the princess."

"The princess? If you're talking about the Prime Minister's daughter she's not a princess."

"Whatever. . . . Can I?"

Kevin shrugged. "Well, I sure as hell won't stop you."

Kevin didn't know why he had said that, but it was too late to issue a retraction. Stacy quickly moved onto Kevin's lap, grabbed him behind the neck and pulled his lips to hers. Kevin closed his eyes and, for a moment, forgot about everything else in the world. Stacy nudged her tongue into his mouth, where it was graciously accepted. While engaged in mouth to mouth combat, Stacy began to unbutton Kevin's shirt. He didn't resist. She pulled it open and began caressing his chest. Then, she pulled her halter top over her head, exposing her exquisite breasts. Kevin stuck a nipple in his mouth and began to stroke it with his tongue. Stacy moaned in delight. She got up and started to pull off her shorts.

"I knew you'd come around," Stacy moaned.

Suddenly, Kevin was hit with a moment of sobriety. He

let Stacy go.

"Come around?" he asked.

"I mean—"

Kevin sat up and pushed Stacy away. "You planned this?!"

A stunned Stacy watched as Kevin quickly got dressed. "No, it's not like that," she moaned. "Paula…"

"Paula? Did you and Paula have some kind of bet?"

"Well, sort—"

"I can't believe this!" Kevin said as he searched the room with a glance. "What do you have? A camera? A tape recorder?"

Suddenly his eyes focused on the hutch in the corner of the room. The door was slightly ajar. He stormed over to it and pulled it open. A video camera was set on the middle shelf. The door had been closed just enough to conceal the camera in darkness but not block a clear view of the sofa. Kevin ejected the tape and stormed through the house to the front door.

"Oh, Kevin. Don't leave. Let me explain."

He laughed. "Right, like it would make a difference."

Once outside, Kevin started to run. He didn't stop until he'd gone several miles. He finally found himself in front of his church, St. Elizabeth Seton Catholic Church. He went inside and knelt in the Chapel. *What is this, Lord—some kind of a test? The mind is strong but the body is weak. Is that it? I've been trying to live my life the way you would want me to, but it's so hard. It's just so hard and I'm so tired of fighting. It seems like everyone is out to derail me, even you. Why did you bring me Kiran only to take her away? I don't understand. You know, it would be so easy just to give up—oh so easy. Help me, Lord. Please, help me and give me strength to go on.*

# Chapter 7

The following week, Kevin got a telephone call from an excited Agent Simmons. He insisted Kevin come down to FBI headquarters the following morning. Although Kevin asked him what was up, Simmons wouldn't discuss it over the phone. All he would say is that they might have found one of the men in the photograph Kevin had picked out. Kevin didn't know how he felt about the possibility of the capture of the man who shot him. He was just starting to get over all of the horrible trauma he had experienced. Now, if there was a trial, he would have to relive it all over again.

Kevin arrived at FBI headquarters precisely at nine the following morning. As he was waiting to speak to the receptionist, Agent Simmons walked in the front door.

"Oh, you're here, right on time, Kevin. Thanks for coming down. Let's go back to my office."

"Sure," Kevin replied.

He followed Agent Simmons down a long corridor to his office. As he stepped inside, he was impressed how clean and orderly it looked. He had thought most cops were slobs. Then he remembered–this was the FBI.

"Have a seat."

"Thanks. So you found the guy, huh?"

"We think so. The Port of Spain police put out an all-points-bulletin on both the persons you identified from the mug shots the other day. Their pictures were also printed in Trinidad's national newspaper, the *Daily Express*. It wasn't long before the police were getting tips on where they might find one of the guys. It turns out he's a security officer for a local shipping company."

"Oh really? What about the other guy?"

"Funny you should ask. It turns out both pictures are of the same person. He apparently used an alias and had been arrested and booked under both names. That's why we're certain this is our man."

"So, did they arrest him?"

"Not yet, but they've located him."

"What's the problem? Why don't they nab the bastard?"

"Trinidad is a democracy, like the United States. They have a constitution and due process, just like we do. They can't just go arrest someone unless they have solid evidence. I'm afraid your photo ID isn't going to cut it."

"So what are they going to do?"

"Well, as a matter of fact, that's why I've called you down here today. They want you to go to Port of Spain, so you can identify the guy in a lineup."

"Oh shit. You've got to be kidding. When do they want me to go?"

"Right away."

A cold wave of uncertainty washed over Kevin. He was stunned. The thought of going to Trinidad had never even occurred to him. He briefly considered the ramifications of the FBI's unexpected request. He didn't know why, but he didn't have a good feeling about it.

"Right away? But I've already missed so much school this year. I can't afford to miss any more."

"You can make up your studies later. This is more important, don't you think?"

Kevin stared silently at Agent Simmons. Still in shock he began to collect himself. "How long will it take?"

"A week or ten days is all. They'll need you to do the lineup. Then you'll testify before a grand jury or magistrate—or some other official. I'm not exactly sure what their procedure is there, but it's similar to ours."

"What about the trial? Will I have to be there for that?"

"Probably, but that will be months off."

Uncertainty now turned to anger. *I've already risked my life to save the Prime Minister–now they want me to turn my life upside down? I can't believe this!*

"Crap! . . . What if I refuse?"

"Well, they could extradite the suspect to the United States for trial, but the government doesn't want to do that. They want to have a quick trial and then hang him–to set an example and send a powerful message to other dissidents. They can't force you to come to Trinidad, but the Prime Minister has notified the State Department that it is of the utmost urgency that you come. As a matter of fact, I've got a letter for you from the Prime Minister himself."

"You're kidding. He wrote me a letter?" Kevin asked–his anger now giving way to curiosity.

Agent Simmons opened his middle drawer and pulled out a letter on the Prime Minister's stationery, secured with his official seal. Kevin took it from him and looked at it with a tinge of excitement.

"You might want to open it and see what it says," Agent Simmons suggested.

"Do you have a letter opener?" Kevin said now smiling. "I don't want to damage it. This will definitely have to go in my scrapbook."

Agent Simmons opened his middle drawer again. This time, he pulled out a letter opener.

"Here you go," he said as he handed it to Kevin.

"Thanks."

After Kevin opened the envelope, he pulled out the letter and began reading it. Suddenly, his eyes lit up, he smiled broadly at Agent Simmons and said, "When do I leave?"

Kevin couldn't wait to get home and show the letter from

Prime Minister Shah to his mother. He was so happy, he could hardly contain himself. He had to share his joy with someone. Luckily the traffic on Central Expressway had died down. Rush hour was over. He raced home, going seventy-five most of the way. He came to a screeching halt in front of his house, ran to the front door and rushed inside.

"Mom! Mom! Where are you? I've got incredible news."

Kevin raced into the laundry room, where his mother was loading the dryer.

"Mom, there you are. Guess what?"

"What, honey?"

"I'm going to Trinidad."

"What?"

"I've got a letter from Prime Minister Shah. You want me to read it to you?"

"Of course," she said, amused by her son's exuberance. "Don't keep me in suspense."

Kevin began to read the letter.

*Dear Mr. Wells,*

*I want to apologize for not personally thanking you for saving my life at the Caribbean Trade Conference. Unfortunately, at the time I had urgent matters of state that needed my immediate attention. I trust my daughter conveyed to you my sincerest thanks for your courageous deed.*

*I know you have already done so much for me, my family and for the people of Trinidad-Tobago. Accordingly, it is with great reluctance that I send you this letter asking your help once again. You are the only person who can testify as to the identity of the scoundrel who would have deprived our people of their elected Prime Minister. I need you. The people of Trinidad-Tobago need you to come to Port of Spain—to do your duty as a citizen of democracy to insure justice is done.*

*Of course, I would insist that while you are here, you stay at my home, as my guest. While I will be busy tending to my duties as Prime Minister, my wife and my daughters will give you all of their attention, so that your stay will be most enjoyable.*
*I will anxiously await your reply.*

*Sincerely,*

*Ahmad Shah*

Kevin looked up excitedly to see his mother's response. "So what do you think?"

Mrs. Wells hesitated. "I don't know what to say. I hate for you to leave the country. I don't know anything about Trinidad. Is it safe?"

"Of course. I'll be staying with the Prime Minister for godsakes. Anyway, I've got to go. Did you catch the gist of the last paragraph?—I will have all of Kiran's attention while I'm in Trinidad. That's so incredible! I never thought I'd ever see her again and now I'm going to spend ten days with her. I can't believe it! I'm so excited I can hardly stand it!"

"I know you're excited, Honey, but you've only met this girl one time. You've only been with her for five minutes. Why are you so infatuated with her?"

"I'm not infatuated with her, I'm in love with her. She's an angel, a goddess. All I can think about is being with her!"

Mrs. Wells frowned and started to respond but Kevin interrupted her.

"For awhile, I thought I would never see her again. I was almost resigned to living a life of misery without her, but it must be our destiny to be together. I mean, how can you explain what has happened? There's some divine intervention here, Mom. You can't deny it."

"I don't know, Kevin. What if she doesn't love you? I

mean, she barely knows you."

"She will. I know she will."

"I don't want you to get hurt, honey. You've got to be more realistic about this. Don't expect too much. You should talk to your father. He went with a few girls before he met me. I'm sure he thought he was in love too."

"I'll talk to Dad, but there's nothing he could say that will change the way I feel."

"Well, if you do go to Trinidad, you should get to know Kiran before you start planning your future. Take it slow. She may be an entirely different person than you think."

"I'll be careful, Mom, don't worry."

"I *will* worry, I'll be scared to death every minute you're gone."

Kevin smiled warmly, then put his arms around her again. "There'll be nothing to worry about. I'll be perfectly safe. I'll call you every couple days."

"You better call me everyday."

"Okay, everyday."

# Chapter 8

Kevin gave his mother a kiss and hugged his father before boarding American Airlines Flight 272, bound for Miami. He was leaving a day early. Unexpectedly a new set of tickets and a revised itinerary arrived from the Trinidad Travel Office moving up the day of departure by one day. He didn't mind this as it meant he'd see Kiran a day sooner. It was nine a.m. and the flight was scheduled to arrive just before one in the afternoon. Kevin was excited, but a little scared, because he had never been out of the country before. He knew nothing about Trinidad and had no idea what to expect. After the usual long taxi to the DFW Airport runway, the plane finally took off.

Once airborne, everyone got a continental breakfast from the flight attendant. Kevin ate everything. He sat back and read the newspaper he purchased just before boarding the plane. After a while, he put the newspaper on the empty seat beside him and laid back to rest. Before long, he fell asleep and began to dream.

In his dream, he re-lived the assassination attempt. He felt the sting of the bullet piercing his flesh and the excruciating pain that had driven him into unconsciousness. Then the dream shifted. He was in front of his house. He stepped out of his car. There were blue and white lights flashing on a patrol car. He could hear the police radio, then a crowd of reporters surrounded him. They were yelling questions at him—so many questions. The camera lights glared in his face. He stuck his hand in front of his eyes to shield them. Then someone grabbed his arm. He pulled away and began to run. He ran inside nearly gagging from the stench. He hurried through a crowd of men in the living room, up the stairs and walked cautiously toward his room. Then he saw her, "No... no—"

The stewardess put her hand on his shoulder. "Sir, are you all right? Would you like a cold drink?"

Kevin opened his eyes and looked up at her. "Huh? . . . I'm sorry, what did you say?"

"A cold drink? Would you like a cold drink?"

He sat up and blinked his eyes. "Oh, yeah, uh huh, Coke, please."

Kevin looked around and noticed people watching him. He turned away and gazed out the window to hide his embarrassment. He felt drowsy. He was pleased to see the stewardess with his Coke—hoping the caffeine would help him wake up.

At twelve-thirty, the pilot announced the plane was making its final descent into Miami. Kevin put his newspaper away and began watching the Florida Everglades below. Precisely at one o'clock, the plane touched down.

Since he had a two hour layover before the BWIA flight to Trinidad and he was hungry, he found one of the terminal cafeterias and got a hamburger. When he was done, he decided to go to a foreign exchange booth and trade some American dollars for Trinidad-Tobago dollars, or TT, as they were called. Then he caught the tram to the international terminal.

At the gate, he showed his passport and ticket to the clerk. She gave him a boarding pass. While he was waiting, he took a good look at the passengers that were getting ready to board the flight to Barbados, and then on to Port of Spain. They were a varied group, primarily of African, Spanish, and Indian descent. Kevin felt strange because, for the first time in his life, he was a minority. Now he was getting a little taste of what it was like to be different. He didn't like it.

After about thirty minutes, it was announced that boarding would begin. The crowd stirred and everyone started scurrying to the gate. Kevin gave the attendant his boarding pass, descended the long ramp to the plane and went aboard. He took his seat, anxious to get underway. The flight was sold out, so he knew someone would be sitting next to him. He watched the passengers file by, wondering who it would be. A tall Hispanic man, weighing at least three hundred pounds, hesitated in front of his row. *Please, . . . keep going.*

Finally a pretty black girl stopped, took a look at the seat number and dropped her carry-on luggage next to Kevin. Relieved, he smiled and greeted her as she sat down.

"Hi."

She didn't respond so he wondered if he should try to talk to her or just mind his own business. Her eyes didn't show any particular interest in him. After a few moments of silence, he couldn't resist the urge to talk.

"You going to Trinidad?" he said.

She looked at him for the first time and gave him a once over. "Yes."

"So am I. Do you live there?"

The young lady gave Kevin an annoyed look and replied cooly, "Yes, I live in Port of Spain."

"What do you do?"

"I'm a teacher."

"Oh, that's great. So what brought you to Florida?"

"I took a holiday. I've got some friends in Miami," she replied and then looked over at Kevin and smiled. "What brings you to Trinidad?"

"Just visiting," Kevin replied not feeling comfortable in divulging the actual purpose of his visit. "What do you teach?"

"History and Government."

"Oh, my favorite subjects. What grade level?"

"Secondary school."

"Hmm. That's cool."

"I hope it doesn't rain too much for you while you're visiting."

"Do you get a lot of rain in Trinidad?"

"Oh, yes. It usually rains everyday. We get about eighty inches per year. I get so tired of it sometimes."

"I don't know much about your country. I went to the library to learn as much as I could, but there isn't much on Trinidad at the Dallas County Library."

"Yes, Trinidad is very small country—about the size of your New Hampshire. We have only a little more than a million citizens."

"Your government was modeled after Great Britain, right?"

"Yes, how did you know that?"

"I read that in a travel book I found at the book store. I also know you have a Prime Minister."

"Right."

"Do you have a king?"

"Oh, no. We don't have a king, thank God."

"I thought, since your government was patterned after Great Britain, that you might."

"No. We have the Prime Minister and Parliament. That's about it, except the courts, of course."

"How many political parties do you have?"

"Quite a few, actually. To understand the political structure of our country, you've got to understand that about forty percent of the country is of African descent and represented by the PNM party. Another forty percent is Indian and represented by the UNC party. Right now the government is run by a coalition between the UNC party and the NAR party. It has been that way for the last five or six years. The PNM used to run the country, but it was ousted in the mid-nineties, in a very close election. There are numerous other minority parties."

"Hmm. Has Trinidad been pretty stable?"

"Oh, yes. There hasn't been any trouble here since the early 1970's, although someone tried to assassinate our Prime Minister when he was in Texas a few months ago."

Kevin took a deep breath.

"Yeah, I know about that. Who do you think was behind it?"

"I'm not sure, but a lot of people don't like how the Prime Minister has embraced the United States and committed Trinidad to the Caribbean Free Trade Agreement."

"Why wouldn't Trinidad want free trade?"

"Oh, I don't know. I guess some people are afraid all the big U.S. companies will come to Trinidad and gain control over the economy. The people of Trinidad are fiercely independent. We like Americans, but we don't want to be controlled by them, or anyone else for that matter."

"I can certainly understand that."

"Well, I hope you have a nice visit to Trinidad."

"I imagine I will."

The young lady laid her head back and closed her eyes. Kevin was starting to get tired as well. He had been up since five in the morning. By this time, the plane had taken off and was heading south over the Caribbean. Kevin peered out the window and looked down at the vast ocean. He was amazed at the large number of beautiful islands that were appearing and disappearing beneath him. Occasionally, he would see a cruise ship or a freighter below and wonder about its destination. The flight attendants strolled the aisle, serving snacks. When he had finished his, he started reading a paperback he had purchased in Miami. Finally, the plane began its descent into Barbados.

Kevin observed the fine beaches and fancy hotels as

the plane landed. He wished he had a few days to check them out. After dropping off quite a few passengers and picking up others, the plane was once again in the air. Kevin resumed reading his paperback. An hour and a half later, the captain announced that he was preparing for the final descent into Port of Spain. The flight attendants gave each passenger a custom's declaration form to be filled out prior to landing. Kevin filled his out and then anxiously awaited his arrival.

As he looked out the window at the island beneath him, he wondered if Kiran would be there to meet him. He figured that would probably be too much to expect. More likely, he would be met by some low-level diplomat, or perhaps a police detective, whose job it would be to transport him the Prime Minister's home. It didn't really matter who met him. Soon he would see Kiran. It was just a matter of time now.

The plane came to a stop. Everyone got up, grabbed their carry-on luggage and began to deplane. Kevin followed the passengers in front of him off the big jet. When he got onto the pavement, he saw everyone was going into a small hangar that had been converted into a customs office. He followed the crowd inside and got in one of the five lines. After thirty minutes, he made it to the front of the line and was called up to a customs official.

"Passport, please," the officer said.

Kevin handed his passport and customs declaration to the officer. He opened it, inspected the declaration and asked, "What business do you have in Trinidad?"

"The Prime Minister invited me. He's supposed to have someone here to meet me."

The officer gave Kevin a skeptical look.

"The Prime Minister? Ahmad Shah?" he asked.

"Exactly."

"How long will you be here?"

"A week or ten days."

"Where will you be staying?"

"With the Prime Minister."

The officer gave Kevin a hard look. "Does he know you're coming?"

"Of course, he invited me."

"You would think someone in the travel office would have alerted us," he said as he stamped the passport shaking his head. "All right. Have a nice stay in Trinidad."

"Thanks."

Kevin walked out of the hanger and followed several passengers into the main terminal of the airport. He looked around, wondering if someone was going to be there to pick him up. He was a little scared, as the airport was very small and kind of run down. The lobby was filled with all kinds of people; African, Anglo, Spanish, Indian, French and Chinese. Most of them were not well dressed, and Kevin, coming from one of the wealthiest communities in the United States, was understandably uneasy. He scanned the lobby for a sign with his name, or someone who looked like a government official.

After fifteen minutes had passed, he decided he had better go get his luggage. He followed the signs to the baggage area and searched through the bags that were stacked up against the wall. When he found his suitcase, he carried it to the middle of the room. There he stood for a while wondering what he should do. After some thought, he decided to go to the front of the terminal and see if his escort might be out there. He followed the foot traffic outside to the front of the terminal. Immediately, he was bombarded by a dozen taxi drivers wanting to take him to his destination. A couple of them grabbed his suitcase and began fighting over it. Kevin got in the middle of them and took it back.

He walked quickly down the sidewalk, waving the taxi drivers off. Looking around anxiously, he saw a sign that read—*Don't ride with un-licensed taxi drivers*. Confused and becoming worried, he began to get angry. *I can't believe this! There should be someone here to pick me up. Jesus, the Prime Minister begs me to come down here, then doesn't have the courtesy to send someone to pick me up.*

When his anger subsided, he started to contemplate what to do if someone didn't come to meet him. He figured he'd have to find a phone and call the Prime Minister's office or perhaps the U.S. Embassy. With another rush of anger sweeping over him, he started looking around for a phone. Not seeing any in sight, he was about to go back inside the terminal when a short, friendly looking black man approached him.

"Kevin Wells?" he asked.

Relief, like a fresh breeze, swept over him. "Yes, that's me."

"Hello, I'm Obatala, I'll be your driver while you're staying in Trinidad."

"Oh, great. Did the Prime Minister send you?"

"The Prime Minister? Oh yes, the Prime Minister is very anxious to see you."

"Oh, good. I've been waiting here for almost an hour."

"I'm sorry, traffic was very heavy. Don't worry though, I'll take you right away to his office."

"Is he there now? It's kind of late. I think you're supposed to take me to his house. I'm supposed to stay there while I'm in Trinidad."

Obatala picked up Kevin's luggage, avoiding eye contact.

"Okay. My car is over here," he said.

Kevin followed him as he made his way through the crowded parking lot to his car. It was a very old Toyota Corolla. Kevin frowned. A cold chill suddenly engulfed him. The exterior was in good condition, but the inside was old and worn out. Kevin hesitated when Obatala opened the door to let him in. *They didn't even send someone in a government car? Give me a break.* He looked skeptically at

Obatala but not wanting to appear rude, he said, "Boy, this is really an antique. I have a 1985 Mazda that I thought was pretty old. What year car is this?"

"It's a 1971model."

"1971?"

"Right."

"Oh, then this obviously isn't a government car?"

"Oh, no, I own it myself. I bought it used in 1976. It has been quite reliable."

Kevin shook his head, got in and sat down. *God, this is a poor country. They make everyone use their own cars.* Obatala shut the door gently and ran around to the driver's side. He cranked the engine, but it wouldn't start. Kevin squinted and looked anxiously at Obatala. *I can't believe this.* A few more cranks and the engine finally started with a jolt. They took off and left the melee of taxi drivers behind. Kevin was surprised to see the cars driving on the left side of the street, rather than the right side. It seemed very strange and he was glad he wasn't going to have to drive while he was in Trinidad. Obatala drove fast, weaving in and out of traffic like an Indy driver. Kevin searched in vain for a seat belt.

"So how was your flight, Mr. Wells?" Obatala finally asked.

Obatala's friendly demeanor made Kevin feel a little better. As they talked he became more at ease and less concerned about the odd manner in which he was welcomed to Trinidad. "Fine, I met one of your high school teachers on the plane and she told me all about Trinidad. She was very nice. Talking to her made the trip seem much shorter."

"Yes, we have many fine teachers in Trinidad. My wife is a teacher. She may know her. Did she tell you to what school she was attached?"

"No, I wish I would have asked her, but I didn't. She told me a little bit about your political system, especially the

UNC-NAR coalition and the PNC."

"You mean the PNM. The Peoples' National Movement."

"Yeah, right. All of those abbreviations are kind of confusing."

"Yes they are, until you get used to them. You know the PNM ran this country for over thirty years."

"Thirty years?"

"That's right. It was a great shock when the UNC got control. No one could believe it. Pretty soon the PNM will take back control of the government."

Kevin frowned, shocked by the glee in Obatala's voice. "Oh really? Is that what the Prime Minister thinks?"

"No, he's too stupid to figure out that his time is about up. The NAR will withdraw their support soon and his government will fall like a brick."

Obatala's statement jolted Kevin, the cold chill he had earlier felt returned with the vengeance of a blue norther. "Huh?" he said, suddenly realizing Obatala hadn't been sent by the Prime Minister to pick him up. *Oh shit! . . . Who is this guy and where in the hell is he taking me?*

Kevin didn't want Obatala to know he was scared so he went along with the charade as if he suspected nothing. "Ah. . . . Where does the Prime Minister live anyway?"

"He lives in the bourgeoisie section of town. It's just forty-five minutes from the airport."

*Bourgeoisie? Oh, God. I've been kidnaped by communist. . . .* Kevin bit his lip. He looked back to see if anyone was following them. He couldn't tell with so much traffic. He began to shake, fear overwhelmed him. *Okay, relax. Take a deep breath. Don't let him know you suspect anything. . . .* "I bet everyone was upset when the Prime Minister was attacked in Dallas."

"No, actually a lot of people were wishing the assassin had done his job."

Kevin sunk back in his seat. He felt sharp pains shoot

through his neck and shoulders. His head started to throb. This sure wasn't the reception he had been expecting from the people of Trinidad. He peered out the window of the cab and noted they were traveling through a slum area. He considered opening the door and jumping out of the car, but the thought of being the only white boy in a black slum was not too appealing.

"So, are you staying for Carnival, Mr. Wells?"

"Huh?" Kevin murmurred.

"Carnival. Will you be staying for it?"

"I don't know. When does it start?"

"It starts in about ten days, but next week there will be all kinds of things going on to get ready for it. Do you like the calypso?"

Kevin hesitated. *Okay, get a grip. You're overreacting. Don't be paronoid.* "I don't know. I've heard of calypso, but I'm not really that familiar with it."

"Calypso originated in Trinidad and is very popular here. Before Carnival there are dozens of tournaments and competitions to find the best performers to participate in Carnival."

"Hmm. That does sound interesting. I'd really like to see it."

"If you'd like, I'll take you to see the Calypso competitions at the Queen's Park Savanna this weekend."

"Well, I don't know. I'm not sure what my schedule will be like."

"Just call me if you'd like to go. I'll take you there, or anywhere else, day or night."

"That's really nice of you. If I need any transportation, I'll keep you in mind."

Kevin's anxiety began to wane again as he continued to talk to Obatala. Although he wasn't a supporter of the Prime Minister, he seemed to be a decent person. As the old Toyota made its way through the streets of Port of Spain, Obatala enthusiastically pointed out all of the landmarks of interest and answered most of Kevin's questions about the country. Kevin took in the sights and sounds of the city with great interest. He noticed that overall, the city was old and not well maintained. The people were obviously poor and struggling for survival. For the first time in his life, he began to understand what the term–third world country–meant.

Finally, Obatala pulled into the bourgeoisie neighborhood and advised Kevin that they were coming up to the Prime Minister's residence. Kevin felt better at being in a neighborhood more like his own.

"See, these are the big houses that the rich people of Port of Spain live in."

"Oh really, what does a house like this cost?"

"Most of them are around a million dollars."

"Trinidad dollars?"

"American dollars."

"Really? These houses wouldn't go for more than two hundred thousand dollars in Dallas."

"Prices are high for luxury items in Trinidad."

"I guess so."

Obatala pointed ahead.

"There is the Prime Minister's home."

Kevin looked at the mansion ahead with great interest. It was a fairly new, yellow stucco building, maybe five thousand square feet he guessed. It was nicely landscaped and there was a large swimming pool along the side. A fence totally encircled the residence and two guards were stationed at the front gate. Obatala pulled the Toyota up to the gate and Kevin got out and walked up to one of the guards.

"Hi, I'm Kevin Wells from Texas. The Prime Minister invited me to stay with him for a week or so."

"Kevin who?"

"Wells. The Attorney General asked me to come to Trinidad to participate in a line up. I'm supposed to stay with the Prime Minister while I'm here."

"The Prime Minister is out this evening. There's no one here."

"Well, can I wait for them? I came all the way from Texas. I don't have any place else to go."

"I'm sorry, but no one is allowed to loiter around the Prime Minister's residence. You'll have to move on."

"But, isn't there someone you can call? Like the Attorney General, maybe? He's expecting me."

"I don't have a telephone out here. I'm sorry. Come back in the morning."

"In the morning? Where am I supposed to stay tonight?"

"Come on, Kevin," Obatala said putting his hand on Kevin's shoulder. "I'll take you to the Trinidad Hilton. You can stay there tonight."

Kevin looked at Obatala in disbelief. "How much will that cost? This trip wasn't supposed to cost me anything. I can't believe this! Jesus, I should have never come here."

"See why we need a new government? Prime Minister Shah is a disgrace. He doesn't even know how to treat his own guests. Don't worry though. I'll take you wherever you want to go. Are you hungry?"

Kevin turned and walked slowly to the car. "Yes, actually I am kind of hungry."

"How about a giant steak?"

"Sure, that would be great."

Kevin got back in the car and Obatala took off, heading back toward downtown. When they passed the U.S. embassy, Obatala pointed it out to Kevin. Then he drove down a dark, deserted street and parked in front of what looked like a warehouse. It had a small sign near the door that read: *The King's Place Restaurant*. They got out of the car and went inside. The interior of the busy restaurant was ornately decorated in red and gold drapery and linens. A hostess directed them to a table. They sat down and began to look at the menu.

"I think I'll go for the ribeye," Kevin said. "What are you going to have?"

"Oh, nothing. I'll just wait for you to eat and then take you to your hotel."

"Nonsense, I'm buying. What do you want?"

"Oh, I couldn't impose. I'm just your driver."

"I don't care, order something."

Obatala hesitated, but finally picked up the menu and started to study it. It wasn't long before the waiter came and asked for their orders.

"I'll take the ribeye, medium," Kevin said.

"Give me the prime rib," Obatala added.

"Is the prime rib good here? I was considering that too," Kevin said.

"It's excellent here. This place has the best steaks in Trinidad."

"I hope you're right."

"Just wait, you'll see."

"Will you take me to the U.S. Embassy in the morning? I think I'll go there and try to straighten this mess out. They knew I was coming, so they should be able to help me make contact with the right people in the government."

"Yes, of course. I'll pick you up at eight-thirty, unless you want to stay at my home tonight?"

"Stay with you?"

"Yes, my wife would be pleased to keep you. Our house is modest, but we have an extra room, since my brother is away."

"Your brother lives with you?"

"Yes, and his family. But he and his wife are away on holiday. We are watching his three children."

As the two men were talking, the waiter brought their steaks. They started eating and continued their conversation.

"Do you have your own children?"

"Yes, three."

"Oh my God, you've got ten people living in your house?"

"Unless my mother-in-law is visiting, then we have eleven."

"I think I better stay at the hotel, I wouldn't want to impose."

"Whatever pleases you, but it wouldn't be a bit of trouble. Really. My wife's a great cook. She'd fix you up a fine American breakfast."

"That's really nice of you, but I couldn't impose. She must have her hands full, with both you and your brother's kids, not to mention working."

"I help her as much as I can, when I'm not on the job myself."

"So, do you make a good living as a taxi driver?"

"I do quite well. I do best during Carnival. I make half of my annual income during the two weeks when all the tourists come."

"Really? Carnival must be some celebration here. I wish I could stay for it, but I think I'll be leaving about the time it starts."

"You should stay, there's nothing like it in the world."

After dinner, Kevin paid the check with the Visa card his dad lent him for the trip, then they headed for the Hilton Hotel. When they arrived, Kevin went up to the front desk to see about a room. A tall, thin desk clerk was on duty.

"I'd like a room please," Kevin said.

"I'm sorry, but we're full tonight, you know, with the Calypso competition and all."

"Really. Shoot. Are there any other hotels around where I could stay?"

"You might want to try the Holiday Inn. I'll call them, if you like?"

"Great."

The desk clerk called the Holiday Inn, but they were full too. He tried several other places, but none of them had a vacancy. Kevin was beginning to panic. *Where in the hell am I going to stay? Damn it. I can't sleep in the street–not in this god-forsaken country. Should I stay with Obatala? He seems nice, but who the hell is he anyway? He obviously doesn't work for the Prime Minister. Oh, God. What is going on?* Kevin looked back worriedly at Obatala, who was waiting to see that he got a room. He thanked the desk clerk and walked back to the car.

"Well, I hate to impose on you, but it seems there's not a hotel room available anywhere tonight. Are you sure your wife won't mind if I stay with you?"

"No, no. It is our pleasure to have you. Come, we'll drive home right away. You must be very tired."

"I *am* beat. It's been a very long day."

As the old Toyota rattled along the bumpy streets of Trinidad, Kevin desperately tried to analyze his situation. Obatala seemed friendly, but he could imagine the conditions he must be living in. He was grateful he had a place to stay and someone to drive him wherever he wanted to go, but he was still apprehensive. He closed his eyes and prayed that he would make it through the night.

When they arrived at Obatala's home, it wasn't nearly as bad as Kevin had imagined. It was small, but very clean. Obatala's wife and several of the children were sitting in the kitchen when Kevin walked in. A woman stood up to greet him.

Obatala said, "Kevin, this is my wife, Cetawayo."

Kevin nodded and said, "Nice to meet you, ma'am."

"These are my children, Kemba, Taiwo and Atiba."

"Hi, guys," Kevin said as he shook each of their hands.

"I don't know where everyone else is, but they'll show up eventually."

Kevin gave the children a hard look, then glanced at Cetawayo and Obatala who were holding hands. "Boy, you've got some good looking kids. Let me see, do they take after their mother or their dad?"

"They're look quite a lot like their father, actually," Cetawayo replied.

"I hope you don't mind having me stay here tonight. I can't believe there isn't a single hotel room in the entire city."

"Yes, I'm afraid it will be that way until Carnival is over. But don't worry. You're welcome to stay here."

"Thank you. . . . So you're a teacher?"

"Yes, I am," Cetawayo replied.

"My mom's a teacher. She teaches math."

"Oh, I'm not good at math. I prefer liberal arts."

"Really? So do I."

"So how do you like our country so far, Kevin?"

"Oh, it seems really nice, but I just got here. I haven't had time to enjoy it yet."

"I think you'll like it."

"I'm sure I will."

"Kevin got stood up by the Prime Minister," Obatala noted. "He was supposed to be staying with him tonight."

"The Prime Minister? Why would you be staying with him?"

"I met his daughter while they were in Texas a couple of weeks ago. They invited me down here."

"Oh, the Indian girls, they love white boys," Obatala said.

Kevin laughed, "Is that right?"

"Yes, without a doubt."

"Well I hope Kiran likes me, she's very beautiful."

"She's a manipulator like her mother," Cetawayo advised. "Be careful."

"How do you know that?" Kevin asked.

"That's what they say in the *Express*. She always manages to get what she wants, no matter what the cost."

"The *Express*?"

"It's our primary newspaper, the *Daily Express*."

"Well, you can't believe everything you read, I guess,"

Kevin said. "I hope they're wrong."

"Okay," Cetawayo said, "we should let Kevin get some rest. He's had a long day. Come on Kevin, I'll take you to my brother's room."

"Thank you. You've all been very kind."

Cetawayo took Kevin to a small room with a double bed. It was covered with pictures and memorabilia of the family. Kevin said good night and closed the door. As he was getting undressed, he couldn't help but look at the dozens of pictures of the family that decorated the room. He looked at a picture of the kids swimming in the public pool, another of them playing cricket and a family portrait taken in Queen's Park. Kevin picked up the group picture and sat on the end of bed. He couldn't believe he was in some taxi driver's home, in the middle of Trinidad. He chuckled. If his mother knew where he was right now, she'd die.

As he continued to study the picture, he squinted to get a better focus on Obatala's brother. A cold chill suddenly engulfed him as he recognized the face. *Oh, my God! This can't be happening. It's not possible. Please, Lord, . . . no. I can't be sleeping in Ray Mohammed's bedroom!*

# Chapter 9

The iron gate began to retract, allowing the black Mercedes to enter the Prime Minister's driveway. The driver pulled the car through the gate and into the garage. The Prime Minister and his family got out and walked to the side door. Anamica, the Prime Minister's personal secretary fumbled around in her purse until she finally found the key to the inside door. She opened it and they all went inside. Anamica went straight for the Prime Minister's office to check for messages. The red light on the answering machine was blinking, so she hit the play button. The Prime Minister, who had followed her to his office, stood at the door to listen before going to bed.

"Beep. . . Beep. . . Beep. Ahmad–Sharad here. Sorry to call you so late, but we've just been informed by the U.S. Embassy that Kevin Wells arrived in Trinidad today! We have no explanation as to why he came early. We're looking for him right now, but have yet to find him. He's not at any of the hotels in the city. We've checked them all. We're in the process of calling hospitals and the city jail. I'm afraid a kidnaping can't be ruled out."

The Prime Minister smashed his fist against the doorjamb.

"Damn it! How could this happen! Who made the arrangements for Mr. Wells? I want an explanation, now!"

Anamica leaped into action.

"I'll call the director of the travel office immediately," she assured him.

A minute later, there was a knock at the door. A servant

answered it and escorted a slim, medium height male into the house.

"Ahmad, I'm glad you're back," Sharad said. "Did you get my message?"

"I'm afraid so," the Prime Minister replied. "How could this happen? This is pitiful. We invite a national hero to our country and he gets kidnaped. Can you imagine how the leaders of the PNM will be howling when they hear about this? They couldn't be responsible, could they?"

"I seriously doubt it. It would be suicide for their party if they were behind it. Besides, it goes against all the principles they espouse. No, I believe it's the work of the NDC."

"You're probably right. Those lunatics would do anything to embarrass me."

"So what do want me to do now? We've checked all the hotels, hospitals and police stations. He's nowhere to be found."

"Are you sure he really is in Port of Spain?"

"Yes, we've got his customs declaration and the customs agent has identified him from a picture we showed him."

"Damn it! How could this happen? Someone's going to pay for this!" the Prime Minister screamed. "What did you tell the U.S. Embassy when they advised you he was in Trinidad?"

"I told them there must have been a change in plans and I was sure he was with you. I told them I would find out for sure and let them know."

"If you tell them the truth, they'll inform his parents and then it will all be over. My God! Something like this could bring down our government."

"I have news, sir," Anamica said as she walked in.

"What is it?"

"One of our guards has advised me that a young American, matching the description of Mr. Wells, stopped by here earlier tonight, but they thought he was just a tourist. So they sent him away."

"Oh! How idiotic! Bring me the guard!"

"One more thing, sir"

"What?"

"I have made a determination as to why Mr. Wells came to Trinidad a day early."

"Tell me. Don't dilly dally, woman."

"Someone canceled the travel reservations that we had made for Mr. Wells. I can only surmise they sent him an alternative itinerary, with the appropriate airline tickets. He would have no reason to suspect that he was being deceived."

"Damn it! Don't we have any security in the travel office? See if you can find out who canceled those reservations, but first bring me the guard."

"Yes, sir."

"We've got to find him before morning, Sharad. If we don't, we'll look like we're incompetent. Oh God! Can you believe this rotten turn of events?"

"No, it's very unsettling."

"I was so certain that, with a quick arrest and trial of Ray Mohammed, the people of Trinidad would rally behind the UNC and finally make us the majority party. But now, my plan may destroy us!"

"Don't panic, Ahmad. We've been through worse situations than this. We'll figure something out."

Anamica entered with the guard.

"Here is Mr. Jain, the guard I spoke to you about."

"Good. What is this about the young American coming by here tonight?"

"Yes, sir. He came by around six-thirty. I checked the guest log and it did not show that anyone was expected."

"What did he tell you?"

"He said he was supposed to stay with you tonight. I told him you would not be in all evening, so he should come back in the morning."

"Mr. Jain, do you read the newspaper or pay the least bit of attention as to what is going on in our country? Didn't you recognize that this was Kevin Wells, the man who saved my life?"

"I'm so sorry, sir. It just didn't register, I guess. I'm totally humiliated. Please forgive me."

"No–I can't be surrounded by idiots. You are relieved of your duty. Report to your commander for further orders."

"Yes, sir."

Mr. Jain left and Anamica followed to begin the task of determining who had canceled Kevin's reservations. The Prime Minister walked over to an overstuffed chair and collapsed.

"I need a drink. Somebody get me a drink! Forget the drink, bring me the bloody bottle! Bring one for Sharad too."

"No, thank you, Ahmad. I must go and direct the search for Mr. Wells. Forget the bottle, you should go to bed. No matter what fortune lays before us, you can bet you will need all of your strength to deal with it tomorrow. Go to bed, Ahmad, go to bed."

Sharad Mishratt and Ahmad Shah had been close friends since secondary school. They had struggled together to make it to the top of the UNC. They worked ten long years for their party, until it finally took power. Just a year ago, Ahmad had unexpectedly been chosen as Prime Minister when the elected Prime Minister became ill. He immediately appointed Sharad his attorney general and he quickly became his most trusted confidant.

"I will. Don't worry, Sharad. I'll be all right. I'll see you in the morning."

"Good night, Ahmad."

A servant brought Ahmad a bottle of rum. Ahmad unscrewed the cap, took one swig and then another. After a few minutes of reflection, he went to bed. Anila was waiting for him anxiously.

"Have they found Kevin?" Anila asked.

"No, but they will. They have to. Otherwise, we're lost. Our coalition with the UAR isn't strong enough to withstand such a scandal."

"I'm so worried, Ahmad. Kiran and Deviane are quite upset too. They were so much looking forward to entertaining this Kevin boy."

"They won't be disappointed. Sharad will find him. He's never let me down before."

Ahmad lay back in his bed. Anila came over and put her head on his shoulder. He began to stroke her long black hair. Anila was a beautiful woman, a beauty queen who had gone to work for BWIA as a flight attendant. He had met her while traveling and fell in love with her immediately. She didn't respond to him at first, as he wasn't the handsomest of men, but his persistence finally won her over. One night, her flight took her to Caracas. Ahmad managed to be there while she had an overnight layover. When she got to her hotel room, it was filled with twelve dozen roses. In one of the arrangements, there was a card from Ahmad asking Anila to dinner. She accepted. From that day forward, she began to take this young suitor seriously. A year later, they were married and Anila had been very happy ever since.

Anila was very outgoing and loved society. She was the perfect politician's wife, always on top of every social event and involved in every charity imaginable. Many said she was as much responsible for Ahmad becoming Prime Minister as he was himself. Now, Ahmad was scaring her with this talk of the government's downfall. She knew it would happen one day, but it was too soon, there was so much she had yet to do.

"It isn't fair," she began to sob, as she contemplated her world falling apart.

"Go to sleep, Anila. Don't cry. Sharad will find him. I know he will."

# Chapter 10

Kevin's mind went into a tailspin. *What is Obatala up to? Did he lure me here to kill me? But why did he take me to the prime minister's residence? That doesn't make any sense. Wait a minute, of course, he must have known the guard would chase me away. He knew there were no hotel rooms at the Hilton. It was all a scheme to gain my trust so I wouldn't resist.*

"Oh, shit. I'm a dead man! Oh, God, I can't believe this."

Kevin fell back onto the bed and stared at the ceiling. He remembered seeing a telephone in the living room. Perhaps he could sneak in there and make a phone call. Then he realized he wouldn't know who to call. Obviously, they didn't have 911. He wouldn't know how to explain where he was anyway. Besides, several of the kids must sleep in the living room. It would be rather difficult to get in there and make a phone call without being detected.

Kevin finally decided to push the bureau in front of the door, so no one could get in during the night without waking him up. After he had done that, he searched the room for weapons. All he could find was a cricket bat so he placed it on the bed next to him. He was determined to stay awake all night, but he was so tired he started to doze off almost immediately. His head fell to the side momentarily, until he caught himself and straightened up. He rubbed his eyes and then stretched, trying to stay awake. Suddenly, he heard someone walking in the hallway in front of his room. He got up and grabbed the cricket bat, ready to do combat.

His eyes were glued on the doorknob, but it didn't move.

He finally decided no one was coming in, so he sat back down on the bed. He looked at the window and suddenly realized he was a sitting duck for a gunman looking in from the outside. Quickly, he rolled off the bed onto the floor. He pulled off the bedspread and laid it out to sleep on. Then he took a pillow and laid back, wondering if he'd make it through the night. He finally succumbed to his exhaustion and fell asleep.

The next morning, Kevin woke up with a headache and a sharp pain in his back. He looked around the room momentarily disoriented. Then the memory of his perilous predicament started to come back. He sat up quickly and looked around. The bureau was still in front of the door, so it was apparent to him that no one had tried to enter during the night.

After considerable deliberation, Kevin decided he had no choice but to let Obatala play his cards. If he had wanted to kill him, he could have already done it. Besides, if he *were* going to kill him, he certainly wouldn't do it in front of his wife and children. After putting the bureau back in its place and straightening the room, Kevin opened the door.

The aroma of sizzling bacon was in the air. Kevin walked cautiously out of the bedroom, down a short hallway and into the kitchen. Cetawayo was in the process of cooking breakfast. She smiled at Kevin when she saw him.

"Did you sleep well, Mr. Kevin?"

"Pretty well," he said forcing a smile. He scanned the room quickly.

"Good. I understand you've got a big day ahead."

"I don't know. I'm not so sure anymore. I may go back to Texas if the Prime Minister doesn't get his act together."

"Come, sit down. Are you hungry?"

He nodded. "Yes, famished."

Kevin sat down and Cetawayo set a plate in front of him.

As he started to eat, Obatala walked in the room. Kevin looked up. *Okay, now what? Do I confront you or play dumb? What in the hell do you want with me?*

"Ah ha, you're up," Obatala noted.

"Yes. Good morning," Kevin said.

Obatala smiled broadly. "Yes, isn't it. How do you feel? Did you get a good night's sleep?"

"Pretty good."

"How is your breakfast?"

Kevin looked at Cetawayo and smiled. "Very good. I wasn't expecting an American breakfast."

"Well, Cetawayo wanted you to feel at home."

Kevin's head began to throb. He rubbed his temples.

"Are you okay?" Obatala asked.

Kevin looked up. "I guess," he said, taking a deep breath. "Listen, you don't have to pretend anymore. . . . I saw the picture of your brother in his room. I know who he is. So, obviously, my being here isn't by chance, is it?"

Obatala looked anxiously at Cetawayo. She turned and walked back to the sink. He took a deep breath and looked back at Kevin. "Okay," he said as he sat down next to him. He began in a low voice. "I want to apologize for tricking you into coming to my house, but I had no choice. I had to talk to you before you met with the police."

"Why?"

"It's my brother, Ray Mohammed. I know you're here to identify him as the person who shot you and tried to kill the Prime Minister."

"How did you know that?"

"The government is not very good at keeping secrets, I'm afraid. There was a story about you coming here two weeks ago. I checked with some friends in the Attorney General's office and they told me it was true."

"So, what was so important that you had to kidnap me? Why didn't you just write me a letter?"

"My brother is a good man. He has a great wife and

wonderful children."

"So wonderful he tried to assassinate the Prime Minister, not to mention shooting me in the back."

"You don't understand. I'm not sure how it happened, but somehow Ray got involved with the NDC. It's a radical party that thrives on anti-American propaganda. Its leaders are ruthless scoundrels that would just as soon slit your throat as shake your hand."

"Yeah, I've heard of them."

"They don't believe in democracy. They have no morality. They will do what ever it takes to take over the government so they can create a dictatorship. Ray fell for their propaganda that several big U.S. companies controlled Trinidad and that the Caribbean Free Trade Agreement would only help increase America's stronghold on the Trinidad economy. He was brainwashed into thinking that by killing the Prime Minister, he would be saving the country from American imperialism. My brother is very impressionable and very naive. He was chosen for the job because he was an expert marksman in the Trinidad army."

"So you think, by bringing me here and telling me all this, that I'd feel sorry for Ray and his family and fail to recognize him when I saw him in the lineup?"

"Something like that."

"Well, despite everything that has happened, I like you, Obatala. You seem like a decent man and you've got a good wife and nice kids, but I can't lie to the police to protect your brother. It wouldn't be right. I feel badly that he has ruined his life for a bunch of hoodlums, but there's nothing I can do about that."

"Please, Kevin. The Prime Minister wasn't killed. You've recovered from your injuries. Now you are a quite famous lad. Would it hurt to let Ray go? He just made a mistake. Please give him a chance."

"You're asking me to commit perjury and risk going to

prison myself? Why should I do that? It would be stupid on my part."

"You don't have to lie, just tell them you're not sure if he's the one. No one can fault you if your memory is not perfect."

"Stop the lying!" Cetawayo screamed. "Why don't you just tell Kevin the truth?"

Kevin looked at Cetawayo.

"If you don't tell him, I will. . . . I'm so sorry, Kevin, to have to tell you this. Obatala was sent to pick you up and to take you to Ray, so he and his friends could kill you. He only went along with it because he knew if he didn't pick you up, someone else would. He figured he could hide you here. He knew Ray wouldn't kill you in front of me and the children."

Kevin just looked at Obatala. Then he shook his head, pushed out his chair and stood up.

"I think it's time you took me to the American Embassy. I'm sorry about your brother. I really am, but he's a grown man and he's responsible for his actions. I appreciate the fact that you protected me from him, but do you really want him to get away with what he's done? I don't think you do."

"Are you going to turn me in for kidnaping you?"

Kevin smiled and replied, "What do you mean? You took me into your home when I couldn't find lodging. You fed me and entertained me. That's hardly kidnaping. I *am* curious though–how you managed to get me here a day early."

"It was simple. Anyone can call the airlines and cancel reservations."

"Right."

"Well, I called the airlines and canceled your reservations. Then I bought you a new ticket for a day earlier. Do you remember getting the new tickets in the mail?"

"Yeah, there was a letter from the Attorney General

saying the dates of the trip had been altered slightly, and that these were my new tickets."

"See how easy it was? I just made up a letterhead and signed the Attorney General's name."

"That's incredible."

"I just wish I could have stopped Ray from going to Dallas. I tried, but he wouldn't listen. His heart is so full of hatred. I worry about his children."

"Luckily, they'll have you to raise them. They may be better off without your brother."

Obatala didn't respond, but only hung his head. Kevin left the room to get his luggage. Before he left, he thanked Cetawayo for her hospitality and said goodbye to the children. It took about twenty minutes for Obatala to get through rush hour traffic and make it to the American Embassy. Obatala dropped Kevin off a block away and drove away. Kevin walked down the street and into the embassy, hoping his second day in Trinidad would be a vast improvement over his first. If it wasn't, he vowed to be on the next plane back to America.

# Chapter 11

Kevin saw a receptionist seated just inside the doorway. He paused a second to look at the beautiful interior of the building, then proceeded to her station. She looked up and he smiled at him.

"Hi, I'm Kevin Wells. I'm having some trouble making connections with the Prime Minister. I wonder if you could help me out?"

"Did you say Kevin Wells?"

"Yes."

"Oh, thank God! Everyone's been looking for you. I've already had three calls in the last hour. Sit down. Let me tell the Ambassador you're here. Oh, what a relief."

The receptionist punched four digits on her telephone and waited.

"Sir, he's here. Kevin Wells is sitting right here. He just walked in," the receptionist smiled gleefully at Kevin. "He's coming up to get you. Where in God's name have you been? Everyone has been worried sick about you."

Kevin looked to the left when he heard the floor creak as the Ambassador walked briskly into the reception area. He was a tall, heavyset man with gray hair and a round face. He was flanked by two aides, and Sharad Mishratt.

"Mr. Wells. I am so relieved to see you. There's been a nationwide search for you. We feared you had been kidnaped."

"Kidnaped? Oh, no."

"Well, where have you been?"

"When I arrived yesterday, no one was there to meet

me so I got a cab and went to the Prime Minister's house. They told me to come back in the morning. I had the cab driver take me somewhere to eat."

"We heard the guard turned you away last night. He's already been demoted for such stupidity."

"Demoted? Oh, that wasn't necessary."

"So where did you stay? We checked all the hotels."

"All the hotels were full, so the cab driver took pity on me and let me crash at his place."

"You've got to be joking? Who was this cab driver?"

"Gee, I don't know. He had some African name. I never did quite catch it."

"This is unbelievable. If the wrong people had found out you were out there alone, you could have been killed."

"Killed? Who would want to kill me?"

"Well, I'm afraid the FBI didn't come totally clean with you, Kevin. I think you have a right to know though, since it's your life on the line here."

"Know what?"

"There are a lot of people here in Trinidad, who would like to see you dead. You see, there's a new anti-American political party that's got everybody stirred up over the Caribbean Free Trade Agreement. It's believed they were responsible for the attack on the Prime Minister's life. You're the only one who can prove the connection, so they would like you dead."

"Oh wonderful! No one ever told me my life would be in danger! My parents would never have let me come if they had known that."

"If you would like, I'll put you on the next plane back to Miami."

Kevin thought for a brief moment of Kiran and how close he was to being with her. He didn't feel scared anymore—now that he was at the embassy. *I can't leave without getting to know Kiran. What if she is the woman I've be looking for all these years?*

"Well, the government can protect me, can't they?" he heard himself say.

Sharad spoke up."Absolutely, Mr. Wells. Our government will take the utmost precaution to see that you're safe at all times."

"Forgive me, Kevin," the Ambassador said. "This is Sharad Mishratt, Trinidad's Attorney General. He's been up all night supervising the search for you."

The Attorney General bowed slightly and continued. "The Prime Minister has instructed me to tell you, so you will feel completely safe, that he will have his two daughters, Kiran and Deviane, travel with you at all times."

Kevin's eyes lit up. *At all times?* "What are we waiting for then? Let's go."

The Attorney General smiled triumphantly and motioned for one of his men to take Kevin's luggage. Kevin followed them outside to several black Mercedes parked on the side of the embassy grounds. Kevin got in the back seat of one of the cars with the Attorney General, and they were off.

The three cars drove north, in the direction of the Prime Minister's residence. They traveled out of downtown, past Queen's Park. After fifteen minutes or so, they arrived at the Prime Minister's home. The steel gates opened and the car drove into the garage. Kevin was excited, as he knew he was close to seeing Kiran. It wouldn't be long now until they were together.

"Come on in, Kevin," Sharad said. "The Prime Minister is waiting for you in his office."

Kevin followed Sharad through the kitchen, down a hallway and into the Prime Minister's office. The Prime Minister jumped to his feet as Kevin walked in.

"Oh, my God! Mr. Wells, you don't know how happy I am to see you. We had feared the worst. Are you okay?"

"Sure, I'm fine."

"I heard a taxi driver kept you last night?"

"Yes, he and his family were very nice."

"You must tell me who he is, so I can give him my personal thanks for keeping you safe."

"Well, I'd like to, but I don't remember his name. It was a kind of a different name. I just don't remember it."

"Well, could you point out where he lives?"

Kevin laughed.

"Are you kidding? I don't know Trinidad at all and he went on so many different streets. There's no way I could ever find it again."

"Well, that's a shame. I should have liked to reward him." The Prime Minister thought for a second and then said, "Well, Sharad, we won't be needing you until Monday, so you may go. Thank you for working so hard to find Mr. Wells. Go home and go to bed."

"Thank you. I'll do that."

Sharad shook Kevin's hand, nodded to the Prime Minister and then left.

"We've planned a full weekend for you here in Trinidad, Mr. Wells. My daughters will accompany you around Port of Spain. I think they are even going to take you to the beach. You do like to swim, don't you?"

"Oh yes, absolutely. As a matter of fact, I'm on the swim team at my high school."

"Are you? Then I won't need to send along a lifeguard, I guess? Ha! Ha!"

"No, I wouldn't think so."

"What's your event? Is that what you call it? I followed the swim team a little at Harvard, when I was there in the late sixties."

"Breast stroke mainly, but I do a little diving too."

"Oh, I bet the girls would like to see you dive. Maybe you can put on a little exhibition for us at the pool, before you leave?"

"Sure, if you'd like."

"Fine. You must be tired. Why don't I have someone take your bags to the guestroom so you can get settled and take a nap before lunch? I think the girls have something arranged for this afternoon."

Kevin smiled and replied, "Thank you. I'm looking forward to seeing your wife and daughters."

"Good then, lunch will be at twelve-thirty. See you then."

"Great."

The Prime Minister pushed a button on his desk. Before long, a servant came and showed Kevin to his room. He deposited his luggage next to the bed and looked around. It was a spacious room, ornately decorated in Indian decor, with a private bathroom attached. Kevin looked at his watch and noted it was ten-thirty a.m. He figured he had plenty of time until lunch, so as the Prime Minister had suggested, he laid down for a nap. Not wanting to be late for lunch, he set the alarm on his watch for noon. Kevin didn't realize how tired he was until his head hit the pillow. He fell asleep immediately.

As he drifted from his conscious state he found himself back in Dallas at the convention center. He looked into the orchestra pit. There was Ray Mohammed staring at him. He ducked out of the side door. Then he saw the laser dot on the Prime Minister's head. He started running, dodging the Secret Service Agent he lifted his arms and yelled for the Prime Minister to get down. Then he felt the sting of the bullet and the excruciating pain in his lung. He couldn't breathe, he began to gasp for air. When he opened his eyes he looked up and saw Ray Mohammed ready to plunge a knife into his heart. No! Don't do it! Please. . . . ."

Beep! . . . Beep! . . . Beep!

Kevin sat up, shaking and breathing heavily. After shutting off his watch, he looked around the strange room. He shook his head and breathed a sign of relief. *It was only a dream.* Looking down at his watch, he confirmed it was noon. He hustled out of bed and headed for the shower. The pressure wasn't nearly as strong as it was back home, so he made it a little hotter than usual. As the steaming water ran over his body, his head began to clear and his thoughts turned to seeing Kiran. Then a sudden sinking feeling overcame him. *What if she doesn't like me? Even if she does like me, what if she doesn't love me the way I love her?*

When he was finished with his shower, he quickly dressed and headed downstairs to the dining room. On the way he heard a strange kind of singing coming from a door slightly ajar. He peered inside. A cute young girl, about his age, was seated at a desk watching a small TV set. Kevin didn't recognize her but figured it must be Kiran's sister. Curious as to what she was watching he coughed. She jumped.

"Hello," Kevin said. "I'm sorry. I didn't mean to startle you.

The girl smiled and stood up. "Kevin. Hi. . . . I can call you Kevin, can't I?" she asked.

"Of course, you must be–?"

"Deviane," she advised. "I'm so glad you finally got here. We were worried sick about you yesterday. Everyone thought the NDC had kidnaped you."

"I'm sorry I caused everyone so much concern. . . . What are you listening to?"

"It's that maggot, Malcolm Mann. He's having a big rally at King George V Park."

"Oh, who's Malcolm Mann?"

"He's the leader of the National Defense Coalition."

"Oh, the NDC."

"Right. I don't know how he put a political party together so fast. It seems to have sprung up overnight–right about the time Daddy announced he would be spearheading the drive for a Caribbean Free Trade Agreement."

"You're interested in politics, I take it?"

"Not by choice, but since the assassination attempt, I'm very interested in my father's enemies."

"I can imagine. So, what do you know about this

Malcolm Mann guy?"

"He's a leftist fanatic, an admitted Cuban sympathizer and a no good hoodlum. Everyone knows he's into organized crime, gambling and drug dealing. The problem is he's a great orator and he knows how to manipulate a crowd."

Yelling and screaming came from the small TV set. Kevin and Deviane looked at it. Deviane bent over and turned up the sound.

"What kind of music is that?" Kevin asked.

"Calypso. It's our traditional music played by a pan band."

The music stopped. Malcolm Mann's voice echoed over the PA system. Kevin and Deviane listened intently.

*"Friends and fellow patriots. Thank you for coming tonight!" Malcolm said.*

He held his hand up to his ear and screamed.

"Ahmad...! Ahmad...! Are you watching this? Do you see the people pouring out into the streets?"

As the crowd screamed its approval, he continued.

"This is what the people of Trinidad think of your free trade agreement. . . . Rubbish! Do you think the people are stupid, Ahmad? Do you think they don't understand why America is pushing free trade in the Caribbean? Ha! We know about the American imperialistic snake, Ahmad. Don't we friends?"

Many in the crowd yelled, "Yes!"

"Would America give a damn about Trinidad if it were not for the oil under Cocos Bay?"

"No!" the crowd yelled in unison.

"My friends, do you think America is the great democracy of the world? Well, it's a lie! The people of America are but pawns of the big Wall Street Business Cartel. They are brainless couch potatoes who have pawned their minds for giant screen TVs, the Internet,

Rolex watches and fancy clothes. The American people are so many billions of dollars in debt to the Cartel that they have become zombies, working two jobs in order to be able to pay Citibank its twenty-one percent interest. Did you know the average American has credit card debt of over twenty-five thousand U.S. Dollars? That's over a quarter million Trinidad dollars! . . . Is this what you want for Trinidad?"

"No!" The members of the crowd shouted.

"Citizens of Trinidad, watch out for the American imperialist snake. It comes in the night and feeds on your crops, steals from your storehouses and beguiles your children. Because you don't see or hear it, you don't fear it, but beware; if you let it, one day it will strangle our Trinidad!"

"Death to the imperialistic snake!" someone yelled.

"As you know, we have formed the NDC to protect Trinidad from foreign intrusion. We are dedicated to preserving our traditions, our culture and our true democracy. I say true democracy, because we don't want American styled democracy here in Trinidad. Did you know that in America more than half the people never vote? It's because the people there have come to realize that voting is futile. It doesn't matter if the Republicans or the Democrats are elected, they both do the bidding of the Cartel.

"Do you know what will happen if you open the door to the crocodiles of Wall Street? They will consume our small businesses and what they don't want they will spit into our bankruptcy courts. They have mountains of capital to work with and their magicians of Madison Avenue will lure our people into believing that only American products are worth having. We won't have a shadow of a chance to compete with them. If we allow free trade, our nation will soon fall, not to tanks and stealth bombers, but to the American imperialistic snake. Take heed, Ahmad. Trinidad is not going to sell out to the devil of the North! The NDC will not allow it!"

The crowd jumped up yelling and screaming.

"Listen to the people, Ahmad. They don't want America's fast food, football or their loose women. Isn't that right, comrades? Do you want the Big Mac?"

"No!" the crowd yelled.

"Would you like your children to grow up like Ken and Barbie?"

"Nooo!..."

"How about Madonna? Do you want her to be a role model for your daughters?"

"Nooo!..."

"Should we be spending the Sabbath watching American football instead of talking to God?"

"Nooo! ..."

"You are right. I thought not. Listen my friends, I have written a little calypso song to our beloved Prime Minister. It's the least I could do as a memorial to him, since his government will soon be falling like rocks in an earthquake. It's called; *Oh Ahmad, You Have Sold Your Soul,* and here is how it goes."

The band started playing and Malcolm began to sing.

*Oh Ahmad, now you've sold your soul,*
*Just to bring to Trinidad, the damn Super Bowl.*
*Why did you bow down with your nose upon the floor?*
*You should have just said; No! Do not come ashore.*

*Why did you forsake, our beloved Trinidad?*
*The people are quite shocked, and very, very mad!*
*We're just a little island in the Caribbean lake,*
*Why did you feed us to the imperialistic snake?*

*Oh, Ahmad, now you've sold your soul,*
*Just to bring to Trinidad, the damn Super Bowl,*

*Why did you bow down with your nose upon the floor,*
*You should have said; No! Do not come ashore.*

*To get yourself elected you pledged equality,*
*Freedom of the press, the end of mediocrity,*
*Now we know, however, your promises were but a ruse,*
*To make you Prime Minister, an office you now abuse.*

*Oh, Ahmad, now you've sold your soul,*
*Just to bring to Trinidad, the damn Super Bowl,*
*Why did you bow down with your nose upon the floor,*
*You should have just said; No! Do not come ashore.*

*A hundred years we've prayed, for this wondrous day,*
*The Lord would give us, the hope of Cocos Bay,*
*Oh, Ahmad, it's time to stop the charade,*
*The citizens of Trinidad, don't want free trade!*

"No Free Trade!" the crowd screamed as they came to their feet.

"No Free Trade! No Free Trade! No Free Trade!"

Malcolm stopped and took a bow as the crowd roared its approval. The master of ceremonies came to the microphone.

"Thank you, ladies and gentlemen."

"No Free Trade!" the crowd continued. "No Free Trade! No Free Trade! No Free Trade!"

"Thank you, thank you. . . . Ahmad, are you listening?" the master of ceremonies said. "Citizens of Trinidad, Malcolm Mann. Malcolm Mann, a great patriot. Wasn't he fantastic?"

Deviane turned off the radio. "What a bastard. I'd like to riddle his body with bullets."

"You think he sent Ray Mohammed to kill your father?"

"Obviously. . . . He's the reason you got a bullet in your

back."

Kevin shook his head. "Bastard."

Deviane smiled. "So, how *is* your back?"

"Fine. I've fully recovered, I think. . . . I've never heard someone sing a speech before. Is that normal?"

"Yes, it is a tradition of some of the political parties in Trinidad to voice their concerns in Calypso."

"Hmmm. That's very interesting. So you have to have a good voice to go into politics in this country?"

Deviane laughed. "It helps, but not everyone campaigns that way. Daddy doesn't."

"Interesting. I guess I've got a lot to learn about your country."

"I know, it must seem strange to you. . . . So, I've been dying to ask you—How did it feel to be on Leno? I couldn't believe you kissed that slut, Uma Thurman. Did you know she posed for *Playboy*?"

"Yes, I heard that, but I wouldn't exactly call her a slut."

"Any woman who would expose her body to every male pervert in the world is a slut. She makes money off her body, just like a whore. She's a disgrace to every decent woman in the world."

Kevin gave Deviane a startled look. After a thoughtful moment he replied, "I guess that's true. Since I'm a man, I would tolerate a woman showing off her body more than a woman would, but you're right. She sold her body for money and fame. I'm afraid there's no morality in America anymore. Everything is about money and profit. If it sells, then that makes it okay."

"I'm afraid it's not just in America. It's all over the world, including Trinidad. It's pretty sad. I wish there was something we could do about it."

"Me too, but I'm afraid it would be like trying to swim up a river—we'd soon tire and probably drown."

"I suppose," Deviane replied.

Kevin gave Deviane a pensive look. He asked, "You

couldn't be too much younger than your sister, could you?"

"We're thirteen months apart."

"So you're what, seventeen?"

"Good guess, actually, next month I'll be eighteen."

"So, Kiran is already nineteen?"

"That's right, she just had a birthday. How old are you?"

"I'm eighteen. I should be graduating from high school in a few months, but I've missed so many days of school, I'll probably end up going to summer school."

"Do you regret what you did?"

Kevin hesitated and then replied, "No, not really. Actually, it's been kind of exciting."

Deviane smiled warmly. "You're lucky you didn't get killed. I don't think I would have been so brave."

"Well, if I had time to think about it, I might not have been so brave myself."

They both laughed. Hearing conversation in the hallway, Kevin and Deviane got up and stepped outside. Kiran and her mother, Anila, were walking down the stairway. Deviane took Kevin's hand and said, "Come on. It's time to eat."

They hustled down the stairway and entered the dining room. Kiran smiled at seeing Kevin but her smile quickly faded at seeing Deviane holding his hand. Kevin saw the disapproving look and immediately let go of it. The two sisters glared at one another.

"Kevin, come here I want to give you a hug," Anila said.

Kevin did as he was told and put his arms loosely around Anila. She hugged him tightly, kissed him on the cheek and then began to cry.

"Oh, Kevin, if it wasn't for you, my Ahmad would be dead. You don't know how many times I've thanked God for bringing you into our lives."

"Well, I'm just glad I was there at the right time."

"It was so brave what you did. I told Father Souza to say a special prayer for you at Mass tomorrow. You are

Catholic, aren't you?"

"Yes."

"Good. I hope you will come to Mass with us."

"I'd be honored."

Anila put her hand on Kiran's arm.

"I see you've met Deviane and you know Kiran, of course."

"Yes, we met briefly. Hi, Kiran."

"Hello, Kevin. How are you feeling?"

"Fine. I've fully recovered, I think."

"Good. We've been so worried about you, and then you disappeared last night."

"Well, I'm sorry I had everybody so concerned. I actually had an interesting evening. I stayed in a house about the size of your garage. There were two families living there, with six children."

"Oh, how dreadful," Kiran said. "I don't know how you could have stood it. I would have died."

"It wasn't so bad. It was clean and everyone treated me like I was part of the family."

"You don't have to be rich to be happy," Deviane interjected.

"Speak for yourself," Kiran laughed.

"Okay, girls. Let's not get into one of your silly arguments. I'm sure Kevin isn't interested in listening to you two squabble. Now, everybody sit down, your father should be here soon. Then, we'll eat."

"So where are we taking Kevin today, Mother?" Deviane asked.

"Well, I thought we'd go to the Royal Botanical Gardens and the National Museum."

"What about the beach? I thought we were going to the beach," Kiran said.

"Not today, darling, we don't have time today. Tomorrow, you girls can take Kevin up to Blanchisseuse Bay, after Mass."

"That's so far away. Why don't we just go to Maracas Bay?" Kiran asked.

"It's not so crowded there. It will be safer," Anila replied.

"Yes, lets go to Blanchisseuse Bay, so I can show Kevin the caves," Deviane said.

"I don't know if you should go in the caves. That might be too dangerous, honey."

"You've never been in them, Mother. How can you say they're dangerous?"

"It's dark in the caves, the ground is very rough and there are deep pits and crevices. You could fall and get hurt, even killed."

"They're not so dangerous. I've been in them a dozen times. Sometimes without a torch."

"Well, if I'd have known it, I wouldn't have allowed it," Anila replied.

"That's why I didn't tell you," Deviane laughed.

"Oh, you're so terrible, Deviane. What am I going to do with you?"

"Nothing. Just let me take Kevin in the caves."

"No, we'll save the caves for another time," Anila said. "Anyway, if we were to take Kevin to a cave, we should go to the Aripo caves. They are much larger and more beautiful."

"Oh yes. Can we do that, Mother?" Deviane asked.

"I don't know, it's up to Kevin."

"Kevin, wouldn't you rather go shopping at the mall than go to a stupid cave?" Kiran asked.

Kevin hesitated and then laughed.

"Actually, the caves kind of sound interesting, but I'd like go to the mall too. I need to pick up some souvenirs to take back home."

Deviane smiled and gave Kiran a gleeful look.

When the Prime Minister arrived and they were all seated, Anila motioned for everyone to be quiet, while she said grace.

"Bless us, our Lord, for these, our gifts we are about to receive from your bounty. And thank you, Lord, for delivering Kevin into our lives, and bringing him safely to our table. In the name of the Father, the Son and the Holy Spirit, Amen."

"Amen. Let's eat, I'm starving," the Prime Minister said. "Kevin, do you like Indian food?"

"Oh yes, I love it. There's a good Indian restaurant in Dallas called India Palace. I go there with my mom and dad all the time."

"Well you're in for a real treat, Kevin," Anila said. "We have a wonderful Indian cook. He'll fix you anything you want."

"Great, I'm looking forward to it."

"So, tell us about yourself, Kevin," the prime minister said. "We want to know all about you."

Kevin shrugged. "Well, I'm a biology major at Plano High School. I'm on the debate team and I'm in ROTC."

"Excellent, a military man. Do you plan to have a career in the armed forces?"

"No, I just want to serve my country for a few years."

"Ah ha! It must be politics then. I was on the debate team at Harvard. It prepared me well for my political career."

"Maybe, I really haven't decided yet."

"Well, you need to make up your mind, Kevin, so you can prepare yourself for your chosen profession. When I was your age I knew I wanted to be Prime Minister and I spent every waking hour preparing myself for the day that I would get that opportunity."

Anila looked at the Prime Minister, and said, "Ahmad, you hardly know Kevin. You shouldn't be lecturing him. He's our guest."

"He saved my life, Anila. Kevin, you don't mind if I treat you like part of the family, do you?"

"No, not at all," Kevin replied. "I'll gladly listen to any

advice you have for me."

"You just made your first mistake, Kevin," Kiran said. "Before long Daddy will be running your life."

The Prime Minister half smiled and said, "Ah! Did you hear that Kevin? Such disrespect from my own flesh and blood. Would your father let you get away with something like that?"

Kevin smiled. "Probably, he's pretty easy going."

The Prime Minister stood up and shook his head. He said, "Well, I'm going to turn these ladies over to you Kevin. I've had enough of them for one day. Good luck."

"Thank you, Sir," Kevin said as the Prime Minister left the room.

After lunch Anila, Kiran, Deviane and three bodyguards accompanied Kevin to the Royal Botanical Gardens. To reach the gardens, it was necessary to climb a steep hill.

When they reached the top, they stopped and looked down at the spectacular display which included a waterfall, babbling brook, twisting walkways, gigantic trees, bushy shrubs, finely manicured hedges and thousands of brightly colored flowers.

"Wow! Look at that," Kevin said.

"Isn't it beautiful?" Anila sighed.

"I guess so," Kevin said and then smiled at Kiran.

She returned the smile and then turned to look down into the garden again. Kevin gazed at her soft elegant face and thought back to his dreams about her. She belonged here, surrounded by nature's splendor. He wondered how he was going to capture her heart in the short time he could be with her. After they had walked a little way down into the gardens, they came upon several benches.

"Let's sit a spell," Anila said. "I'll have one of our security men get us a Coke or some lemonade."

Anila sat down and Kiran took a seat on another bench.

"Fine," Kevin said and then sat next to Kiran.

Deviane hesitated and then sat next to her mother.

"Where do you go to school, Kiran?" Kevin asked.

"We go to a private Catholic school in town. It's run by a Jesuit order."

"How long until you graduate?"

"Actually, I've already graduated."

"Oh, really? So what are you going to do now?"

"I'd like to go to college in the United States."

"Do you know what college you want to go to?"

"Not yet. Maybe Harvard or Stanford."

"You have to have good grades to get into colleges like that."

"Well, one of the benefits of being a Prime Minister's daughter is you can get unlimited access to tutors."

"Oh, really. Have they helped you a lot?"

She smiled wryly. "Uh huh. "They're a big help—Particularly when they get the exam questions ahead of time."

"Oh, I guess so," Kevin laughed. "So, what will you study?"

"I don't know. Liberal arts, I guess."

"Hmm."

"What are *your* plans after you graduate?" Kiran asked.

"I haven't decided if I want to go to law school or medical school. I kind of like politics, so the law would be the best way to go if I wanted to become a politician. Realistically, my political philosophy is not very popular these days, so politics may be out of the question."

"I'd love to marry a politician. I want to be just like my mother. She has the perfect life."

"Really?"

Kiran's eyes began to sparkle. "Yes, she knows everyone and they all adore her. She gets to go to all the good parties and social events, of course. Oh, and you should see her clothes."

"Doesn't she get tired of being in the limelight all the

time?"

"No," Kiran replied. "She loves it. She likes reading about herself in the newspaper."

"Yeah, I guess it is kind of neat to pick up a newspaper and see your picture."

"That's right. You know how that feels now, don't you?" Kiran said.

"Yeah."

"Not only does everyone respect and admire my mother, but she's a big help to my father too. She knows everyone of any importance to Trinidad. She knows how to get them to do what she wants."

"Yes, I can imagine. Your mother is quite a woman. I really like her."

"She likes you a lot, too."

"I hope so. You know, maybe you and I will end up going to the same school."

Kiran turned quickly and smiled at Kevin.

"That would be nice. It would be great to have someone I knew there. If you give me your address before you go, I'll write you when I know for sure where I'm going."

"Okay. I'm not sure I could get into Harvard or Stanford. The competition to get into those schools is pretty tough."

"I bet you can."

"Here are your drinks," a security guard interrupted. He handed Kiran and Kevin a drink and then turned to walk away.

"Thank you," Kevin said.

Kiran took a sip and then looked up at Kevin.

"You're going to love Blanchisseuse Bay. It's where lovers go to be alone. Sometimes, if you walk along the shore, you'll stumble across them making love."

"You're kidding?"

"No, it's so funny when that happens."

*Kevin suddenly imagined he and Kiran naked on the*

beach. *The warm tropical sun beating down on them as they made love on a blanket of pure white sand. Kiran moaned quietly as Kevin rocked back and forth to the beat of the pounding surf. Suddenly, a wave splashed over them, but they paid it no mind. Kevin lifted himself up slightly and gazed at Kiran's luscious pale breasts. He leaned down and kissed a nipple and then began caressing it with his tongue. She opened her eyes and beckoned him to bring her joy. He thrust himself, harder and harder, deeper and deeper until he felt the tension in her body melt away as she reached a blissful climax.*

Kevin sighed, "Oh, God!"

"What did you say?" Kiran asked.

"Huh?" Kevin said as he was jerked back to reality. "Oh. . . . Nothing."

"Okay, kids," Anila said. "It's getting late, let's go see the National Museum now."

Kevin started to get up, but realized there was a distinct bulge in his pants. Deviane noticed his plight and giggled. Kevin blushed, sat down and took another sip of his drink. After a moment, he was able to get up and continue on. Anila and Kiran looked at Deviane, wondering what was so funny.

When they arrived at the National Museum, Kiran and Deviane took Kevin, arm in arm, to the Cazabon exhibit. Anila excused herself to go talk to a friend, who managed the museum. Kevin felt exhilarated with two beautiful women pampering him. For a moment, he thought he was dreaming again, but a sudden twinge from the wound in his back convinced him he was quite conscious.

Kevin had fully recovered from the gunshot wound, but every once in awhile, he felt a sharp pain. The doctors told him that this was a normal part of the healing process and not to worry about it. Nevertheless, it was painful. When it occurred, he would usually close his eyes and let out an audible groan. Although he managed to restrain himself from groaning this time, Deviane felt the sudden tension in his body.

"Kevin, are you all right?"

"Yeah, it's nothing. Just a little lingering pain from the gunshot wound."

"Do you want to sit down?"

"No, it's fine."

Kiran seemed oblivious to Kevin and Deviane's conversation. She had her mind on a handsome young man, who was standing in front of a statue. Kevin noticed her gazing at the lad. He wondered who he was and why she was so interested in him. Deviane pulled on his arm to remind him she was talking to him.

"That's Roger Harvey, the British ambassador's son. He loves Kiran."

"What?" Kevin said.

"He does not," Kiran protested. "We just went to a dance together, that's all."

"Uh huh," Deviane chuckled.

Kevin felt a jolt of jealousy as he watched Kiran and Roger smiling and flirting with each other. Deviane seemed pleased and pulled Kevin away from Kiran.

"Go ahead, Kiran. Go see your friend. I'll take Kevin to the Pre-Columbian Exhibit. We'll meet you there later."

Kevin started to protest and then thought it would be impolite, so he reluctantly followed Deviane down some stairs, into another part of the museum.

"Did you know Columbus discovered Trinidad, just as he did America?"

"Oh really? He was a busy guy."

Deviane smiled and continued.

"It happened six years after he discovered America. You've had six flags over Texas, right?"

Kevin suddenly quit thinking about Kiran.

"What?" he asked.

"Didn't you have six flags over Texas?"

"Right."

"Well we've only had four flags over Trinidad. I bet you can't guess which ones they were?"

"Hmm. Well, I would say Britain, France and Spain, but I'm clueless on the fourth."

"The Dutch flag, silly."

"Oh. Are you a history buff or something?"

"No, I used to give a tour here."

"Did you really?"

"I worked here last summer. It was kind of fun."

"I always wanted to work at Yellowstone. I love the Rocky Mountains."

"Oh, I'd love to see the Rocky Mountains. The highest mountain we have here is Mt. Aripo. It's only three thousand feet high."

"Oh, man. How would you like to go to the top of a fourteen thousand foot mountain?"

"Can you breathe that high up?"

"Yeah, the air is a little thin, but you get used to it."

"I'd really love to do that sometime."

"Well, talk your dad into letting you and Kiran come visit me. I'll take you to Colorado. You'd love it."

"Would you really?"

"Of course. It would give me an excuse to go myself. If you come in the winter, I'll teach both of you how to ski."

As Kevin and Deviane entered the Pre-Columbian Exhibit, they saw that Kiran was already there, waiting patiently.

"Where have you two been? I've been waiting here five minutes."

"Kevin just invited me to Texas. He's going to take me to Colorado and teach me how to ski."

"You're invited too, Kiran." Kevin added.

Kiran stiffened and replied.

"I would never go skiing, it's too dangerous. I don't do

things if there is a strong probability of injury."

"Well, that's okay. A lot of people just come to see the beauty of the mountains in the winter. You can sit by a big fire, drink coffee and relax during the day. At night, they have lots of parties. It's really a beautiful place."

"Hmm. That could be fun, perhaps."

As the threesome were about finished viewing the many exhibits contained in the museum, Anila rejoined them.

"I'm sorry I took so long. I hadn't seen my friend for some time. She insisted I have a cup of tea," Anila said.

"That's okay, Mother. You timed it perfectly," Kiran said.

"Well, good. I'm hungry. What do you say we go home and have dinner?"

"You got my vote," Kevin said. "I'm starving."

That night, the Prime Minister was unable to have dinner at home with the family. When he arrived home later that evening, he asked Kevin to join him in his office for a cup of tea. Kevin was curious as to why the Prime Minister wanted to speak with him alone. He figured it was something to do with the lineup on Monday, but he wasn't sure. He wondered if he had done something wrong. He feared the Prime Minister had noticed his keen interest in Kiran and was going to warn him to leave her alone. He was a little scared as he entered the Prime Minister's office.

"Kevin, come in. Sit down."

"Good evening, sir."

"I'm sorry I missed you at dinner. I trust you had a good day?"

"Oh, yes."

"Did my family take good care of you?"

"Absolutely, they pampered me all day. It was wonderful."

"Good. Well, I called you up here to discuss some serious business. As you know, Sharad will be here Monday morning. He will take you to the prosecutor's office to view a lineup."

"Right."

"In the last few weeks, we've learned that this new NDC party was, most likely, behind the assassination attempt."

"That's what the Ambassador told me."

"Yes, and Ray Mohammed is the number two man in the NDC."

"The number two man?"

"Yes. So if he is indicted, we will have good cause to put an end to the NDC."

"Well, I hope it all works out."

"It's all up to you, Kevin. The NDC is full of rats and scoundrels. We must put a stop to them!"

"If he's the one I saw in Dallas, then I'm sure I'll recognize him."

"What I'm saying is, if you're not so sure, it's alright. Go ahead and ID him. We know for sure he's the one."

"You want me to lie?"

"No. No. Of course not, but if there is a little doubt in your mind, I wouldn't worry about it. This man is evil and his party is evil. You would be doing Trinidad a favor if you helped put him behind bars."

Kevin was silent. An uneasy feeling came over him. For the first time, he wondered what would happen if he couldn't identify the assassin. He'd be a hero if he did, but if he couldn't do it, he could kiss Kiran goodbye.

"If he looks like his photograph, I'm sure I'll recognize him."

"Fine. I'm glad we have an understanding."

Kevin squirmed in his chair. He suddenly thought of Obatala and Ray's innocent children. *What would become of them*? He wouldn't identify Ray unless he was positive he was the assassin. *But what if preserving his integrity meant sacrificing the only woman he might ever love?*

"I couldn't lie, sir. I'm sure you wouldn't want that. I'm

just saying I would be really shocked if Ray Mohammed wasn't the assassin. I wouldn't worry about Monday."

"Of course, I wasn't suggesting–"

"No, of course not."

"So, Anila tells me you've got an eye for Kiran."

Kevin began to blush.

"Is it *that* obvious?"

"Well, it wasn't to me, but my wife has a keen sense about those things."

"I do like her a lot, but let me assure–"

"No, it's not necessary. I trust you implicitly. After all, you saved my life, and now you're going to save Trinidad. What better son-in-law could a father ever want for his daughter? If you want Kiran, she's yours. I'll arrange everything."

Kevin suddenly felt faint. Had he been standing, he would have surely fallen over. Suddenly, his dream had become a reality, but instead of joy, he felt like he'd been hit by an Amtrak train. This isn't the way he wanted to have Kiran. He wanted her to fall in love with him and give him her unconditional love and devotion. If the marriage were arranged, he wouldn't know if she truly loved him. This wouldn't be the perfect marriage that he had so desperately sought.

"But, I'm not sure Kiran even likes me, let alone would want to marry me."

"Well, you needn't concern yourself about that. She will trust my judgment. If you want her, she's yours."

# Chapter 12

The next morning, Kevin didn't want to get out of bed. He was confused and scared about what was happening to him. He loved Kiran, at least he thought he did. He desperately wanted to make her his wife, but he didn't want her as a reward for saving Ahmad or, God forbid, payment for bearing false witness. He wondered if Kiran knew what was going on.

*Did she know that she was being used by her father for his political advantage? If she did know, would that knowledge turn her affections away from him? If he took her to be his bride, would she always wonder about his love?*

Kevin was sick. He almost wished he hadn't come to Trinidad.

He put on a pair of jeans over his swimsuit and threw on a Super Bowl XXX T-shirt he had bought in Phoenix when his dad took him to the Super Bowl. He wished his father was there to give him some advice. Finally, he decided he would have to confront Kiran and find out how she felt about him. He had to know. If she didn't have a strong interest in him, then he'd have to forget her and continue his search. Fate had not given him much time to win her love. His destiny may have already been sealed.

The Prime Minister sent a half dozen security police with Kevin and his daughters. He didn't expect any trouble, but he wasn't about to take any chances. The small motorcade left Port of Spain and headed north on Saddle Road. The narrow highway wound its way up and over the coastal mountains. This part of Trinidad was a tropical rain forest, abounding in vegetation and wildlife. At the summit of the pass, there was a lookout that provided an incredible view of northwest Trinidad. Deviane insisted the motorcade stop to take a look. As they drove up, they saw a half dozen black men selling coconuts and various other tropical fruits. Another man held a small stringed instrument resembling a ukulele.

"Come on, Kevin," Deviane said. "This will be fun."

"Have you heard any calypso yet?" Kiran asked.

"Well, just what Deviane was watching on TV the night I first got here."

Kiran gave Deviane a dirty look. Deviane ignored her and got out of the car. Kevin followed her and they were immediately surrounded by the men. Kevin was a little tense at first, but seeing Kiran and Deviane quite at ease made him feel better. The middle aged vocalist directed his attention at Kevin.

"Welcome to Trinidad, have you heard the music of our land yet? The calypso?"

"No, not yet," Kevin said as he looked at Kiran and Deviane, who were laughing.

"Well then, I will sing you a song about yourself and also reveal to you a glimpse of the future," the vocalist promised and then began singing;

*You're a wise young man from far away,*
*Most certainly the USA,*
*You love your country with all your soul,*
*You live in Phoenix and you like to bowl.*

Kevin and Deviane began to laugh. Kiran smiled. The other men were dancing to the music with great rhythm. The security police were watching and looking around for anything out of the ordinary. The calypso singer continued;

*With bright blue eyes, a pretty smile,*
*Ladies, yes, they do beguile,*

*Love abounds you as we speak,*
*now's not the time to be meek.*

*If innocence is the lure,*
*Are you sure that she is pure?*
*The road ahead is fraught with peril,*
*It all began with a long black barrel.*

*As you pray to the Lord above,*
*You should look for peace and love,*
*By your side your lover lies,*
*Yet you fail to hear her cries.*

*Now, if you liked this Calypso song,*
*Then it certainly would not be wrong,*
*To do something not so rash,*
*Like leaving this poor soul, a little cash!*

Everyone laughed and gave the performers a round of applause. Kevin pulled out his wallet and handed the man a five dollar bill. He took the money, bowed and waved as Kevin and the girls got back in their cars to continue the drive to Blanchisseuse Bay. Kevin was intrigued by the song and asked one of the security guards for a piece of paper and a pencil so he could write it down before he forgot it.

"That was really good. I'm glad we stopped," Kevin said. "What did you think, Kiran?"

"It was cute."

"Do you believe that he could see into the future?"

"No, that's impossible."

"I believe some people have that gift," Deviane said.

"Yeah, how did he know it all started with a long black barrel?"

"It was just a coincidence," Kiran said. "If he's so perceptive, why did he think you lived in Phoenix."

"True, he's obviously not a football fan. I guess the people of Trinidad don't follow the Cowboys," Kevin said.

"No, but there are a lot of NBA fans here," Deviane said. "Cricket and soccer are the most popular sports."

"Soccer is getting popular in the United States. I played a lot of soccer when I was younger."

"So did I," Deviane said. "I love soccer."

"Do you like any sports, Kiran?" Kevin asked.

Kiran thought a moment and then replied.

"Croquet is fun."

"Hmm. I played that a couple times, with my dad, when I was really young. You might like horseshoes. That's big in certain parts of West Texas. Then there is buffalo chip throwing and watermelon seed spitting."

Kiran looked at Kevin and frowned.

"That's disgusting!"

"Yeah, I guess it is. Actually, I've never done either of them."

"I'm glad. I assumed you were civilized."

Kevin laughed.

"The people in Texas are a little crazy sometimes. Hey, we do have something in common. Isn't that an armadillo going across the road?"

"Uh huh," Deviane replied. "We've got lots of them here."

"Really? I thought only Texas had armadillos. See, you learn something new everyday."

Around eleven-thirty a.m., the motorcade arrived at Blanchisseuse Bay. As promised, the beach was beautiful and deserted. The temperature was a balmy eighty-two degrees. There was a light breeze from the north and the sky was clear. Deviane bolted out of the car, ran down to the water and started splashing around in it. Kevin watched her with great interest, but stayed back to help unload the trunk. Kiran grabbed her large beach purse and walked gingerly through the sand to the edge of the water. She looked around for the best spot and then began laying out a blanket. Kevin finally joined her with the picnic basket.

"Isn't it wonderful out here?" Kiran said.

"Yeah, it is," Kevin replied as he pulled off his shirt. Kiran took an approving look at Kevin's wide shoulders and hard stomach. Then she kicked off her shoes, untied the straps on her cotton dress and let it drop to the ground. Kevin felt a surge of excitement as he saw her exquisite body, covered only by a modest yellow bikini.

"You want to go for a swim?" he smiled and asked.

"No, I don't like to swim that much, I just like to lay out."

"Oh. How about a walk on the beach then?"

"Sure, that would be fine."

Kevin took Kiran's hand and began walking with her down the beach. Deviane walked by and said, "Come back soon, I'm hungry."

Kevin didn't respond as his mind was on Kiran. For the first time, he was enjoying the warmth of her soft, slender hand. As they strolled down the beach, he looked over at her and spoke.

"You know, Kiran, after you kissed me in the hospital the day we met, I haven't been able to keep my mind off you."

Kiran glanced over at Kevin to catch the expression on his face. "Really? I'm surprised a simple kiss would have such an effect on you. You must have had a dozen girls by now, if what I've seen on television is true."

"Some guys, most guys take what they can get, but I'm not that way. Is it true that I was the first man you ever kissed?"

Kiran laughed. "Well, I should be honest with you. That's my father's fantasy. I've kissed before."

Kevin was disappointed by this revelation but then he thought a moment and replied, "That *was* kind of hard to believe. I'm not so surprised. So how did my kiss compare to the ones before me?"

Kiran smiled. "It was interesting, but you held back."

"True, I was in a state of shock with the President there, and then your appearance was such a total surprise."

"Shall we try again?"

Kevin's eyes lit up like a fuse on a firecracker. He nodded. Kiran turned and put her arms on his shoulders. He slid his hands behind her back and pulled her body to his. They kissed, tenderly at first, feeling each other's breath, rubbing their lips together tentatively, until a sudden rush of passion exploded within them. With their lips firmly locked, their tongues frolicked joyfully as they pressed their bodies ever so close. They felt so exhilarated that neither could bear to bring the kiss to its inevitable conclusion. Finally Kiran pulled away. They stared at each other silently for a moment, both breathing heavily.

"Well, you get an A-plus. That was much better than the last time," Kiran said. "Wow!"

Kevin took a deep breath. "That was incredible. I've never experienced anything like that before."

"I'm glad you liked it. It will make our marriage better if there's passion between us," Kiran laughed.

Kevin swallowed. "Our marriage?"

"Isn't that what you want? Didn't you ask my father for my hand?"

"Well, yes. Kind of."

"Then you've got your wish. I will marry you."

"You will?"

"Yes. On one condition."

"What's that?"

"I want to live in America. My father will try to convince you to live in Trinidad, but I want you to take me back to Texas."

"That's it?"

"Well, I want you to be a politician, not a doctor. I want so much to be like my mother, the wife of an important government official. Don't you think I'd make a good first lady?"

"First lady?" Kevin laughed. "That's kind of a long shot, don't you think?"

"Oh, you're too modest, Kevin. The Ambassador said you could be President of the United States someday."

"He said that? Huh. . . . Well, if it's that important to you, I'll give politics a try. But, I may not be successful. Politics is very competitive in America."

"You will be successful, I just know it."

Kevin took a deep breath, trying to figure out if Kiran was for real. This should have been the happiest moment in his life, but he felt sick inside. He suddenly remembered something his father had said to him once—Be careful what you ask for, you might just get it.

His mind was racing as he continued to walk down the beach. He couldn't believe Kiran had consented to become his wife. It had all happened so fast, he was in a state of shock. After a few minutes of contemplation, however, the anticipation of marrying Kiran and spending the rest of his life with her dispelled all the anxiety he had been feeling. He knew he was a very lucky man. *Don't look a gift horse in the mouth. This is what I wanted and now I've got it! Thank you, God.*

He turned and smiled at Kiran. "You've made me the happiest man alive, Kiran. I'll be a good husband, I promise!"

Kiran smiled and laughed. "I know. That's why I agreed to marry you. I'm going to enjoy being your wife. But, we need more practice kissing, don't you think?"

Kevin smiled gleefully, opened up his arms and embraced Kiran. They kissed passionately for several minutes, until Kiran finally broke away and spoke.

"Umm. You're getting better and better each time. We could do this all afternoon, but, I'm afraid we better get back. Deviane won't eat without us and she'll be complaining all afternoon if we don't return soon. Besides, I think we've given the security police enough of a show for one day."

Kevin smiled and reluctantly let go of Kiran. She turned and started walking back to where Deviane was waiting. Kevin followed her a few paces behind, still in a state of shock. When they finally made it back, Deviane was taking in some sun. She too, had on a bikini and looked quite exquisite. Kevin suddenly felt embarrassed to look at her, now that he had made a commitment to Kiran. He turned, looked out to sea and took a deep breath of he salty air.

Kiran slipped her dress on and said, "I'm going to go to the ladies' room, Kevin. I'll be right back. We can eat then."

He turned around and smiled. "Sure."

Kiran left and headed for the bathhouse which was situated about two hundred yards down the beach. Kevin watched her lovingly as she walked away.

"Kevin, will you rub some suntan lotion on my back? I can't reach it," Deviane said.

"Huh?" Kevin said as he turned and made eye contact with Deviane.

"Suntan lotion. I don't want to get a burn."

Kevin hesitated as he felt a flurry of guilt come over him. He didn't know what to do. He didn't want to offend Deviane, but he didn't want to betray Kiran either.

Deviane turned over and smiled.

"She won't mind. Come on. I can't reach my back or I'd do it myself."

Kevin shrugged and picked up the bottle of suntan lotion. He watched her as she unbuttoned the top to her bikini. He poured some lotion on his hand and began to rub it gently on her back. As he felt her smooth, silky skin beneath his fingers, he felt an excitement that shocked and embarrassed him. Suddenly Deviane turned over exposing her naked breasts. Kevin quickly turned away.

"Deviane!"

"Oops!" She laughed. "I'm sorry, I forgot I had unbuttoned it. Jesus, you must think I'm terrible. Please forgive me"

"It's okay, I just don't want Kiran to get the wrong idea. You won't mention this to her will you?"

"No, of course not."

"She just agreed to marry me. I really love her and I don't want anything to come between us."

"Marry you? No! You can't be serious."

Kevin squinted. "Yes, quite serious."

"But, she doesn't love you."

"How would you know whether she loved me or not?"

"She's my sister. Believe me, I know. . . . I bet she made you promise to take her to America, didn't she?"

"Well, she did mention that, but that's no big deal. I wouldn't want to live in Trinidad anyway. . . . No offense to your fine country, but–"

"What else does she want?"

"Just that I be a politician rather than a doctor."

"See, she doesn't care about what you want, just about herself. She's always been that way. I'd marry you without condition. We could live anywhere you like, and I wouldn't care what career you choose, as long as we were together."

"But I love Kiran, not you."

"You just think you love her. She doesn't love you, I promise. She didn't tell you she loved you, did she?"

"Well, not exactly."

"Kiran is very honest. She won't lie to you. She may evade your questions, but she won't lie. If she loves you, she'll tell you so. You should ask her if she loves you."

"I'm not going to play games with her. She wouldn't marry me if she didn't love me."

"Oh, Kevin, you're so naive. I'm not saying she won't be faithful to you, I'm sure she will, but you two don't have anything in common. You'll be living together, but your minds will be apart. You won't be happy."

Kevin stared at Deviane, not knowing what to say to

her. He was stunned by her opposition to the marriage and her apparent interest in him. *It's probably just gratitude for saving her father's life. Why else would she care about me? I can't let her distract me from Kiran. I've searched for too long for the right woman to let anything get in my way.*

"Deviane, I'm in love with Kiran and I'm going to marry her. I'm sorry you're against it, but I'm sure it will be wonderful marriage."

When Kiran returned, they opened the picnic basket and began to consume the fare that had been provided them. Kevin felt badly knowing Deviane was so dead set against their marriage. After lunch, the three sunbathers sat and enjoyed the warm sunshine. A cool breeze coming in from the ocean made it quite pleasant. After a while, Deviane got up and looked toward the ocean.

"Let's take a swim."

Kevin got up eagerly and replied, "That sounds like fun."

Kiran looked at them.

"You two go ahead. I don't like to swim in the ocean. The salt hurts my eyes and it will take me a week to get my hair clean again."

Deviane smiled and started running toward the water. Kevin wanted to swim, but he didn't want to leave Kiran alone. He decided not to go. He watched her run toward the beach.

"Aren't you going, Kevin?" Kiran said. "She shouldn't be out there alone."

Kevin knew she was right. He nodded to Kiran and started running after Deviane. When she reached the water she ran out as far as she could and then collapsed into the surf. Kevin quickly caught up to her and started swimming and playing in the water around her. Before long, they were having a water fight and laughing and giggling like a couple of children. Kiran seemed oblivious to what was going on. Her mind was obviously occupied by something of greater importance. When the two swimmers got tired, they returned and sat on the blanket next to Kiran to dry.

"How was the water?" Kiran asked.

"Very pleasant, you should have come with us," Kevin said.

"I was thinking about our wedding. I would like to have it at the botanical gardens. It is so beautiful there."

Kevin felt an unpleasant sensation in the pit of his stomach. He was worried. What would his parents say when he told them he was getting married. It seemed so strange to have Kiran talking about their wedding. He hardly knew her. He twisted his neck slowly to release the tension that was rapidly working its way into a headache.

"That would be nice, as long as it didn't rain," Deviane said.

"True, that would be a worry, but if we have it during the dry season, we should be okay."

"When is the dry season?" Kevin asked.

"In January, usually," Kiran replied.

"A January wedding, hmm. That will be okay, I guess. We'll have to wait a year before we start college. After the wedding, we'll have eight months before the term begins. Wait until I tell my parents that they've got to come to Trinidad to see us get married. Oh, God, won't they be surprised."

"How will you support me?" Kiran asked.

"What?" Kevin said suddenly realizing he hadn't even thought of that minor detail.

"How will we live?

"Ah. . . . Well, unfortunately I'm not rich. I'm sure my parents will pay for my college. Do you think your parents will pay for yours?"

"Yes, of course."

"Good. Then all I'll have to do is get a part time job, so we'll have money for rent and food, right? If we come up short, I can always get a student loan."

"We shouldn't borrow, I wouldn't like being in debt."

"I agree. We'll just live on whatever we can scrape up. It will be fun."

Kiran looked over at Deviane.

"Deviane, will you be my maid of honor?"

Deviane looked like she had been stung by a jelly fish, She looked away, then back at Deviane without saying a word. Then she got up, put on a T-shirt and slipped on some sandals. Kiran watched her, waiting for a response. After she regained her composure, she turned back and smiled.

"If you actually do get married,  I'll be your maid of honor," she said and then looked at Kevin. Their eyes met. . . . "And when I get married, will you be mine, . . . no matter who I marry?"

Kevin gasped under his breath. He turned away and took a deep breath.

Kiran looked at him and frowned, "Of course, Deviane. Even if you marry some peasant, I'll be there at your side."

"Good, then it's settled."

Kevin shook his head, then turned to Kiran and said, "Kiran, let's take another walk on the beach. I want to see the caves."

Kiran looked down the beach to where Kevin wanted to go.

"Okay, but we're not going in them."

"I know, I just want to see where they are."

"I'll take you, Kevin," Deviane said.

"No, I'll take him," Kiran snapped. "Come on, Kevin."

"You better put on some shoes, it's very rocky by the caves," Deviane advised. "Some of the rocks are razor sharp too. I've cut my feet on them before."

"Oh, really? I guess I'll put on my sneakers then," Kevin said. "Where are your shoes, Kiran?"

"In my bag, will you get them for me?"

"Sure," Kevin said and then went over to the beach bag. He pulled out Kiran's sandals and handed them to her.

After Kiran put them on, she got up and they began walking down the beach, hand in hand.

"I feel like I'm dreaming," Kevin said.

"What do you mean?" Kiran asked.

"When I came here I wasn't– I didn't–"

"What?"

"I was hoping to spend some time with you, so you would get to know me. You know, so you might fall in love with me. Realistically, I didn't think it would happen, but I was determined to try. I'm so amazed that it happened so fast."

"They don't have arranged marriages in America, do they?"

"Huh?"

"Arranged marriages. Your parents don't pick your wife, do they?"

"No."

"Well, we don't have arranged marriages exactly, but parents play an important role in deciding who their children will marry."

"Really?"

"Yes, they choose a spouse for you, but you can reject their choice if it doesn't feel right."

"Is that so?"

"Uh huh."

"You mean, your father decided you should marry me?"

"Yes. He said it would be a good marriage and that I should seriously consider it. I thought about it and I think he's right. It will be good for us to be married."

"But what about love? Do you love me?"

"I hardly know you, Kevin. I like you a lot. I feel good when I'm with you. I love kissing you, but I'm not exactly sure what love is."

"I love you."

"How do you know?"

"I can just feel it. From the moment I first saw you, I just knew you were the woman I wanted to be with the rest of my life."

Kiran laughed.

"I'm glad you love me. I'm sure I'll grow to love you too. Maybe I do love you, but don't realize it. God, Kevin, I don't know. It doesn't matter, my mother didn't love Daddy at first, but she does now."

Kevin stopped, sat down and stared out into the ocean. Kiran sat next to him and put her arm around him.

"Do you still want to marry me?" Kiran asked.

Kevin looked at Kiran and sighed.

"Oh, God, yes! I love you. I just want you to love me as much as I love you."

Kiran put her head on Kevin's shoulder.

"It will come, I'm sure it will come. Don't worry," she whispered.

After Kevin and Kiran left, Deviane laid back and took a long, frustrated breath. She grabbed a book and started thumbing through it. A minute later, she threw down the book and looked around for one of the security guards. She wanted to know the time. She scanned the beach, but no one was around. *That's odd.* She stood up and put her hand above her eyes to shield them from the glare. In the distance, she could see the three cars that had brought them to the beach, but there were no security guards to be seen. A sudden chill darted down her spine. She could sense that something was wrong.

Then she heard it—the chilling sound of a helicopter gunship. She whipped her head around toward the sound and saw it. Soldiers were dropping off the chopper and sliding to the ground on ropes.

She started running down the beach to warn Kiran and Kevin when the helicopter opened fire and the first of the three government cars exploded. The jolt knocked her to the ground. As she was trying to get up, two more explosions rocked the beach. After a second, she looked up, only to see flaming debris falling to the ground. Panic-stricken, she began to run. Suddenly, three soldiers came out of nowhere and started chasing her. She shrieked in terror.

Kevin and Kiran were standing, trying to figure out what was happening. Alarmed at seeing three men chasing Deviane, Kevin took off to help her. As he approached, he realized her pursuers were carrying guns. When she reached him, he grabbed her hand and started running with her. As they approached Kiran he yelled.

"Run, Kiran, run!"

Kiran started running along the beach as fast as she could. The men chasing them were tall, lean and obviously in good shape. They began to get closer and closer. Suddenly, several more men came at them from the main road.

"Up ahead! The caves!" Deviane yelled. "Follow me and we can lose them in the darkness."

Kevin was starting to tire and Kiran was already lagging behind. Only Deviane seemed to be up to the physical challenge confronting them. As they got to the entrance of the cave, she directed them to hold her hand. She would lead them safely through the cool darkness. Kevin and Kiran followed Deviane blindly into the depths of the earth. They could see nothing. The ground was rocky and they often stumbled.

"Watch out for the stalactites hanging from the cave's ceiling. Hit one of those and it could knock you out."

"I don't know how I'm supposed to see them," Kiran complained.

After a while, Deviane stopped.

"Why are we stopping?"

"We're safe here for awhile," she said.

"Good." Kevin said. "But how are we going to get out of here?"

"I don't know."

"What?"

"I know these caves pretty well, but I've never been this far back without a flashlight. One of the games we used to play was 'bat eyes.' We'd shut off our flashlights and see how far we could get without light."

"Wasn't that a little dangerous?" Kevin queried.

"I guess it was, but we always turned on our flashlights way before we got to the bottomless pit."

"The bottomless pit? . . . Oh, Jesus, where is that?"

"I think it's just ahead."

"How do we get around it?"

"There's a narrow path around its perimeter."

"Oh God, Deviane. Why did you take us in here?" Kiran said.

"What choice did I have?"

"Can we get by it?" Kevin asked.

"Yes, just take my hand and stay close to the wall to your left."

They all got up and started to creep along the wall of the cave. Deviane led the way with Kiran in the middle. About half way across Kiran slipped on a wet rock and fell toward the pit.

"Ah!" Kiran screamed as she tried to grab hold of Kevin for dear life. Kevin grabbed her arm and jerked her back toward him.

"I've got you, Kiran, relax," Kevin said. "Don't make any sudden moves."

Kiran began to cry. "Get us out of here Deviane. I don't like it in here."

"I will. It's not too much farther. Just quit crying. It's not going to help."

After they had made it around the bottomless pit safely, they stopped to rest.

"Who were those men?" Kevin asked.

"I don't know," Deviane said.

"Did they kill our security police?" Kiran asked.

"I'm afraid so," Deviane said.

"Don't you think they'll go find some flashlights and be back here to get us?" Kevin asked.

"Right, but we'll be long gone by that time."

"Where are we going?"

"After we rest a minute, we'll sneak out the back entrance to the cave and hide in the forest until someone comes looking for us."

"What do you think they want with us, Deviane?" Kiran asked.

"I don't know for sure. I suppose it could be a ransom."

"Or it could be political," Kevin added. "They may be after me, to keep me from identifying Ray Mohammed. It wouldn't be the first time they tried."

"What do you mean?" Deviane asked.

"I didn't tell anyone before, but the reason I was missing on my first day in Trinidad was I had been kidnaped."

"What?" Kiran said. "You were kidnaped? What do you mean? Why didn't you say something?"

"The kidnapper was actually trying to save me from the NDC. They had intended to kill me. In fact, if it weren't for him, I'd be dead right now. He was such a good person, I didn't want him to get into trouble. So I kept my mouth shut about it."

"I can't believe this," Kiran said. "That means, if they find us, they'll kill us!"

"Maybe not. If they wanted us dead, they could have killed us on the beach." Kevin replied. "No, I think they want us as hostages."

Suddenly there were voices in the distance and flashes of light. Deviane jumped up and said, "It's time to go. Just hold my hand and we'll be out of here in just a minute."

Kevin grabbed Deviane's hand with one hand and Kiran's with the other. They made their way through the darkness slowly, until they could see a light in the distance and finally emerged into the forest. The sudden blast of sunlight blinded them. They shielded their eyes with their hands until they had adjusted to the light.

"Follow me," Deviane said and then turned, hiking toward the foothills.

Kevin and Kiran walked hand in hand behind Deviane. It wasn't easy walking through the rugged rain forest, particularly for the girls, who were in sandals. Before long, Kiran began to complain.

"Slow down, Deviane. My feet are killing me."

Deviane stopped to give Kiran a chance to adjust her sandals. After a minute, she started walking again. She led them inland, along a small stream, for several miles. It was beautiful country. Had the circumstances been different, it would have been a pleasant hike. They continued on until they came to a small clearing overlooking a waterfall. It appeared to be a popular camping site, judging from the scattered remnants of many campfires. The three weary travelers stopped to rest and discuss how they were going to avoid capture.

"It's getting late. Before long, it's going to be dark. We better start thinking of how we're going to protect ourselves tonight," Kevin said.

"We're going to have to sleep in the forest?" Kiran asked.

"Unless someone rescues us real soon, I'm afraid so."

"What about the animals?" Kiran asked.

"I don't know. What kind of animals are out here?"

"Oilbirds and armadillos, mostly," Deviane replied. "Maybe some agoutis and deer. Nothing too threatening."

"Good, I'll make us a lean-to for protection from the rain," Kevin said. "You two gather some leaves or something soft for us to sleep on. Later on, I'll make a fire."

"How are you going to do that?" Kiran asked. "We don't have any matches."

"Luckily, I was a Boy Scout. If I can find the right kind of rock, I can strike it against my pocket knife and get a spark. Otherwise, I'll have to use a bow and a stick, which is much harder. It might take a while, but I'll have a fire started eventually."

"I'll get us some coconuts to eat," Deviane said.

"Where?" Kevin asked.

"There are coconut trees everywhere. I'll just look around. Maybe I can find some on the ground."

After an hour of hard work, the three campers had built a pretty credible shelter. Kiran was lying on a bed of leaves, watching Kevin trying to make a fire. Deviane was sitting on a big rock at the edge of stream, eating some coconut. Kevin had prepared a bed of dry, shredded leaves and built a wooden frame around it. In the river he had found a suitable rock. He struck the rock again and again against the edge of his knife. Sparks began to fly into the dry leaves. After several minutes, one of the sparks ignited a leaf. Kevin immediately began to blow on the smoldering embers. The oxygen made the fire spread to the other leaves. Before long, smoke was rising from the bed. Suddenly, the entire bed of leaves burst into flames. Kevin jumped up and took a bow.

"What did I tell you? Am I good or what?"

"That was brilliant, Kevin," Deviane said. "Good job."

"A match would have been much simpler," Kiran laughed.

"Hey, I didn't know we were going camping or I would have brought some."

"This is kind of fun," Deviane said. "We should do this more often."

"I'm game," Kevin said.

"I prefer dinner and the theater, thank you," Kiran noted.

"I wonder if Daddy is out looking for us?" Deviane asked.

"Of course he is," Kiran said. "He's probably got a thousand men out searching for us right now. Tomorrow we'll try to find a telephone so we can call him. There has to be someone living out here, somewhere.

"We'll have to be careful," Kevin said. "The NDC unit may still be out there looking for us. I imagine they're pretty pissed off that we got away."

"Do you think it's safe for us to sleep tonight? What if they're looking for us right now?" Deviane asked.

"You're right," Kevin replied. "We'll take turns sleeping. Someone needs to be awake at all times. You two go to sleep now. I'll wake Deviane at midnight and Kiran can take over at four. If you hear anything at all, wake whoever's sleeping."

"Do you think it's wise to keep a fire going?" Deviane asked.

"Hmm. You're right. I thought it would keep the animals away, but we probably should douse it. It could lead the NDC to us. Damn, I'm not used to being stalked."

"What are we going to do if they come? We don't have any weapons," Kiran noted.

"We'll have to run," Kevin replied. "We can't let them catch us. If they killed our security police, they won't hesitate to kill us, too."

As Kevin was about to throw water on the fire, the skies opened up and it started to pour down rain. The girls immediately scrambled under the lean-to, with Kevin close behind.

"Wonderful," Kevin said. "This is all we need."

# Chapter 13

Early Sunday evening, the Prime Minister and Anila were having a small dinner party. Guests at the party included the Attorney General and the United States Ambassador, both accompanied by their wives. Also attending was Walter Wellersby, a special emissary from Washington. They had planned the event to discuss the prosecution of Ray Mohammed and the other leaders of the NDC. They met at Michael's, a popular restaurant in the suburbs. As they drank cocktails and nibbled on some appetizers, they discussed the upcoming arrest of Ray Mohammed.

"It will be tomorrow morning, when he leaves his house, probably around eight. We'll transport him to the police station where Kevin Wells will be ready to identify him immediately. I've assigned our best investigators and our top prosecutor to interrogate him. Hopefully, he'll implicate Malcolm Mann and the rest of the hoodlums that run the NDC," the Attorney General said.

"I seriously doubt if he'll say anything," the Ambassador replied. "By now, he must have an attorney on standby. He's got to be worried about being arrested. I'm really surprised he came back to Trinidad after the assassination attempt. He can't be very bright."

"Perhaps he knows something we don't," Mr. Wellersby said.

The ambassador looked at Wellersby. "Perhaps he does," he replied.

"When are you going to inform the press about what's coming down?" the Ambassador asked.

"We've called a news conference for noon tomorrow," the Attorney General replied. "We'll advise the press that we've arrested a suspect in conjunction with the assassination attempt on Prime Minister Shah and the shooting of Kevin Wells. Whether we elaborate any further depends on how much Ray Mohammed talks."

"If you go after the NDC, do you have a contingency plan in case there is violence?" Wellersby asked.

"We don't expect any trouble, but as a precaution, our military will be put on alert at midnight tonight. We currently have all of the NDC leaders under surveillance. If they try anything, then we'll pounce on them like a lion on a caribou."

Several waiters arrived to serve the dinner salad. As they were working, Anamica came in, hurried up to the Prime Minister and whispered something in his ear.

"What?" the Prime Minister said as his face became grim.

"No!" he said and then slammed his fist on the table. "This can't be!"

Anila, having overhead Anamica, let out a scream and began to cry. The Prime Minister put his arms around her to comfort her.

"What's wrong, Ahmad?" the Ambassador asked.

"Someone has kidnaped our two daughters and Kevin Wells!"

"Oh, Lord!" the Ambassador said. "You've got to be joking."

"They've killed six security officers and bombed their cars. I must leave at once. Sharad, let's go."

The Prime Minister and the Attorney General made a hasty exit from Michael's. Ahmad was visibly upset by the news. Anila was in such a panic, she had to be assisted out of the restaurant.

"Oh, Ahmad, what are you going to do?" she moaned. "They have our Kiran and Deviane. You've got to find them!"

"I will. Calm down. I'll find them and bring them home to you safely."

"Do you think the kidnappers will hurt them?" the Ambassador asked.

"No, I'm sure they want them as hostages."

"Who would do something like this?"

"I'm sure it's the NDC. They're the only ones that would resort to kidnaping to get what they want. But, they've made a big mistake. Now, I'm going to see to it that every last one of them hangs. Believe me, the bastards will pay for what they've done!"

Ahmad and Sharad were escorted to a waiting helicopter by security police. Within minutes, they were airborne and flying toward the capitol building.

"Let's go straight to Blanchisseuse Bay," Ahmad said. "I want to see if they've found out anything yet."

"That wouldn't be wise," Sharad replied. "You need to go to your office, where it is safe. If the NDC is really behind this, they may be looking for another opportunity to assassinate you. I'll get my best men out there. They'll find out what happened and track down the cowards responsible for this outrage."

"Don't fail me, Sharad. These are my children, my own flesh and blood. They are the reason I've fought so hard to get to the top. I'm looking forward to the day when they'll fill our house with grandchildren."

"Believe me, Kiran and Deviane are like children to me too. I will not sleep until they are home safe with their mother."

"Anila will die of grief if we lose them."

"We won't lose them. We don't even know for sure that the kidnappers have them. They may have escaped."

"Do you think that's possible?"

"To be honest, it's not likely, but with Kevin there, it might be possible."

"Deviane is very cunning and she knows the terrain quite well, perhaps they did escape, Sharad!"

"I will order a search first thing in the morning. What about the press? What should I tell them?"

Ahmad thought for a moment.

"We'll wait for the news conference tomorrow. If God wills it, we'll have them back safely. If not, we'll ask every citizen of Trinidad to search for them. This is a small country. It will be difficult for the traitors to hide their hostages."

The helicopter started its descent onto the roof of the capitol building. As soon as it landed, Ahmad and Sharad rushed inside. General Pelton met the two leaders as they entered the building.

"Mr. Prime Minister, we've put the military on full alert. Since we had already planned an alert at midnight, we should be well prepared for anything that might happen."

"Excellent. Has anything else occurred, other than the kidnapping?"

"No, sir. We've had no reports of anything unusual."

"Has anyone claimed responsibility for the kidnapping?"

"No, sir."

"Are there any witnesses to what happened out there?"

"No, sir. It's a complete mystery. Late in the afternoon, we lost radio contact with the security police escorting your daughters and Mr. Wells. We immediately dispatched helicopters that reached the scene within minutes. When they got there, the beach was deserted, except for three burning vehicles and a few items on the beach."

"What items?"

"Some towels, clothing and a picnic basket."

"They must have been swimming when the assault occurred," Sharad said. "What about tracks? Could you tell how many there were from the footprints?"

"Yes, sir. There appeared to be six men in combat boots running on the beach, perhaps chasing your daughters and Mr. Wells. The footprints stop at the water's edge, near the north perimeter of the beach."

"The caves. Did anyone search the caves?" Ahmad asked.

"No, sir. We weren't aware of any caves."

"Get someone out there tonight to search the caves. They may have hidden there. Deviane knows the caves well. She may have led them in there to hide."

The general barked some orders to a subordinate and he ran off.

"There's someone there now, so I'll radio for them to search the caves immediately. I'll advise you of what they find the minute they report back."

"Thank you, General. You may go. Keep me appraised of what's going on?"

"Yes, sir," the general said and then turned and left.

"Oh, Sharad, pray they are in the caves. They've got to be in the caves."

# Chapter 14

The headquarters of the NDC was fully manned and operational. Hundreds of NDC members were scurrying about, getting ready to handle their first assault on the Shah government. Once they had their hostages safely stashed away in the basement of their headquarters, the game would begin. The Prime Minister would face a stinging attack for allowing Kevin Wells to be kidnaped, thus jeopardizing the prosecution of Ray Mohammed. Such incompetence would lead to a no-confidence vote and the end of the Shah government. The NDC would deny any involvement in the kidnaping and join in the call for the Prime Minister's resignation.

While the battle to form a new government was raging in Parliament, the NDC would strike. With the help of a small Cuban mercenary army waiting on standby, the NDC would seize all government buildings, the television and radio stations, and arrest, or kill if need be, the Prime Minister and all other members of the current government. Leaders of the NDC believed that with anti-American sentiment increasing each day, the people would rally behind the NDC once it was in power.

When they had gained control, they would rationalize the use of force to seize power by simply pointing out the urgent necessity to stop American economic aggression in the form of the Caribbean Trade Agreement. They would argue that Trinidad was about to suffer irreparable damage if the agreement went into effect, and by the time a new government could have been formed, it would have been too late. When the dust settled and an election could be held, the NDC would claim itself the savior of Trinidad and would win an overwhelming mandate at the polls.

Unfortunately, phase one of the NDC's grand scheme had not gone well. At eight p.m., Malcolm Mann was in an emergency meeting with his lieutenants.

"This kind of incompetence is unacceptable!" Mann screamed. "Hundreds of Trinidad patriots have been carefully planning this operation for over a year. Now the plan may have to be scrapped, before it even gets off the ground. All because a highly trained assault unit couldn't catch three unarmed teenagers on the beach. Damn them! I want the commander of that unit arrested and thrown in jail. I will not tolerate failure!"

"Sir," Ray Mohammed said. "They couldn't have gone far from the beach. It was getting dark, so they must be somewhere close by in the forest. We can still get them."

"How?" Mann asked. "As we speak, government troops are crawling all over the area. I don't have to tell you that if they find Kevin Wells, it could be the end of our party and we all may wind up at the end of a rope."

"We've got party members and supporters who live in that area. We could send them home to search for Kevin Wells and the Prime Minister's daughters. Since they live there, the government troops will have to let them in the area. All we have to do is find them before the government does."

"It's a interesting idea, but just as soon as it gets light, they will find them quickly. We may not have enough time. Even if we do find them, how will we get them out of the area with government troops surrounding us?"

"We won't wait for daylight. We'll start our search now. Our people know the area. The darkness will not hinder them. Once we capture them, we'll drive them to a safe location and bring them out by helicopter."

"All right, unless someone has a better idea, we'll implement Ray's plan. Assemble all these members you speak of, so we can brief them and send them on their way. Start calling our other soldiers in the area around Blanchisseuse Bay and give them their instructions. For the sake of Trinidad we must succeed!"

Twenty minutes later, a dozen men stood in front of Malcolm Mann. He looked them over carefully and then addressed them.

"I've called you before me to enlist your help in saving our beloved Trinidad. This will, no doubt, be the most important mission in your lives. If you are not successful, America will soon control our economy. As you know, we planned to have the Prime Minister's daughters and Kevin Wells as hostages by now. Somehow, they escaped our grasp and may be hiding in the forest near Blanchisseuse Bay. You all know this area well, so we need you to put on your civilian clothes and go home. We have enough men for three four-man search parties. You've been issued night vision equipment, which you'll need to use in your search. You should all have weapons at your homes, which you can use in the operation. One last thing, we'd like the hostages brought back alive. However, if that's not possible, then kill them. If you do nothing else, you must kill Kevin Wells! If the government finds him, all is lost!"

The men quickly dispersed, leaving Malcolm and Ray Mohammed alone in the conference room. Ray took a deep breath.

"What if they do fail?" Ray asked.

"I've arranged for you and I to have political asylum in Cuba, so don't worry."

"What about our comrades? What will be their fate?"

"They will surely hang at the hands of Ahmad Shah. He will show no leniency. Since we have attacked his family, no one will blame him."

"Can't we do anything to protect them?"

"No, they are expendable. When we return, we will get others to take their places."

Ray said nothing as Malcolm packed up his briefcase and left the conference room. Ray thought for a moment and then hustled off to his office. He picked up the phone and dialed his home number.

"Hello."

"Cetawayo?"

"Yes."

"Is Jane in?"

"Yes."

"Get her for me. Immediately, it's urgent."

"Yes Ray, right away."

Cetawayo ran into Jane's bedroom and told her to pick up the phone. Then she went back into the kitchen and started to put the kitchen phone on the receiver. She stopped and slowly lifted the phone to her ear so she could hear the conversation.

"Jane, you must pack your bags. Get the children ready. We may have to leave the country tonight."

"What's wrong?"

"The plan has failed, the Prime Minister's daughters and Mr. Wells have escaped. They're hiding out in the forest near Blanchisseuse Bay. The army is all over the area and will surely find them by morning. When they do, they will arrest me. I don't have to explain the consequences of that to you."

"Oh no, Ray! What are we going to do?"

"Malcolm has arranged political asylum for us in Cuba, but we must leave before daybreak."

"Oh, Ray! I don't want to live in Cuba. This is terrible."

"Don't argue, Jane. We have no choice. Do what I say and someone will pick you up at three, okay?"

"Damn it, Ray!"

"I'm sorry. I'd go without you, but I'm sure you'd be arrested too. You have no choice. We have to leave the country."

"All right, we'll be ready."

Jane and Cetawayo hung up the phone at the same time. Cetawayo quickly went about her business. Soon, Jane came into the kitchen and sat down.

"So, was that Ray?" Cetawayo asked.

"Yes."

"Is everything all right?"

"Of course, he's just not coming home tonight. He's got to go out of town on some business. He wants me and kids to meet him in San Fernando early tomorrow morning. We'll have to leave early to get there in time. We'll try not to wake you when we leave."

"Can I help you pack?"

"Sure, I could use some help."

Later, when Jane had left to run an errand, Cetawayo picked up the phone and dialed a number.

"Hello."

"Obatala, you must come home now. I've got some news, but I can't discuss it over the phone. Come quick, while Jane is out!"

"What kind of news?"

"I don't have time to explain, just come home."

"All right. I'm on my way."

# Chapter 15

Kevin watched Deviane as she laid down and tried to go to sleep. The makeshift lean-to would do a credible job at keeping her dry, but he knew the bed of leaves would do little to insulate her from the cold, damp ground. The prospect of an NDC unit lurking about wouldn't sooth her nerves much either. All in all, it would be difficult for any of them to relax enough to sleep. Deviane rolled over on one side, shifted around, then rolled back to her other side. Kevin wished he could do something to make her comfortable, but he could think of nothing. Finally, she sat up and gave him a frustrated look.

"Why don't you sleep now, Kevin? I'm not tired enough yet."

"I doubt if I'll be able to sleep at all tonight. Too much has happened today. I think I've had an overdose of adrenaline."

"Kiran seems to have fallen asleep."

"Good, we'll let her sleep until four. Then you and I can get a few hours sleep before daybreak."

"You want some more coconut juice?"

Kevin frowned. "No thanks, I've had my fill of it for awhile. We don't drink much coconut juice at home."

"It's good for your kidneys," Deviane laughed.

"Really, my kidneys are fine, thanks."

"Do you think the NDC will search for us in this weather?"

"They probably don't have any choice. I suspect this place will be crawling with your father's troops at daybreak."

"Maybe we should think about what to do if they find us."

"That makes sense. You have any ideas?"

"Well, if we could make it to the main road, our troops should be there."

"How far is to the main road, do you think?"

"I would guess about three miles."

"Do you know how to find it?"

"I think so, but it would be difficult in the dark."

"Well, if we hear anything, we'll follow you and keep our fingers crossed that you've got a good sense of direction."

"Don't worry, I do. I always manage to get where I'm going."

"So I noticed."

"At least so far."

Their eyes locked. Kevin could see the desire in Deviane's eyes. She wanted him and Kevin knew it. Despite his love for Kiran he was tempted. Something was drawing him to her–her confidence and determination to have him. He turned away, trying to control his excitement.

"You know, Kevin. I wouldn't mind if you had both of us."

"What?" Kevin chuckled.

"Why don't you marry both of us?"

"You may not mind, but I have a feeling Kiran might object."

"She wouldn't mind. We're sisters, we're used to sharing things."

"I think that would be slightly illegal."

"We could live in Utah."

Kevin started laughing and then stopped when he realized Deviane was serious.

"Deviane, even if I did love you both it wouldn't be fair to you or Kiran if I did that."

Deviane crawled over next to Kevin and put her arms around him.

"You don't think you could satisfy both of us, is that it?"

"That's a distinct possibility, I think you need a man all to yourself."

"And you're that man," Deviane said as she gently kissed him. Kevin closed his eyes as a rush of excitement overwhelmed him. For a moment he savored her sweet lips unable to resist her. She broke away and smiled, savoring his helplessness. Then she slipped her head down on his neck and gently bit him. Kevin moaned in joyful bliss until Kiran stirred. He drew back.

"Stop it!" he whispered. "What do you think you're doing? I told you I love Kiran."

"You don't love her."

Kevin shook his head. "How could you possibly know whether I love her or not?"

"I just do, trust me."

Deviane suddenly got to her feet and peered into the dense jungle.

"What's wrong?" Kevin said.

"I thought I heard something."

Kevin got on his feet and stood behind her. "What is it?"

"Be quiet."

A second later, they both heard the distinct sound of men walking in the mud. Deviane knelt down and shook Kiran.

"Kiran. Get up. We've got to go."

Kiran let out a moan and rolled over.

"Wake up!" Deviane hissed.

Kiran sat up quickly and rubbed her eyes.

"What?" she said.

"Shhhhh," Kevin grabbed her hand and pulled her up. "Come on, we've got to go. Someone is coming."

Deviane started hiking. The rain had stopped, but the ground was wet and slippery. Kevin heard the chilling sound of soldiers marching in the distance. He looked back at the moon-lit forest to see if he could get a glimpse of the soldiers. Deviane was on a direct path to the road, but it became obvious as the rhythm of the soldier's boots got louder and louder, that they weren't going to make it in time.

"We're going to have to run for it," Kevin said. "In a minute, they'll be close enough to shoot us."

"You're right, let's get moving!" Deviane said as she began to run as fast as she could through the forest.

Kevin followed, pulling Kiran along as best he could. Before they had gone a hundred yards, Kiran stumbled and pulled Kevin down with her. He picked her up quickly and started to run again.

"Come on, Kiran. We're almost there."

She began to run, but stumbled again and screamed in pain as her ankle twisted beneath her.

"I can't run anymore, Kevin. I think it's broken."

Kevin gazed at Kiran lying helplessly in the mud. Suddenly he saw one of the soldiers come out of a clump of trees. He bent down, picked Kiran up and began to run with her in his arms. The sound of gunshots pierced the silence of the night. Kevin heard the trail of the first bullet as it passed several feet from his right shoulder. Motivated by fear of imminent death, he ran as fast as he could with Kiran holding herself tightly against his chest. He vividly remembered the excruciating pain he had felt when Ray Mohammed's shot hit him in the back. He didn't relish the idea of experiencing that kind of pain again.

Hearing Deviane ahead screaming that she could see the road, he stopped briefly and turned to check the position of his pursuers. At that same moment, a bullet exploded from the barrel of an NDC rifle and hit Kiran directly in the chest.

"No! Nooo!" he cried out.

Kiran went limp in his arms. Blood poured from her

wound. Kevin looked back and realized that if he didn't keep going, he was a dead man. He ran with all the speed he could muster, constantly aware of the eyes of his pursuers on him. His feet were bleeding from running through the rocks and thorny brush and his back was breaking from the dead weight of Kiran's body. At any moment another bullet might pierce through his back and bring him down. He could only hope that the silence ahead meant that Deviane had reached the road and was waiting for them. He pressed on, hearing another gunshot and hearing the bullet's trail barely miss him again. Finally he reached the road.

Deviane was carefully scanning the highway, but there was nothing visible in either direction.

Kevin stopped next to her. "Now what?"

"I don't know," she whispered. "Where are the troops?"

"Shit! We'll be sitting ducks on this road. We'll have to go back into the forest and try to lose them."

Even in the moonlight, he saw the color drain from Deviane's face as she saw her sister lying limp in his arms. "Is Kiran, okay?"

"I don't know. She's been hit. I can't tell if she's breathing."

As they pondered their next move, a bullet hit the pavement next to Deviane.

"Kevin! We're going to die!"

Just then, they saw headlights coming quickly down the road. Kevin and Deviane didn't move, seemingly paralyzed by the light.

"What if it's NDC men?" Deviane said.

"If it is, then it's all over for us."

Just as the speeding car got to them, it came to a screeching halt and the door flew open.

"Get in! Hurry up before they put a bullet in you."

"Who are you?"

"It's Obatala, don't you remember me?"

Deviane opened the front door, climbed in quickly and closed it behind her. She sunk down as low as she could, so she wouldn't be an easy target. Kevin jumped in the back seat and laid Kiran down, with her head in his lap. He found a rag on the floor of the back seat and pressed it against Kiran's wound, trying to stop the bleeding. She was in and out of consciousness, moaning and thrashing from the pain of the bullet wound. Just as Obatala started to accelerate, a bullet pierced the side window, shattering it into a million pieces. The old Toyota struggled to gain speed. The NDC unit reached the road and directed a barrage of gunfire toward the fleeing vehicle, but it was out of range.

"What are you doing here?" Kevin asked.

"Cetawayo overheard Ray telling his wife that they were searching for you up here. I figured you might need some help."

"You figured right. If you hadn't come along we'd be dead."

"How's Kiran?" Deviane asked.

"She's breathing, but she's lost a lot of blood. We need to get her to a hospital."

"The nearest hospital is behind us," Obatala noted. "If we turn around, we'll run right into the NDC death squads."

"Death squads?" Kevin said.

"Yes, Malcolm Mann has ordered that you be killed rather than allowed to escape."

"Shit! She'll die if we don't get her to a hospital."

"Maybe not. I know a midwife who lives about ten miles from here. She may be able to stabilize her until we can get help."

"A midwife? What would she know about treating a bullet wound?"

"She worked in the hospital for years and has a lot of medical training. She probably knows as much about medicine as many of the doctors who practice at the hospital. She retired from nursing and became a midwife so she could stay at home. I think she's our best bet."

"I guess we don't have much choice."

"No, you don't."

As Obatala's car sped along the winding mountain road, Kevin stroked Kiran's hair. Periodically, he put his head on her chest to be sure her heart was still beating. Deviane looked on anxiously, frequently wiping tears from her eyes.

"How did you get past the government troops, Obatala?" Kevin asked.

"Oh, I just made up a little story."

"It must have been a good one. What did you tell them?"

"I just said that twice a week I had to pick up an old woman who had kidney disease. I said she had to go into town for her dialysis treatment. If they didn't let me through, she would die."

"Hmm. That's pretty creative, but didn't they wonder why you would be taking her in the middle of the night?"

"As a matter of fact they did ask me that. I told them she was a pauper and could not pay for her treatment. The only time the hospital would let her use it for free, was in the middle of the night."

"That was quick thinking. I don't know how you could have thought of such a great story so quickly. I'm impressed."

"Actually, it's true. There is such a woman, but tonight's not the night I pick her up."

"How much longer will it be?" Deviane asked.

"Not far, another five minutes and we'll be there," Obatala replied as he gazed at Deviane's nearly naked body. "Are you cold? I brought some clothes."

"Yes, the rain gave me a chill. I'm freezing to death."

"Kevin, there's some jeans and a T-shirt in the back. I brought some sneakers too. I heard you were swimming when the attack occurred, so I assumed you would be short on clothing."

"You're a wonderful man, " Deviane said. "You saved our lives."

"You can call me Obatala."

"Why would you risk your life for us?"

"Did you tell them anything about me, Kevin?"

"Just that you saved my life when I first got here. This is getting to be a habit."

"You see, Deviane, I am ashamed to say it, but Ray Mohammed is my brother. He was always a good boy, but somehow he got in with Malcolm Mann and the NDC. They have poisoned his mind. I tried to get him to quit and stay away from those hoodlums, but he wouldn't listen to me. Since I can't save my brother, I thought perhaps I could save Trinidad."

"It's hard to believe that you and he could be brothers. You're so good and he's so evil."

"It's a strange world we live in. Okay, here is the road into Miss Victoria's house," Obatala said and then turned the car onto a dirt road. "We'll be there in just two or three minutes."

Obatala drove the cab up to the front door of Miss Victoria's house. It was three o'clock in the morning. He banged on the door until the porch light came on. A heavyset black lady peered out the window. Obatala waved at her to open the door. Finally recognizing him, she quickly unlatched the door and opened it.

"Obatala, my word, what are you doing here in the middle of the night?"

"It's the Prime Minister's daughter. She's been shot."

"Good Lord! Bring her in here and put her on the sofa."

Kevin carried Kiran into the house and laid her on the sofa as instructed.

"Oh, look at her, she's as pale as a ghost. I see she's lost a lot of blood. I'll get an IV running and then clean that wound."

Miss Victoria ran into the other room and quickly returned with an IV rack. She skillfully inserted a needle in Kiran's arm and started the IV.

"She's not breathing too well, get that oxygen bottle out of the closet."

Kevin ran over to the closet and pulled out one of several oxygen bottles and brought it to her.

"Here you go."

"Okay, put this mask over her nose and attach that hose onto the oxygen bottle."

Kevin did as he was told. When he had finished she said, "Okay, turn it on before she dies on us."

Kevin turned it on. "Okay, it's opened all the way."

"Now, watch her a minute while I get some hot water and disinfectant."

She left for a moment and when she returned she began to clean Kiran's wound. Everyone watched her intently as she worked.

"She needs to get this bullet out of her soon."

"What about your cellular phone, Obatala?" Kevin asked. "Can't you call the Prime Minister's office and tell them where we are? They could have a chopper here in ten minutes."

"I considered that, but the NDC will be searching for cellular transmissions. There's not much activity at this time in the morning. If we used the phone, I'm sure they'd pick up our call right away."

"We've got to get Kiran to a hospital immediately," Deviane pleaded.

"We'll have to risk it," Kevin said.

"All right, but I hope they get here fast."

"They will," Deviane promised.

"Okay, I'll go get the phone."

Obatala went outside and retrieved the phone from his car. He brought it in and handed it to Deviane.

"I'll call my father's private line, so we'll get straight to him."

She dialed the number and waited. It rang twice and then someone picked up.

"Yes," the Prime Minister said.

"Daddy, it's Deviane."

"Deviane, where are you? Are you all right?"

"I'm fine, but the they've shot Kiran. We need to get her to a hospital immediately."

"Oh my God! Where are you? I'll send a helicopter right away."

"I don't know, I'll put Obatala on to tell you."

"Who?"

"Obatala, he's a cab driver," she said and then handed the phone to Obatala. "Here, Obatala, speak to my father and tell him where we are."

Obatala took the phone.

"Hello, sir. We are eight kilometers north of Blanchisseuse Bay. There is a small dirt road that goes off to the right, just past the gas station. We're about a half-mile down that road. It's a small, white frame house with a green roof."

"Okay, someone will be there immediately."

The phone went dead. Obatala set it down on the kitchen table and took a deep breath.

"I hope they get here fast," Kevin said.

Deviane walked over to a small desk in the corner of the room. On the desk were a lamp, a bible and some rosary beads. She picked up the rosary beads and asked, "May I borrow these for a moment."

"Of course, I think your sister could use a little divine intervention right now."

"Thank you," Deviane said and walked over and knelt next to Kiran.

Kevin watched Deviane pray a moment and then walked over and put his hands on her shoulders. After a second, she got up and embraced Kevin. They held each other and waited to be rescued. Miss Victoria took Kiran's pulse and checked her blood pressure. Then in a motherly gesture, she ran her hand through Kiran's fine black hair. Deviane began to weep.

"Come on, child. Just hang on a little while longer," she said.

It was less than fifteen minutes, but it seemed like an eternity before the sound of a helicopter could be heard in the distance. Kevin ran outside with Deviane right behind. He jumped up and down, waving frantically at the chopper, but in the darkness they couldn't see him. Finally, he went over to Obatala's car and turned the lights on and off. The chopper suddenly veered toward them and landed a hundred yards away. Kevin and Deviane ran over to the chopper and met the medics as they jumped out. They pointed to the house and yelled that Kiran was inside. The medics pulled out a stretcher and carried it across the field and into the house.

"What's her condition?" the paramedic asked.

"She has a bullet wound in the chest, her breathing is difficult and she needs blood," Victoria replied.

"How long has it been since she was hit?"

"Forty-five minutes," Kevin said.

The paramedics loaded Kiran on the stretcher and carried it back to the helicopter.

"There's another chopper, five minutes away, that will pick you up and take you back to the capital. We're going to Port of Spain General Hospital. Good luck."

The chopper rose slowly into the air and then headed off over the forest. Kevin and Deviane watched it disappear and then waited in anticipation of their rescue.

Suddenly, two headlights appeared, moving up the dirt road leading to Miss Victoria's place. Kevin and Deviane ran back toward the house to warn Obatala, but before they got halfway there, another set of lights appeared, coming from the other direction. The two cars intercepted Kevin and Deviane. A half dozen soldiers jumped out and surrounded them. Obatala and Victoria looked out the window in horror as they watched Kevin and Deviane being bound and gagged and thrown into the back of a jeep. Obatala suddenly felt sick, his worst nightmare had become reality. Phase one of the NDC plan to seize control of the Trinidad government had been successfully carried out.

# Chapter 16

It was raining heavily when the helicopter arrived at Port of Spain General Hospital. A special team of doctors had been assembled in anticipation of the arrival of the Prime Minister's daughter. Kiran was immediately rushed to the casualty department. When her condition had been stabilized, she was taken into surgery for the removal of the bullet. Ahmad and Anila waited anxiously in a private waiting room. Sharad and Anamica checked in periodically to see how they were doing, and to keep them appraised of any new developments.

"I can't believe my baby is having a bullet taken out of her chest. God, Ahmad, how could you let this happen?"

"What do you mean? I had them heavily guarded. I never suspected the sleazy cowards would launch an all out attack on my children! Jesus! I used to have a little respect for Malcolm Mann, but now I know he's nothing but a spineless cockroach!"

"Why don't you arrest him?"

"I'd like to, believe me. Unfortunately, at this moment I have no proof he's responsible. I guarantee, though, just as soon as we can tie him to the assassination attempt or this kidnaping, we'll put him behind bars, where he belongs."

"What if Kiran dies, Ahmad? She's so young."

"She won't die. She's a strong girl."

"I can't stand this, Ahmad! I can't stand just sitting here not knowing if she's going to live or die."

"She'll be all right, relax!"

For nearly an hour, Ahmad and Anila waited impatiently for news. Finally the doctor walked into the room.

"Mr. Prime Minister?"

"Yes."

"Your daughter is out of surgery. We've removed the bullet and she's in the recovery room. She was a very lucky girl. The bullet narrowly missed her heart."

"Oh, thank God!" Anila sobbed. "So she's going to be okay?"

"Yes, it's fortunate they were able to get her to Miss Victoria when they did. She lost a lot of blood and may not have made it without her help."

"Who is Miss Victoria? I want to personally thank her," the Prime Minister said.

"She's a midwife who's been practicing up in the north for as long as I can remember. A lot of folks still use her to avoid having to come to Port of Spain and pay for a hospital visit."

"Anamica, make a note for me to stop by and visit her one day."

"Yes, sir."

"Is she awake, doctor? Can we see her?"

"No, we better let her sleep awhile. Why don't you come back about noon tomorrow? She should be awake and feeling much better by then."

"Oh, I'm so relieved. Thank you, doctor," Anila said.

"I'm happy that I could be of service. I hope your other daughter is okay."

"Speaking of Deviane, has the other helicopter brought her back yet?"

"I'll call immediately and find out," Anamica replied and then started to leave the room.

As she was leaving, Sharad entered.

"Ahmad, you won't believe this."

"What?"

"When the second helicopter arrived, Deviane and Mr.

Wells were gone. They've been kidnaped!"

"Oh no! No!" Anila screamed and began crying.

Anamica quickly came over and held her.

"Are you sure? How could that be? What happened?"

"Miss Victoria said the NDC arrived right after Kiran had been taken away. They bound and gagged them and threw them into a jeep. She and Obatala managed to slip out the back door and into the forest without being seen. She said the NDC jeep headed south, toward Arima."

"Oh, God!" Anila wailed.

"Are we in pursuit?"

"Yes, of course, and we've got a blockade on the road ten miles north of Arima."

"Good. I wonder how they knew where to find them?"

"It was the mobile phone, sir. They must have intercepted Deviane's call to you."

"Damn it!" the Prime Minister yelled.

Tears welled in his eyes. He struggled to keep from crying.

"I know, Ahmad. I know."

"I'm going to take Anila home. Call me if you hear anything."

"I will. What about the news conference?"

"Cancel it! Until we know Deviane and Kevin's fate, I don't want to talk to the press."

"Should we tell them about the kidnaping and that Kiran is safe?"

"No, tell them nothing. They'll have to wait."

"Some of what happened may have already leaked out. They'll be asking lots of questions."

"I know. They always ask lots of questions, but they'll just have to wait another day, until we can sort things out. I can't deal with them now, okay?"

"Yes, Ahmad. Of course."

****

The two jeeps raced along the narrow highway towards

Arima, with Kevin and Deviane bound and gagged in the back seat. The sky was starting to lighten with the approaching dawn. Suddenly, the jeep veered off the main highway onto a dirt road. It stopped five minutes later. Kevin heard the door open and a hand reached in to pull him roughly from his seat.

Moments later, he was assaulted by the wind and the roar of helicopter blades as he was lifted into the chopper and thrown onto a seat. He heard Deviane's muffled screams as she was also forced aboard. The helicopter rose quickly and flew low to the ground, toward its destination.

Kevin was paralyzed with fear. He knew the kidnappers had orders to kill him. They would have reason to keep Deviane alive. She could provide them a good ransom, but he was only a liability. He was the one person who could bring down the NDC. He wondered why he was still alive.

It wasn't long before the helicopter made its descent. Once on the ground, the two hostages were led to an elevator and taken down several floors. They were led down a hallway and put in a room. When their blindfolds and gags were removed, and their hands untied, a half dozen young soldiers were surrounding them. Without a word, they were left alone in the small, concrete, windowless room. In the far corner there was an old mattress thrown on the ground. In another corner, a dirty toilet and a sink.

"Where are we?" Deviane asked in a quivering voice.

"Who knows? We could be anywhere. I think we flew back toward Port of Spain, but I'm not sure."

"I wonder how Kiran is doing? I hope she's okay. I can't believe she got away and we didn't."

"I guess using the mobile phone wasn't such a hot idea."

"At least it saved Kiran."

"I hope it did. She didn't look so good when we left her."

"She'll make it, won't she, Kevin?"

"I think so. Miss Victoria had her stabilized at least."

"I hope so. I am so scared."

"I know. So am I. Why don't you lie down? You must be exhausted."

"Actually, I *am* exhausted. That mattress is looking pretty good right now."

"I'd like to take a nap too, but I'm starving. I wonder if they plan to feed us?"

"I assume they will eventually."

Deviane walked over to the mattress and lay down. It didn't take her long to fall asleep. Kevin watched her awhile, running the events of the last 24 hours through his mind over and over again. Finally he succumbed to his exhaustion, lay down beside her and fell asleep. Hours later he awoke and found her cuddled next to him with her head on his shoulder. He was afraid to move as he feared it might wake her up, but she was already awake.

"I've dreamed of sleeping with you," she said. "But not like this."

"You have?"

"Yes, ever since you were on Jay Leno. Kiran and I both have had a crush on you. I was so mad when my father let Kiran go visit you. I knew you'd fall in love with her and then I wouldn't have a chance."

"I'm sorry, I had no idea. . . . Where did you learn that vampire move anyway? I've never felt anything like that before."

"I read about the technique in a magazine, *Twenty-four Ways to Drive Your Man Wild!*"

"Twenty-four?"

"Yeah, that was number 11."

"Jesus! What kind of magazines do you read?"

"All of them. Even Cosmopolitan and all the teenage slut magazines. I hate being naive or ignorant about anything."

"Hmm. I don't think you have to worry about that. You're already a lot smarter and more knowledgeable than most girls I've met."

"Does that bother you?"

"No, I like a smart girl."

"Even one who may be smarter than you?"

He laughed. "Well, I haven't met that girl yet, but I wouldn't care either way."

Deviane chuckled. "Good. A lot of boys don't like me because I have a brain."

"Yeah, I can believe that. A lot of my friends are like that too. It's pretty stupid."

The two prisoners pondered their plight for several minutes in an uneasy silence. Deviane closed her eyes and clutched Kevin tightly. Kevin stared at the blank wall as if in a trance.

"I can't believe I'm going to die before I ever get married," Deviane said.

"We're not going to die, don't talk like that."

"How will we ever escape?"

"Your father will rescue us, I'm sure."

"If he can find us."

"If he doesn't find us, then we'll have to figure out a way to get out of here on our own."

"But, how?"

"People escape from prisons everyday. We'll just have to be observant and resourceful. We'll figure something out."

"What if we don't?"

Kevin took a deep breath. "Then at least we won't die alone."

Deviane lifted her head and looked Kevin in the eyes. After a moment of silence she smiled.

"You're right. Having you with me when the end comes will make it so much easier to bear."

Kevin took her hand and gave it a tender squeeze. She

smiled and then wiped away a tear that had started to run down her cheek. Finally she laid back down and closed her eyes. Soon she was asleep.

Kevin watched her as she slept. His mind was whirling–pondering her apparent infatuation with him and trying desperately to come up with a plan, a strategy for their survival. Finally, he gave in to exhaustion and fell asleep.

*He was in Texas now, living the assassination attempt once again. Feeling the sting of the bullet piercing his flesh. Reeling from the pain that finally drove him to unconsciousness. Then he was in front of his house.*

*He stepped out of his car. There were blue and white lights flashing on a patrol car. He could hear the police radio, then a crowd of reporters surrounded him. They were yelling questions at him, so many questions. The lights of the cameras flashed. He stuck his arm in front of him to shield his eyes from the bright lights. Then someone grabbed his arm. He pulled away and began to run. He ran inside nearly gagging from the stench. He hurried through a crowd of men in the living room. Then upstairs toward her room. Then he saw her. She was lying on her bed with a white sheet stretched from head to toe. Kevin pulled it down to look at her face. She looked so peaceful, like she was in a deep wonderful sleep. He began to cry. . . .*

# Chapter 17

Ahmad stared at the crowd of reporters outside the entrance to the hospital. He had kept a lid on the situation about as long as he could. He and Sharad had been dodging reporters all morning. Rumors were running rampant. Most reporters were speculating that Ray Mohammed had been arrested and charged with the attempted assassination of the Prime Minister. He would have to have to hold a news conference soon, but first he had to visit his beloved, Kiran. He still couldn't believe what had happened to her. As he and Anila walked in, they were elated to see her smiling.

"Sweetheart! I've been so worried about you," Anila said, cautiously bending over to give her daughter a hug.

"I'm okay."

"You look tired. Your skin is pale," the Prime Minister said.

"I feel kind of weak."

"What do you expect?" Anila said. "You've been shot, for godsakes."

"We were so worried when you disappeared from the beach. What happened?" the Prime Minister asked.

"We were just messing around when all of a sudden, cars started exploding everywhere and men started chasing us. Deviane took us into the caves. From there we managed to escape into the forest."

"Oh my poor darling, it must have been terrible being in the forest all night," Anila said.

"It actually wasn't so bad. We camped at a really pretty waterfall. Kevin built us a lean-to and made us a fire. It was kind of fun, until the death squad showed up."

"The death squad?" the Prime Minister asked.

"Yes, didn't you know Malcolm Mann ordered Kevin killed?"

"What! He ordered him killed?"

"Yes."

"God damn it! That bastard! I'll strangle him with my bare hands! Jesus! If the NDC hurts Kevin or Deviane, I'll see every last member hanged. I swear it!"

"How do you know this, Kiran?" Anila asked.

"After I was shot, some man, a friend of Kevin's, picked us up on the road. He told us."

"Who was he?" the Prime Minister asked.

"I don't know, but if he hadn't come along, we'd all be dead now."

"What do you mean?"

"We were asleep when they showed up. We made a run for the main road, thinking your troops would be there. About half way there, I sprained my ankle. So Kevin had to carry me. It was just before we got to the road that I was shot. Luckily, the man came just in time to help us get away."

"You poor child. What a horrible experience," Anila said. "I'm so glad Kevin was with you two, to protect you."

"He was wonderful. I wouldn't be here now had it not been for him. Where is he anyway? I was hoping he would come and visit me."

Anila frowned. "Oh, Kiran, you don't know."

"Know what?"

"Kevin and Deviane were captured by the NDC!"

"Oh, God. No, no! It can't be! They'll kill them!"

"Maybe not," the Prime Minister said. "If they want to gain public support for their party, it wouldn't look good for them to be murdering innocent people. They'll have to be very careful about what they do with Kevin and Deviane. It's a delicate situation. They probably just want to use them as bargaining chips."

"You've got to find them, Daddy. You can't let them kill Kevin and Deviane!"

"I won't, believe me child. We've got thousands of people looking for them right now. We'll find them and we'll bring the kidnappers to justice. I promise you."

"I don't care about the kidnappers, I just want Kevin and Deviane back safely."

"I know. We'll get them back. Don't worry. I'm going to leave you with your mother now. I must get to work on a statement for the press. They're frantic for information, I've got to give them something."

"Okay, I'll see you later, Daddy."

Ahmad left. Anila and Kiran talked for another half hour, until the nurse suggested Anila leave and let Kiran get some rest. She promised to return after dinner so they could talk and watch television together.

Anila was taken by her security escort from the hospital to St. Andrews Church, where she met with her priest. They prayed together for Deviane and Kevin's safe return. Then she went home to get ready for dinner. She and Ahmad were supposed to have dinner with the leader of the NAR and his wife. The purpose of the dinner was to brief his ally on recent developments and get his advice on how the government should handle the current crisis.

After dinner, Anila returned to the hospital to spend the evening with Kiran. The evening went quickly as they reminisced about past events and speculated about the future. Late in the evening, the Tonight show with Jay Leno came on.

"And now here is the host of the Tonight Show, Jay.... Lennooo."

Jay Leno came out on the stage to the music of the

Tonight Show Band and made his usual run to the audience to shake hands. Then he returned to the stage for his monologue.

"Ladies and gentlemen, welcome to the Tonight Show. We've got a great lineup of guests tonight, including Priscilla Presley, Tom Hanks and singer, Paula Abdul."

The crowd roared its approval and Jay continued.

"In the news tonight, there's a rumor about Kevin Wells. You remember Kevin Wells, the boy who saved the life of the Prime Minister of Trinidad? As you recall, he was a guest on the Tonight Show several months ago. Well, you may have heard Kevin was invited to Trinidad to stay with the Prime Minister's family for a week or ten days. Well, he's down there now and apparently, he and the Prime Minister's two daughters, Kiran and Deviane, were nearly kidnaped."

"Ohhh...," the crowed wailed.

"Yes. They got away though. In fact, rumor has it that Kevin and these two beautiful woman are lost somewhere in a rain forest in northern Trinidad."

"Ewww...," the crowd yelled.

"You may not know this, but Trinidad is where Robinson Crusoe was stranded with his trusted companion, Friday. That's right. Now, I want to ask you, does Kevin Wells know how to get in trouble or what? Come on. This guy gets in the way of an assassin's bullet and becomes a national hero. Now he goes to Trinidad and is nearly kidnaped, but ends up stranded in the forest with two beautiful women. Jesus, I wish I had that kind of trouble!"

The crowd laughed and Jay went on.

"Now, we've done a little checking on Kevin Wells to see what makes this kid tick. We talked to some of his friends back at his high school in Plano, Texas. They tell us that Kevin had a hidden agenda in going to Trinidad. Yes, you see, the Trinidad police believed that he was going down there to finger the Prime Minister's assassin. The

Prime Minister thought he was coming down to accept his thanks for saving his life. Actually, Kevin went to Trinidad in search of a virgin."

"Ohhh...," the crowd yelled.

"Yes. Apparently Kevin is from the old school and believes that a man and wife should be virgins when they get married."

Several of the members of the audience chuckled.

"No, now that's an ideal that's rarely achieved nowadays," Jay laughed, "but a goal all young people should aspire to, right?"

More chuckles from the audience.

"So, as you would expect, he hasn't been able to find a virgin here in America. However, when he found out the Prime Minister's daughter had never been kissed, he became obsessed with the idea of seeing her again. Well now he's got his wish. In fact, he's out in the forest right now with two virgins."

"Ooo...," the crowd screamed.

"You could say he's covering some virgin territory."

The crowd moaned.

"You know, it's really amazing that the Prime Minister of Trinidad was the father of two virgins. But I guess he's the commander and chief of the army, so all the boys in Trinidad knew what would happen if they messed with his daughters!"

The crowd applauded.

"If they didn't get shot, they'd get drafted, right?"

The crowd roared with laughter. "No, seriously, Kevin's a good kid and we hope he and the Prime Minister's daughters find their way home safely. With their virginity intact, of course."

The crowd clapped vigorously.

"Oh, just one last thing. The President announced today that he has added virgins to the endangered species list, so he can get funding from Congress to help in the search to find Kevin and the Prime Minister's daughters."

The audience laughed and applauded.

"Can you believe that Kevin is a virgin?" Anila asked Kiran.

"Sure, he told me he was."

"You've talked about *virginity* with him?"

"More or less."

"What does *that* mean?"

"He's told me how important love and trust are to him and that marriage is sacred. It's pretty obvious what he meant."

"He sounds like your sister."

"You're right. She's got a big crush on him, too."

"Deviane?"

"That's the only sister that I know about, unless you've been hiding something from me, Mother."

"Don't be a wise-ass. Hmm. I had no idea Deviane was interested in Kevin."

"It's too bad, Kevin already asked me to marry him."

"What?"

"Didn't Daddy discuss it with you? He made some kind of deal with Kevin. I guess if he does what Daddy wants, then he gets to marry me."

"Well, I'm going to have a talk with him, right now. I can't believe he would do such a thing and not even talk to me about it."

"No, don't. I've already agreed to it. I told Kevin I'd marry him."

"Are you serious? Do you love him?"

"I don't know, but he's good looking and fun to be with."

"You shouldn't marry him unless you love him."

"You didn't marry Daddy for love."

"Well, that was different. I was poor and I needed someone who could give me security."

"And I need someone who can make me an American

citizen."

"Oh, Kiran, you shouldn't marry just to get away from Trinidad. We'll send you to America to go to school. You may not like it there."

"I'll grow to love Kevin, like you've grown to love Daddy. It'll be okay. You'll see."

"Oh, Kiran, I hope you're not making a mistake."

"The only mistake I've made is letting the NDC kidnap Kevin. If I would have been conscious, I would have made him come with me in the helicopter. I can't believe he's gone."

"Your father will find him, don't worry."

"He'd better. I'll never forgive him if Kevin is killed."

# Chapter 18

Kevin's nightmare was so vivid he awoke and looked around the stark cell. It was dark, the only light that made its way into the room came from a small window above the door. He carefully extricated himself from Deviane's embrace, trying not to wake her up.

Instinctively, he looked down at his wrist to see what time it was. Then, he realized he had left his watch on the beach. Judging from the hunger pains he was feeling, he believed they must have slept four or five hours. That would make it close to noon. He got up, stretched and began examining the room carefully, looking for a clue as to how they might escape.

The small window above the door was the only one in the room. Although it was glass, a careful inspection revealed it to be reinforced by a thick wire mesh. There would be no way to get through it without some sort of wire cutters. Giving up on the small window, Kevin began to examine the walls. Unfortunately, they were solid concrete and provided no hope of penetration. Kevin turned his attention to the ceiling, which appeared to be made of heavy wooden beams. A hardwood floor had been built above it. Finally, he carefully examined every inch of the floor, only to realize that it, too, was solid concrete.

While he was trying to think up a strategy for escape to tell Deviane when she awoke, he heard voices coming toward them. He watched the door as it opened. Three men dressed in military attire stood before him. He recognized one of the men as Ray Mohammed. The commotion woke up Deviane and she sat up to see what was happening.

"Hello, Mr. Wells, I'm Malcolm Mann. I want to welcome you to the National Defense Coalition headquarters."

"What do you want with us?" Kevin said.

"I'm sorry that it has to be this way, but the Prime Minister has left us no choice. You see, he insists on pushing this Caribbean Free Trade Agreement, which would jeopardize Trinidad's independence and destroy its economy. It's obvious the only reason the United States is interested in Trinidad is to get control of its oil. Something has to be done to stop Ahmad."

"I know why you kidnapped me, but how does kidnapping Deviane help you?"

"The Prime Minister isn't likely to launch an attack on us if his precious little daughter might get killed in the process."

"I can't believe you'd use an innocent girl as a shield. What kind of a person are you, anyway?"

"It's not our choice, it's what must be done to rescue Trinidad from the clutches of American imperialism."

"You're kind of paranoid, aren't you? I haven't noticed the people in Mexico complaining much about NAFTA. The Mexican economy is as strong as ever."

"The economy may be strong, but the people are in bondage and they don't even realize it. They think they're free, but really, they're the slaves of Wall Street, just like the American people. I won't let that happen to Trinidad."

"No, you'd just trample all over the Trinidad Constitution and destroy forty years of democracy? You're a real savior."

Ray Mohammed started to lunge toward Kevin, but Mann stuck up his arm to restrain him.

"I don't think you're in any position to be so

sanctimonious," Mann said.

"Well, when a man is about to die, it's no time to be timid, right? I know you ordered my death and I should be shaking in my boots, but somehow, I doubt that would help keep me alive. Why am I still alive, anyway?"

"That's an interesting question. You see, the Prime Minister is on very shaky ground and I don't want to do anything to strengthen his position. The thought occurred to me that if I killed you, he might make a martyr out of you. There's also the possibility that if I killed an American citizen, it might give the United States an excuse to intervene in the current political situation. So, Mr. Wells, I won't kill you today, but just as soon as Ahmad Shah has fallen, I'm going to kick your little virgin ass all over this room and break your neck with my bare hands!"

Malcolm's threats filled Kevin with fear. At any moment his captors could end his life, but he knew he had to be strong if he and Deviane were to survive. He struggled to maintain his composure.

"What makes you think the government will fall?"

"Oh it will fall, Mr. Wells. The Prime Minister is already being perceived as incompetent. He can't even protect a key witness who could solve the assassination attempt on his life. He lets his own children get kidnaped while they're swimming on the beach. Is that the kind of man who should be leading Trinidad? I think not. I suspect his government won't last another week."

Kevin looked Malcolm straight in the eye and replied. "Why don't we quit the bullshit and be honest for a minute. I'm not as stupid as Ray and the other goons you've got surrounding you."

Ray lunged at Kevin again, grabbed his shirt and hit him across the face knocking him to the ground. Deviane jumped on Ray's back, trying to keep him from hitting Kevin again. Ray slung her to the ground, next to Kevin. Malcolm grabbed Ray's shoulder and ordered him to stop. Kevin sat up and wiped the blood off his lip.

"You're going to kill me whether the government falls or not. You can't afford to have me alive." Kevin looked over at Deviane and said, "You can't afford to have either one of us alive now that we've heard your plan to commit treason."

"You're very perceptive Mr. Wells. That's too bad. I was trying to give you some hope so your last few hours on earth wouldn't be so painful."

"Since you're being so thoughtful, how about some food, or is it your plan to starve us to death?"

"No, I told you I was going to break your neck, remember? I'll send down some food in a little while. You'll just have to be patient. This isn't the Hilton, you know?"

Malcolm and his men left the room. Deviane walked over to Kevin and put her arms around him. Kevin didn't respond, but only stared at the door, replaying Malcolm's words over and over in his mind.

He had put up a brave facade, but he had been shaking inside all along. Suddenly, he felt sick to his stomach and had to struggle to keep from throwing up.

"You okay, Kevin?" Deviane asked. "I can't believe how you stood up to him."

"I can't either. It just came out, like someone else was saying it."

"It was you, and I loved it. I'm so proud of you."

"What are we going to do, Deviane? He can't wait to kill us."

"We've got to get out of here somehow."

"How? I've inspected every inch of this room and I don't see any way out!"

"There's got to be a way!"

"But there isn't. Look around, it's solid concrete everywhere. The only thing that's not concrete is the ceiling. Unless you can fly, that's out of the question."

"What about the door? Have you checked the lock?"

"No."

Deviane went over to the door and examined the lock. "This doesn't look too promising."

"I guess we'll just have to relax and wait for your father to rescue us."

"I hate just waiting around and not knowing what's going to happen. I wish I had a book to read or something to keep my mind occupied."

"Maybe they have a prison library," Kevin laughed.

"It's not funny. . . . What if they do kill us? What if this is the last day of our life?"

Kevin pondered Deviane's words. Finally he said, "Well, I guess we should ask for a priest."

"Yes, but they would never send us one," Deviane replied.

"Well, I guess we could confess our sins to each other. I think God would let us do that under the circumstances."

"Since we may die, it would be good for us to get any guilt we've been feeling off our chests."

Kevin nodded. "Yes, I suppose so."

"So how shall we do it?"

"Just pretend I'm a priest. Tell me your sins and ask for God's forgiveness. I'll do the same with you. We'll take turns."

"Oh, I don't know, Kevin. I don't know if I could do that. You're not really a priest."

"You don't trust me? I thought you were in love with me."

"I am, but you're not in love with me. The last I heard you were going to marry Kiran."

"Well, fine. It was your idea."

"Do you promise, if I confess to you all my sins and somehow we get out of here, that you'll never tell anyone what I told you?"

"Absolutely."

"Even Kiran, if you marry her?"

"Even Kiran. I promise, but you've got to make the same

promise to me."

"Of course."

"Okay, you want me to go first?"

"Yes."

Kevin took Deviane's hand and pulled her up from the floor. Then they walked over to the mattress and sat down.

"All right. I've never told anyone this before, but when I was in the second grade, I wasn't too good in math class. One day the teacher pulled a pop quiz. I knew I was going to flunk it, since I hadn't been doing my homework. The kid that sat next to me was a brain and I knew he would ace the test. So, when the teacher wasn't looking, I copied all of the kid's answers. Later, when the teacher confronted me with the fact that all my answers were identical to the boy next to me, I lied to her and swore that I had studied my homework really hard, and the answers were my own."

"Kevin, you little devil!"

"I don't think in this game we should assess blame or ridicule anyone. We're priests, remember? You need to be solemn and tell me if God will forgive me."

"Okay, yes, he will forgive you."

"Really?"

"Yes, silly, that's nothing. Wait until you hear mine. Lets see, when I was about thirteen, my mom was still an airline stewardess. She used to take us girls to exotic places. This particular year, we went to Barbados. We loved Barbados, because the beaches are so pretty and the water is so blue. Well, Kiran and I met this boy from Argentina. He was so cute and fun to be with. I was very jealous, because Kiran was older than I was and always ended up winning the boys we met. I wasn't going to let her do it again. So that night, at dinner, when no one was looking, I put dish washing liquid in her enchiladas. Needless to say, she threw up all night and had to stay home. Since she was sick, I had no choice but to go out with the cute Argentine boy."

"Deviane! I can't–"

"Hey, I thought–"

"I'm sorry. Hmm. I guess God will forgive you."

"You guess?"

"He'll forgive you, relax. Okay it's my turn. Hmmm! Back home, there is this really gorgeous girl that I know. She's a cheerleader and she's very nice, not real smart, but a really sweet girl. Unfortunately, her parents are too busy for her, so she's pretty lonely. Consequently, she doesn't mind going to bed with any guy who's got the time."

"Kevin! You didn't."

"Hang on, let me finish my confession. One day I was on my way home and I stopped to pick up some stuff from my locker. I was feeling kind of depressed. As I turned to leave, there was Stacy. She was so excited to see me, I couldn't be rude to her. She invited me home for dinner. I didn't want to go, but I felt sorry for her. She was so lonely."

Deviane stood up, walked a few steps away and stared at the wall.

Kevin continued.

"Anyway she took me home and we drank too much wine."

Deviane began to cry, "Kevin I can't bear this. Tell me this didn't happen."

"Will you let me finish! Jesus!"

"Okay, go on."

"Anyway, after dinner we started kissing and making out. Pretty soon, my hand was on her breast, things were getting out of control. Then she said something that made me realize I'd been set up. My so-called friends, who were so anxious to corrupt me, had asked Stacy to seduce me. Thank God I had the strength to get up and leave right then, before they had accomplished their objective."

"You touched her breasts?"

"Just for an instant. I curse myself for falling into their trap, but I can't deny that I did. Do you think God will forgive me? . . . Do you think Kiran will forgive me?"

Deviane was silent for a moment. Then she took a deep breath and turned and looked Kevin in the eyes.

"Yes, God will forgive, maybe even Kiran will forgive you but you're on thin ice with me."

Kevin burst into laughter.

"Come on! Me on thin ice? After you laid number 11 on me back in the forest. I think you're the one on thin ice?"

Deviane turned away. "Do you promise you won't laugh at me?"

"Laugh, why would I laugh?"

"Since we're about to die, I suppose I should tell you."

"Tell me what?"

"You know how you've been looking for the perfect woman to marry?"

"Yes."

"Well, I've been on a similar quest for the perfect man. I've been looking for my soul mate just like you. I've never been with a man and now I'll probably die a virgin."

"Don't give up, Deviane. We'll be rescued. I'm sure we will. You'll find your soul mate."

"I know, I already have."

Kevin frowned. "Huh?"

Deviane shook her head. "You are such a typical male, blind and stupid. . . . Jesus! Don't you know I'm your soul mate? You're the man I've been searching for all my life."

Kevin raised his eyebrows. "You're serious?"

"Yes, and if you marry Kiran I'll just die. I suppose I'll have to become a nun and give myself to God. You're the only man I could ever marry."

Kevin gazed into Deviane's beautiful angry eyes in shock. Feelings for her were welling up inside him quickly, but he felt an incredible guilt at the mere thought of betraying Kiran. Confused, he became angry.

"You haven't really known me that long. You don't know anything about me."

"That's not true. I know everything about you. I've read every news story, I've seen you on TV and now I've lived in the same house with you. I've known from the very beginning you were the one."

"My God, if that is true, why didn't know it?"

"You were so infatuated with Kiran you didn't give me a second thought. I knew I had to stop your marriage or we would both be miserable for the rest of our life. That's why I've been trying to seduce you."

Kevin walked away to ponder the situation. *How can I marry Kiran now when I know how Deviane feels about me? It would haunt me every moment of our marriage. Every time I held Kiran, I would think of Deviane. When we made love, I'd see Deviane's face. And if she became a nun it would be twice as bad. And what if she is my soul mate and I am too blind to recognize it?*

*Damn it! I love Kiran, . . . but she doesn't love me, she's admitted it. But she'll grow to love me just like her mother grew to love Ahmad. . . . Deviane loves me but I don't love her. How ironic? Everything is so complicated and impossible. . . . But, one thing is clear–I promised Kiran I'd marry her and I can't betray her. . . . But she doesn't love me. . . . Oh, hell! It doesn't even matter–I'll soon be dead anyway, if Malcolm has his way.*

\*\*\*

Ambassador Rawlins walked into his office and sat down. Sharad and General Pelton were seated in front of the Ambassador's desk. The United States Emissary walked in a minute later carrying a handful of large photographs. He hung one up on an easel and then turned to address the group.

"These satellite photographs were taken early this morning. The area you're looking at is just northwest of Port of Spain, near the city of Carenage."

He pointed to a spot on the photograph and continued.

"This area, right here, is an old abandoned warehouse. Actually, many years ago it was part of a U.S. Naval Base. After the base was closed, it was turned into a warehouse. Ten years or so ago, it was abandoned and no one has been using it since. If you look closely though, you will see a strange sight."

"What?" Sharad asked.

The emissary pointed to the west end of the building.

"Right here. There is actually a helicopter on the ground."

After everyone had studied the photo, he replaced it with another one.

"If you look at this blow-up, it's really quite clear."

He pointed to the helicopter. It was clearly discernible in the second photograph. After a minute, he changed photographs again.

"Now, if we look at the next photograph, taken fifteen minutes later, the helicopter is gone."

"So what are you saying?"

"Well, if you study these photographs closely, you'll also see trucks coming and going from the warehouse. In one of the photographs, there's a boat at a nearby dock, unloading supplies. It looks to me like this could be an NDC installation. It could even be the place the Prime Minister's daughter and Kevin Wells are being held hostage."

"Thank you. We appreciate this information very much. We'll check out this facility immediately."

"Be careful, Sharad. If you storm the place, they may kill them."

"I know. We'll plan our assault carefully."

"Good luck."

"Thank you."

Twenty minutes later, Sharad and General Pelton were in a meeting with the Prime Minister and his Cabinet. The mood was somber since everyone knew how perilous this operation would be. One miscalculation could lead to the death of the Prime Minister's daughter and the one witness who could take down the NDC. Military officers were coming and going as the group went over and over every detail of the operation.

"Ladies and gentlemen," General Pelton said. "let's go over the plan one last time, to make sure everyone has it down cold. At eighteen hundred hours, a half dozen men will enter the facility disguised as NDC recruits. They will gain access with the help of a former NDC soldier who was captured earlier today. He's agreed to help get our men inside in exchange for his life and his freedom. Once inside, the sole function of this advance unit is to secure the prisoners and protect them during the assault on the facility, which will begin at nineteen hundred hours."

General Pelton went over to a map of the warehouse and began describing how the operation would be handled.

"Three helicopter assault teams will be dropped in front of the main entrance to the warehouse. Two teams will blow access holes from each side and another will come in from the roof. The entire operation should take less than fifteen minutes, assuming we catch them by surprise. We'll use the helicopter on the roof to transport Kevin and Deviane back to the Prime Minister's residence."

"What if the advance team doesn't get in?" one of the officers asked.

"Then we'll have to move fast and get to the hostages before they have a chance to harm them."

"Do we know where the hostages are being kept?"

"We're pretty sure they're in the basement. That would be the logical place to keep them, since it would be the most secure location in the facility. You'll need to instruct your men not to be too trigger happy, since it's possible they could be anywhere. The last thing we want to happen is to have one of the hostages killed by our own men."

"Before you leave, ladies and gentlemen," the Prime Minister interjected, "I just want to say to you that the future of Trinidad may well rest on the success of this mission. We're facing the greatest constitutional threat to this nation since it was founded in 1962. If we fail, the government may well fall, and the invidious Malcolm Mann could seize power. Go now, ready yourselves for the operation."

****

"Okay, it's your turn, Deviane."

"Hmm. I can't think of anything else."

"Come on, there must be something else you need to confess. Think back."

"Well–"

Deviane stopped and looked toward the door. The sound of footsteps could be heard in the distance. The door flew open and Ray Mohammed stood in the doorway with another soldier. Ray was carrying a revolver in his belt and the soldier had a rifle. Ray approached Kevin.

The sight of Ray Mohammed angered Kevin. The horror of the assassination attempt came roaring back into his mind. He wished he had some kind of a weapon so he could exact a little revenge. He was frustrated and bitter as the man who had nearly ended his life stood before him.

"I've come back to finish what I started earlier," Ray said.

"What's that?" Kevin asked.

"To teach you a little respect."

"You're wasting your time. I could never respect a cowardly low-life like you."

"Oh, yeah?" he said as he proceeded to smack Kevin across the face and then hit him in the stomach. Kevin doubled over in pain and gasped for air. Ray punched him in the mouth again, knocking him to the floor. Then Ray turned toward Deviane and started unbuckling his belt.

"Now I'm going to show this little virgin what it's like to have a man!"

"No," Kevin screamed as he tried to struggle to his feet. "You can't do that! I'll kill you if you touch her!"

Ray nodded to the guard. The soldier grabbed Kevin and threw him against the concrete wall. Kevin fell on the floor and began coughing up blood. Deviane tried to run over to him, but Ray intercepted her. Holding her by the neck with one hand, he ripped off her T-shirt and threw her onto the mattress. Then he tried to hold her down, while pulling off her jeans. She struggled violently and managed to bite his arm. He cursed at her and slapped her hard across the face. Kevin lunged forward to help her, but the guard hit him in the mouth with the butt of his rifle.

Kevin fell limp onto the concrete and didn't move. Ray fell on top of Deviane and thrust himself inside her. She screamed in pain. Her screams stirred Kevin. He lifted his body, shook his head and then rushed the soldier who was watching the rape with great amusement. Kevin caught the soldier off guard, grabbing his rifle and hitting him hard across the face. The soldier fell to the ground, reeling from the assault. Kevin rushed Ray, hitting him hard across the back of the head. As Ray struggled to his feet, Kevin pointed the rifle at him. Ray went for his revolver, but Kevin pulled the trigger before Ray could take aim.

Ray slumped to one knee and looked at Kevin, moaning with pain. He started to lift his revolver one more time. Kevin fired again and again until Ray Mohammed was dead. Then the guard, who had recovered somewhat from the blow to his head, got up and started charging Kevin. Seeing him in his peripheral vision, Kevin turned, aimed and pulled the trigger. The bullet hit the man in the stomach. He screamed in pain as he grabbed his wound.

By this time, soldiers were rushing down the hallway toward the prison cell. Kevin dropped his gun and put up his hands. Several soldiers entered the room and surrounded him. Malcolm Mann rushed in. He looked at Deviane, who was curled up on the mattress sobbing. He looked at Kevin, knelt down next to Ray and shook his head.

"Ray, you imbecile, look what you've done now! The people will think we're a bunch of pirates. Jesus! I can't believe this! Get them out of here! Send one of the medics down here to take care of these prisoners!"

The soldiers took Ray and the guard away. Malcolm followed them out of the cell and closed the door. Kevin rushed over to Deviane and helped her get dressed.

"Kevin, he raped me! I've been raped!" Deviane cried out. "What am I going to do?"

"Nothing right now, just lie down. The medic will be here in a minute."

"He's ruined my life. Why did he do that? What did I ever do to him?"

Deviane began to wail and moan as she rocked back and forth in utter agony.

"Your life isn't ruined. You'll heal, I promise you."

"Kevin, I've been raped. I'm spoiled. Why did he do it? Damn him! . . . I'm glad you killed him!"

"Deviane, come here," Kevin said as he pulled her into his arms and held her tightly. "Don't think about it. Tomorrow it will be nothing but a bad dream. In time you won't even remember it happened. It hasn't changed the person you are."

"But, how can I forget that I've been raped! It's worse than a bullet to the head. I never thought it would happen to me, oh God, Kevin" she sobbed. "How could he have been so cruel! Damn him! My life is over, I just want to die!"

Kevin held Deviane for a long time, trying to console her. She was so distraught, nothing he could do or say helped. Finally, he laid her down. She curled up in the fetal position and stared at the concrete wall.

As Kevin got up, pain shot through his stomach. His head pounded from the blow he had taken. He felt dizzy and nearly fell down. He put one hand against the wall to steady himself. When he regained his balance, he turned and leaned against the wall. The medic came a few minutes later, with food and water. He looked at Deviane. He remarked that there wasn't anything he could do for her and left.

Kevin sat down next to Deviane, who refused to eat, and gently stroked her jet-black hair.

She didn't move, but continued to stare at the blank wall, her eyes wide opened.

# Chapter 19

General Pelton went to the microphones that had been hastily set up by the media for the news conference. He opened his notebook and began reading to the crowd of reporters.

"At eighteen hundred hours, six men and an NDC defector drove up to a warehouse that had been identified as NDC headquarters. "The defector told the guards that he had some new recruits and needed to bring them down to be processed. The guards did a search and then allowed them to pass. Once inside, the men were led to the armory, where the defector had been assigned. He outfitted them with NDC uniforms, rifles and ammunition. He led them toward the makeshift brig. Unnoticed, they passed by many soldiers and NDC officials, until they reached the corridor leading to the prison cell that held Kevin Wells and Deviane Shah. There, they waited.

"At nineteen hundred hours, six attack helicopters converged on the warehouse. The first two helicopters dropped their squads at the front entrance, where they met heavy resistance. While the NDC soldiers were occupied at the front of the building, two attack helicopters fired rockets, ripping gaping holes in both sides of the warehouse. The helicopters landed and government troops poured into the building, meeting little resistance.

"A fifth helicopter landed on the roof. Eight soldiers jumped out to secure it. As they were scrambling into position, an NDC helicopter suddenly appeared and attacked the government troops who were sitting ducks. The pilot of the government helicopter made a desperate attempt to leave, but before he got a hundred yards from the building, he was hit by a missile. The chopper exploded and fell to the ground. The NDC helicopter immediately landed. Several men emerged from the building and climbed into the helicopter.

"The sixth government helicopter, which had been doing surveillance, made a pass and the pilot opened fire with its machine gun. The chopper was hit but not disabled. As soon as it was off the roof, it turned and headed across the Caribbean Sea toward Casper Grande, a small island off the coast of Trinidad. As the government helicopter started to pursue it, another NDC helicopter appeared from the north. After a short chase, it locked on its target and launched a missile that hit the government helicopter dead-on. It burst into flames and fell into the sea. Both NDC helicopters headed out across the Caribbean Sea and disappeared into the blazing sunset.

"Inside the warehouse, a battle was raging. The government defense team had secured the prison cell. A half dozen NDC soldiers came to retrieve the prisoners and take them to the roof. They were surprised by the intense gunfire that greeted them as they made their way down the hall. Three soldiers were immediately hit and fell to the ground. The others laid low, using their fallen comrades as shields and returned the fire. In less than fifteen minutes, the warehouse was secured. The soldiers, pinned down in the hall, surrendered and two government soldiers escorted Kevin and Deviane to a waiting helicopter. Twenty minutes later, they landed at Port of Spain General Hospital and were rushed into the casualty department.

"That's all I have for now," he said as he closed his notebook. "I'll be back when I get more information. Thank you.

The Prime Minister was waiting in the casualty department of Port of Spain General Hospital when Kevin and Deviane arrived. He immediately went to Deviane.

"Deviane, are you all right?" he asked. There was no response. "What did they do to you, my darling?"

Deviane's eyes were open, but she didn't react to him at all.

"Kevin, what did those swine do my Deviane? She won't talk to me."

"I'm so sorry, I tried to protect her. She's in shock, I think. After they beat her up, they raped her."

"Oh, God, no! I'll kill the bastard who did this! Who was it?"

"Ray Mohammed."

"Damn him! I'm going to track him down and kill him with my bare hands!"

"He's already dead. . . . I killed him."

"How did you manage that?"

"It's a long story."

"Tell me, I want to know!"

"They thought I was unconscious, but I was just dazed. When I heard Deviane scream, I jumped up, surprised the guard and took his gun. Then I shot Ray. I'm not sure how many times. I just kept shooting until I knew he was dead."

"Thank God! I hope by now he's half way to hell!'

"After it happened, Deviane went crazy. I tried to calm her down and console her, but she just lost it. She's been staring into space for hours."

Anila came rushing into the waiting room. Seeing Ahmad's tearfilled eyes, she knew something was wrong. She immediately began to cry.

"What is it? What has happened? Is my baby all right?"

"She's alive," Ahmad said. "She's not seriously hurt, but she's been raped and beaten."

"Oh Ahmad, no, no!"

Two orderlies took Kevin and wheeled him into a

treatment room. Ahmad put his arms around Anila and took her down the hall to their private waiting room. Reporters were everywhere, wanting the details of the raid on the NDC headquarters, but Anamica told them they would have to wait until morning, when General Pelton would brief them on the operation.

Watching Ahmad and Anila reminded Kevin of his own parents. A surge of guilt came over him as he recalled his promise to call them everyday. He found the nearest phone and called home. His mother wanted him to come home.

"I can't come home right now."

"Then we'll come there," Mrs. Wells said.

"No, its too chaotic here. It would just complicate things if you were here. I'll be alright, I promise."

"Oh, Kevin. I'm so worried. I can't lose you too."

"You won't. I'm safe now. I'd like to come home, but I've got to stay and figure things out."

After much reassurance Kevin convinced his mother to stay home. He hung up the phone and laid back in his bed. His mind was still on Deviane. His body ached, he was depressed and he felt terribly guilty over Deviane's rape. *Why did I have to be such a macho smart-ass? Why didn't I just keep my damn mouth shut? Ray might have left us alone, if I hadn't provoked him. Damn it! I was so selfish. It never even occurred to me that Ray would take out his anger on Deviane. Oh God, I am so sorry. Please help Deviane recover. Please Lord, I beg you.*

As he was lamenting over the situation, Kiran was wheeled into the room in a wheel chair. She wore a green hospital gown and no makeup. She looked a little weary too, not the princess he'd first met, but still as beautiful as ever. Kevin felt a warmth radiate through him just being in her presence, but it wasn't the same surge of excitement he had felt before.

"Kiran, I was hoping you'd come to see me. How are you? I've been so worried about you. It was such a relief to find out you were alive and doing well."

"I'm getting better. How are you feeling? You look terrible."

"I'm okay. It's nothing serious, just a few broken ribs. I'm a little sore. . . . How's Deviane?"

"There's no change. She's still just lying there, staring off into space. The doctors finally got her to sleep. They're hoping she'll start to come out of it when she wakes up. I can't imagine being raped like that. I think I would just die. At least you killed the asshole. I'm glad of that."

"You know what's horrible?"

"What?"

"I've just killed a human being, but I feel no remorse. I'm glad he's dead."

"You'll be feeling lots of remorse when you have to tell your friend you killed his brother."

"Oh God! You're right. What will I say to Obatala?"

"I don't know."

"He'll never forgive me. How can two brothers be so different? It's just incredible."

"When you explain what happened, he'll understand."

"Maybe he'll understand, but that won't lessen the pain."

"It must of been terrible watching Deviane being raped. I couldn't imagine it."

"I felt a rage you wouldn't believe. When I saw Ray pull off Deviane's jeans and heard her scream, I just wanted to choke him to death!"

"I'm glad you took the gun instead."

"I don't even know how I got the gun. It all happened so fast. It almost seems now like it was nothing but a bad dream."

"So now what are you going to do?"

"What do you mean?"

"A lot has happened, you may have had enough of Trinidad. I wouldn't blame you if you just packed your bags and got the hell out of this dismal country."

Kevin suddenly realized he had been less than excited to see his bride to be. He gave her a gentle smile.

"Come here," he said. She struggled out of her wheel chair and sat next to him in his bed. "I'm so sorry all this has spoiled such a happy moment in our lives. I love you."

"I was so worried about you," Kiran said, tears streaming from her eyes. "I thought for sure they would kill you."

"And I had no idea whether you were alive or dead. After taking that bullet in the jungle I was sick that I had lost you forever."

"Oh, Kevin! I'm so glad you're safe," she said as she bent over and looked him in the eyes. He smiled and pulled her lips to his.

After a few seconds she lifted her head and said, "So whose kiss was better mine or Deviane's?"

"Huh?" Kevin said as he was blasted with a rush of guilt.

"Kevin, I saw you and Deviane out there in the forest. I wasn't asleep. I know Deviane loves you, and it sure looked like you were enjoying her advances."

"Why didn't you say something?"

"I wanted to see what you would do. You didn't put up much of a struggle for me."

"I didn't want to offend Deviane, or wake you up by causing a commotion."

"It's all right, I know it wasn't your fault. She's been jealous of every boy I've ever dated. I should have warned you."

"She's got some crazy idea that I'm her soul mate."

"Is that so crazy? I know about your search for a virgin."

"What search? What are you talking about?"

"I heard it on Jay Leno. He said you were here in Trinidad because you thought I was a virgin. You wanted the perfect relationship, remember?"

"Virginity is just part of it. Obviously I don't want to marry a girl who has slept with every jock on the football team.

How could there be any trust in such a relationship?"

"True, but what if it wasn't every jock on the football team, but just one jock?. . . . I mean what if a girl thought she loved a man so she gave up her virginity only to find out she had been mistaken?"

"That might be different, it depends on the circumstances."

"So, being a virgin isn't a hard and fast rule."

"No, I never said it was. Everybody just jumps to conclusions. I just want a relationship that's based on love and not sex. Love first, then sex."

"Good, I wouldn't want to marry a man who couldn't forgive. Forgiveness is such a great virtue."

"Yeah. . . . I suppose it is."

Kiran continued, "So, do you remember when we were in the Natural History Museum? Remember the boy I talked to while Deviane tried to charm you?"

"Right."

"He's the one."

"What one?"

"He's the one, you know, that I thought I loved."

Kevin's face dropped. "You were talking about yourself?"

"Why of course. What do think was the point of the conversation? I thought I loved him. We talked of marriage. One afternoon on the beach, where I told you the lovers go, well, we made love there. It was wonderful. . . . Then he dumped me like I was a two dollar whore."

Kevin felt weak. He couldn't believe what he was hearing. He closed his eyes, hoping when he opened them again Kiran would be gone and he'd know he had been dreaming. He opened them. Kiran was weeping.

"I'm sorry, Kevin. I should have told you before we talked of marriage, but I never dreamed virginity would be a concern to a boy from America. If you want to forget our marriage, I'll understand."

"No, no," Kevin said. "If it was just an isolated incident I can understand. It's almost happened to me a couple times."

"Good," Kiran said. "I was starting to get excited about planning the wedding." She smiled, laid her head on Kevin's shoulder and closed her eyes.

"But, there is one thing," Kevin said. "There must be love."

Kiran's eyes opened. She sat up and looked at Kevin. "There will be, it will come, I'm sure."

Kevin took a deep breath. His eyes showed his disappointment.

Kiran got up. "I've got to go. I'll come visit you later."

Kevin didn't respond. Instead, he stared into space.

Kiran motioned for the orderly to take her away.

That night. Kevin couldn't sleep. He was worried sick about Deviane. He wondered what was going on in her mind.

*Was she thinking about what had happened to her? Was she aware of what was going on around her? Was she thinking of him? Was she really his soul mate?*

He tossed and turned and tried to fall asleep, but to no avail. Finally, he could stand it no more. He got up, put on a robe and headed toward Deviane's room. He had been told that he couldn't see her until morning, but he couldn't wait. When he got to her room, Anila was beside her bed. The room was dark, illuminated only by one small lamp in the corner. When she saw him, she opened up her arms and embraced him.

"Oh, Kevin, she didn't move all day."

"Was she awake?"

"Yes, but she's sleeping now."

"I had to come see her. I'm so worried about her."

"Come here. You can sit with her. I need a break anyway."

"Thank you."

Anila smiled at Kevin and started to leave the room. Then she turned and spoke.

"Kevin, I know if it hadn't been for you, I would have lost Kiran. I know you did your best to protect Deviane. I just want you to know that I will always be in your debt and I will always love you, as I would my own son."

"Thank you, Anila. Your daughters have told me what a wonderful mother you are. I hope I will have the opportunity to get to know you very well."

"Yes, I hope so too. Okay, I'll be back in a little while."

When Anila had left the room Kevin took Deviane's hand and squeezed it gently. He bent over her and kissed her softly on the lips. Even in her comatose state, the feel of her sweet lips sent shivers through his body. He stood up and gazed at her, wondering if she would ever regain the joyful, confident spirit that he had grown to love. After awhile, he sat down on the bed beside her and began stroking her long black hair. He ran through his mind every moment they had been together.

*Why hadn't I seen it? From the instant we first met, she wanted me. She loved me, the kind of love I've always wanted. How could I have been so blind? I can't marry Kiran, she doesn't love me. She just wants a ticket to America. But how will I get out of my commitment to marry her without angering her father and mother? I can't do anything that might jeopardize my future with Deviane. She was right, we are soul mates and I love her so.*

After a while Anila came into the room. Kevin had his back to her so he didn't see her. He began to talk to Deviane out loud.

"Deviane, I don't know if you can hear me, but just in case you can, I want you to know some things. First of all I'm not going to marry Kiran. She doesn't love me and I can't live a life without love. I don't know how I'll tell her, but somehow I'll figure out a way. I know now that I love you.

Once I tell her the wedding is off, there'll be nothing stopping us from being together. We can have that perfect relationship that we've both wanted so badly. All you have to do is wake up and get better. Please Deviane, you have to wake up. I love you. I need you."

Deviane coughed and twitched slightly in her bed. Kevin grabbed both her hands and squeezed them, hoping they would suddenly come alive and embrace him. Nothing happened, her body remained limp and lifeless. Kevin turned as he sensed someone behind him. But by the time he looked Anila was gone.

Kevin laid her hands back down and sat in the chair next to her. After awhile, he laid his head on the bed and fell asleep. An hour later, Anila woke him up and sent him back to his room, where he slept on and off until morning.

# Chapter 20

When Kevin woke up the next morning, he was excruciatingly sore. Noticing his discomfort, the nurse brought him a pain pill. He ate his breakfast and then took a hot shower. Ordinarily, he would have been anxious to be discharged since he didn't like hospitals much. However, today he had no such wish because he wanted to be close to Deviane. He was about to go to her room when the Attorney General walked in.

"Mr. Wells, how are you feeling today?" Sharad asked.

"A little sore, but I think I'm going to live."

"Good. I'm glad to hear it. Listen, I need to ask a favor of you."

"Oh really? What's that?"

"We've arrested some NDC leaders and I need you to come down to the courthouse to see if you can identify any of them. You might have seen them when you were kidnapped, or at the NDC headquarters."

"Sure, no problem. How long will it take?"

"Just a couple hours."

"Okay. Can I go see Deviane for a minute before we go."

"Sure, how is she doing?"

"There wasn't any change yesterday. I haven't seen her yet today, so I just want to check on her."

"Okay, I'll wait here."

"Thanks," Kevin said as he hurried out of the room and went down the hall.

When he walked in, the Prime Minister was standing over his daughter, looking at her tranquil face.

"Oh, hi, Mr. Prime Minister."

"You can call me Ahmad, Kevin. After all you're damn near part of the family. Although I wish you'd make up your mind which one of my daughters you love."

Kevin froze. "What do you mean?"

"Anila overheard you last night talking to Deviane. Have you told Kiran how you feel?

"No, Sir. . . . Oh God, I'm so sorry. I had no idea I'd fall in love with Deviane. I really thought I loved Kiran, but as I got to know them both better and I found out Deviane loved me, everything changed."

"It's not your fault. I just thought it would be such a wonderful match, you and Kiran. An American hero and my daughter. I thought it might bring Trinidad and America closer together. You know, soften some of the anti-American feeling that has been so rampant lately. But, it doesn't matter which daughter you marry."

"So, you don't object to me marrying Deviane?" Kevin asked.

"No, I just pray she wakes up soon so she can start planning her wedding."

"Oh God, so do I. She has to wake up. She just has to be my bride."

"So, how do you plan to tell Kiran of your decision?"

"I don't know. I haven't figured that out yet."

"Well, I can have Anila tell her if you wish."

"No, that wouldn't be right. I'll tell her. I'll tell her tonight."

"Good. I've got a cabinet meeting tonight. I don't want to be home when you tell her."

Kevin smiled. "I don't blame you."

"So, Sharad is going to take you to identify some of the NDC pigs, huh?"

"That's what he says."

"Listen, Kevin. We know for a fact that everyone we

picked up was in on the assassination attempt and the kidnapping. I know you might not recognize them all, but so what. Who could challenge you if you did identify them all? We need to rid Trinidad of all these evil men, who would destroy democracy."

"I can't falsely accuse someone, Ahmad. I told you that."

"No, of course not, but don't hesitate to identify anyone who looks the least bit like one of the traitors. We have been carefully watching these people and have put together files on their sinister activities. Ask Sharad to show you the files. You will see that they all belong behind bars or at the end of a rope."

"I'll identify anyone I recognize, don't worry."

"Even if you don't identify them, we have enough on them to put them away for many years. It would just be a lot easier, you know, if you did recognize them. You know what a tough burden the State has to convict someone. This is why so many criminals are let go each year. We can't let these traitors back on the street. Help us out here, Kevin."

"Like I said, I'll identify anyone I recognize."

The prime minister nodded and turned to go.

"Here, I'll leave you with Deviane for a moment, but don't linger, you have important work to do."

"Yes, sir. I'll be brief."

The Prime Minister left and Kevin went over to Deviane. She was awake, her eyes fixed on the ceiling. Kevin waved his hand over her face, but there was no response. He bent down, pressed his lips next to hers, gently caressing them with his tongue, but she didn't move. He stood up, smiled and took her hand.

"Deviane, while I'm gone I want you to forget about all the horrible things that have happened to you in the past few days and concentrate on what a wonderful life we're going to have together, okay? We can't change the past, but the future will be what we make of it. Now that I've found you, I can't live without you. I'll be back soon. I love you."

Sharad took Kevin downtown to the courthouse where the prisoners were being detained. The building was crowded with spectators and members of the press. Sharad ordered the driver to take them into a private entrance underneath the courthouse. They got out of the car and went inside. The building was spacious and ornately decorated. It reminded Kevin of the Texas State Capitol building. They walked down the hall and through a private entrance, guarded by two security police.

"Okay, Kevin, you've seen these two-way mirrors before, right?"

"Sure."

"Well, we're going to bring in five groups of eight men. Take your time. If you see anybody you recognize, let us know."

"Okay."

Kevin sat down and waited for the guards to bring in the first group. As they filed in, he looked them over very carefully.

"The third man on the right, he was a guard I saw when they took off my blindfold at the prison."

"Excellent. Anyone else?"

"No, none of them look familiar."

"All right, bring in the next group," Sharad yelled.

The guards brought in the next group and Kevin scrutinized them as carefully as he had the first.

"I've never seen any of these men before."

"Are you sure, Kevin? I've got the files on these men. Would you like to see them?"

"No, what good would that do? If I don't recognize them, nothing in that file is going to help."

"Didn't the Prime Minister have a talk with you, Kevin?"

"Yes, but I'm not going to lie, it wouldn't be right. I

couldn't live with myself."

"Kevin, these men are traitors. We know they were instrumental in the plot to assassinate the Prime Minister. Do your duty here."

"Let me see the others. Maybe I'll recognize some of them."

"Okay, bring in the next group."

The third group walked in the room. Kevin hoped he would see someone he recognized but none of the men were at all familiar.

"I'm sorry. I've never seen any of them."

"Damn it, Kevin. We've gone to a lot of trouble to find the bastards who were responsible for your kidnaping. Don't you want to punish the men who caused Deviane to be raped?"

"Of course, but Deviane wouldn't want an innocent man dying either. She believes in justice, just as I do."

"And Ahmad and I believe in justice too, but sometimes to obtain justice you have to do some things that are not pleasant. These men, they are all guilty! That's what I've been trying to tell you."

"They have a right to a trial, don't they?"

"Of course, and that's why we need your help. With your testimony they will surely be convicted. Without it they will more than likely go free."

"I won't do it. I'm sorry, it's not right. Would you please take me back to the hospital?"

"You're very naive, Kevin. I hope you understand what you've just done."

"I've done the right thing, that's all that is important."

"We shall see."


Kiran was waiting for Kevin in his bed when he got back to his room at the hospital. Kevin was surprised to see her. He hadn't had time to plan out how he would break the bad news to her.

"Kiran, hi. How do you feel?"

"Horrible, how come you didn't come say goodbye before you left the hospital?"

"I'm sorry, Sharad came to get me and he was in a big hurry."

"But you managed to see Deviane before you left?"

"Right. . . . Listen, Kiran, something has happened to me these last few days. I don't know how to explain it . . . but, well . . . you know, Deviane and I spent some time together while the NDC had us. We talked a lot and got to know each other very well. Deviane loves me. I don't know why, but she does and I've fallen in love with her too."

"You said you loved me."

"I do love you, but I've come to realize that you'll never love me the way I need you to."

Kiran began to weep. "How do you know that! You can't just turn love on and off. It takes time. You never gave me a chance."

"You're right, I didn't but–"

"How could you do this to me! How could Deviane do this to me! How am I supposed to feel when I see you together? Did you ever think of that?"

"Kiran, I'm sorry. I hope someday you'll forgive me."

Kiran turned over in the bed and began crying hard. Kevin came over to her and put his hand on her shoulder.

"It would have never worked for us," Kevin said. "We weren't right for each other. I think deep down you know that. You need to find someone you love and who loves you."

Kiran turned over and wiped the tears from her eyes with a tissue. "I know, but I'm so scared I'll never find that person. I thought you were handsome and such a good person that surely I would fall in love with you. That's why I agreed to marry you."

"I know. But, you've just got to be patient. The right man will come, don't worry."

They embraced and then Kevin left to be with Deviane. He spent the rest of the evening at her side. He held her hand, talked to her, told her stories, whispered in her ear and played with her hair. Finally, at eleven, he decided to turn on the TV. The Tonight Show was just starting.

"Ladies and gentlemen, America's king of late night television, Jaaay Lennno!"

Jay stepped out and took a bow.

"Good evening, ladies and gentlemen. Tonight we have three great guests, Gina Davis, Whoopi Goldberg and the music of the Plain White Sand."

The crowd roared their approval and Jay continued.

"Well, by now you've probably heard that Kevin Wells has been rescued."

The crowd applauded and roared with delight.

"It seems the government launched an all out attack on the National Defense Coalition hideout where they were holding Kevin and the Prime Minister's daughter, Deviane Shah. Fortunately, they were both rescued. However, apparently they were both severely beaten."

"Ohhh. . . . ," The crowd wailed.

"Yes, and poor Deviane is still in shock from the incident. Anyway, I just want to say, we're all praying that both Kevin and Deviane fully recover. Later on, we'll have an NBC News Special where you can see a full report on the raid, together with some actual footage of the assault."

"Can you believe that, Deviane? We're on national, I mean, international television. Damn. Everybody in the world knows about us. You heard Jay, didn't you? The whole world is praying for you to recover. Please wake up, honey. I love you so much. I need you."

Kevin got up and went to the window. He looked out at the beautiful lights of the city and prayed to God to have his Deviane back. Tears ran down his face. He turned and walked back to the bed, picked up Deviane's hand and held it against his cheek.

"If you don't wake up, I'm going to have to become a priest, I guess. If I can't give my life to you, then I'll have to give it to God."

Kevin looked down at Deviane's face and saw a tear slowing running down her cheek. Her head turned. She looked at Kevin and tried to smile.

"You wouldn't be happy as a priest. You love women too much."

Kevin smiled and replied, "I love one woman too much."

Deviane took Kevin's face in her hands and gave him a loving look. "Oh, Kevin, are you alright? I couldn't bear it when they were beating you up."

"I'm fine."

"Are you sure?"

"Yes, the doctors say I'll be as good as new in a few weeks."

"What about Kiran, is she okay?"

"Yes. She was very lucky."

"Good, I'm so relieved. . . . Have you told her how you feel?"

"Yes, she wasn't pleased but I think she knew deep down we weren't right for each other."

"So, will she ever talk to me again?"

"She loves you, Deviane. She'll get over it."

"Do you really want to marry me, even after what happened? I'm not a virgin anymore. How can you even consider marrying me?"

Kevin sighed. "I've never told anyone about this, but there is something you should know about me before you commit to marrying me."

Deviane frowned. "What?"

"It's something that has haunted me for many years. It is so painful there are few nights that I'm free of the horror."

"What is it?"

"I never told you about my sister, Diana."

"No, I didn't know you had one."

"She was very pretty, too pretty. When she was young Dad and Mom protected and sheltered her. I remember going to her ballet recitals and watching her dance. She was like a butterfly, so vibrant and happy. She was a dream sister, so thoughtful and loving. We used to talk for hours and hours, just her and I, about life, our dreams and how we were going to conquer the world. I loved her so."

"What happened, Kevin?"

"She was so naive, so vulnerable and so unprepared for the evil in the world. It all started when she went to junior high school. She was very popular. The boys fought over her and she loved the attention she was drawing. Unfortunately she was too trusting. She assumed everyone, like herself, was pure and honest.

"She went to a lot of parties. Parties where there were older guys, high school jocks and spoiled rich kids. Mom and Dad tried to stop it, but the more they came down on her the more she tried to defy them.

"I was too young to understand what was happening. I knew it was something bad, really bad, but I didn't know how to deal with it. Diana suddenly got distant and didn't have time for me anymore. When she was home, she'd go to her room and lock the door. She'd spend hours and hours on the phone and would only come out to make a hasty exit or grab something out of the refrigerator.

"Then one weekend my parents went to San Antonio for their anniversary. Diana was supposed to watch me. After my parents were gone she arranged for me to stay overnight with one of my friends. I didn't think anything about it until the police called late that night.

"Diana had gotten rid of me because she was planning a party at the house, a big party. I was told there were over fifty teenagers there. Apparently the party went okay for a while. The kids were drinking, smoking grass, doing a little cocaine but nothing really nasty was happening. Then a couple guys showed up with some ruffies. They were looking to get laid and didn't want any resistance. Diana was an obvious target. She was so beautiful and sexy.

"She immediately took a liking to one of the guys and started talking to him. He spiked her drink when she wasn't looking. When she went numb he took her to her bedroom and three of them raped her over and over. Apparently they did the same to two other girls. About midnight the party got a little noisy and some neighbors called the police.

"The police came and searched the house for drugs. When they came to Diana's room they questioned the boys but when they tried to question Diana she wasn't responsive. One of them checked and realized she didn't have a pulse so they called for an ambulance, but it was too late. She was D.O.A. A fatal combination of drugs and alcohol."

"I got a call to come home immediately. When I got there the police and news reporters were swarming all over the yard. I was only eleven years old. It was pretty scary. The reporters kept asking me questions but I didn't understand what they were talking about. Finally a cop took me by the arm and escorted me into the house. He told me to wait but I knew something was wrong upstairs. I ran up the stairs to my sister's room. The room was a shambles, then I saw a white sheet covering a body. I was shaking badly when I pulled down the sheet to see who it was. It was Diana, cold and blue, her eyes wide open. I fainted."

"Oh my God, Kevin. I'm so sorry."

Kevin began to cry. "So you see, I have good reason to feel the way I do about casual sex, I've seen how destructive it can be. How a life can be destroyed. It's not just a joke like most people think."

"I know, Kevin. I know. I'm so sorry."

Kevin wiped the tears from his eyes. "So I don't care about what happened to you. Anyone can take but only you can give. And you're going to give yourself to me, and only me, and that's what's important. Nothing has happened to change what exists between us. I love you. I will always love you, no matter happens to either of us."

Deviane smiled. "See, I told you we were soul mates."

"Yeah, it took me awhile to figure that out. I'm not as smart as you are, but I can live with that."

"Good, because I won't ever let you forget it."

Kevin smiled. "I need a kiss. I've been dying to kiss you."

"Haven't you kissed me a hundred times the past two days?"

"Yeah, maybe, but I think it will be more satisfying if we both participate."

"Oh, alright. Come here, I'll give you a kiss you'll never forget."

"You sure you have the strength?"

She smiled. "Oh, I can probably manage."

Kevin leaned down and Deviane gave him a long, delicate kiss. Then she slid her face down and sunk her teeth gently into his neck.

"Hmmm! Ahhh! Ohhh . . . . , God! What was that?!"

"That was the Vampire Maneuver, Number two of *Twenty-four Ways to Drive Your Man Wild!*"

"You mean I've got twenty-two more to look forward to?"

"Uh huh. . . . But that will have to wait. You better go find my mother and tell her I've regained my sanity. I know she's been worried."

"Right. . . . I'm so happy, Deviane. I love you so much!"

"Me too."

# Chapter 21

The next day, Kevin, Deviane, Kiran and Anila were talking in Deviane's room. It was midday, the sun was shining brightly and the mood was one of joy and happiness. Deviane was sitting up and Kevin was sitting on the side of her bed. Anila and Kiran were sitting in chairs, facing Deviane. Everyone was particularly happy, because word had just come in that the Prime Minister had just survived a no-confidence vote.

"I want the bridesmaids to wear yellow gowns," Deviane said. "Yellow is my favorite color."

"I didn't know that." Kevin said.

"There's a lot you don't know about me, Kevin. But you'll have plenty of time to learn, don't worry."

"I'm not worried. I'm the happiest man alive."

"Where do you want to have the wedding, Deviane?" Anila asked. "At the Cathedral?"

"I don't know. I haven't had time to think about it."

"Why don't you have it at the Royal Botanical Gardens?" Kiran suggested.

"I'd love to have it there, but are you sure you wouldn't mind?"

"No, God knows when I'll get married. Have it there if you like."

"It's so beautiful there. Would January be okay, Kevin?"

"Sure, whatever pleases you, honey."

"Good, it's set then." Anila said. "We'll have it the last week of January at the Royal Botanical Gardens. I'll call the manager tomorrow and reserve it."

"How many people do you think will come from Plano to the wedding, Kevin?" Kiran asked.

"Oh, probably not more than a dozen or so. My family is pretty small."

"Well, it doesn't matter, you've made hundreds of friends here in Trinidad," Anila noted.

"I know, the people of Trinidad have been so nice to me. I really like it here."

"I hope you'll stay and make your home here, Kevin," Anila said.

"We haven't really given that much thought yet," Kevin replied.

"We're going to school in the United States, and then we'll see what happens," Deviane added.

"Well, there's no rush to make a decision."

"Where do you want to go to school?" Anila asked.

"I've been looking at UCLA and Stanford out in California, but Deviane may have her mind set on another college. It doesn't really matter that much to me, as long as we're together."

"I like UCLA, but we should consider Columbia or Yale too," Deviane said.

"Fine, there are a lot of good colleges to choose from," Kevin replied.

"In a couple of weeks, when you two are feeling better, I want to have an engagement party for you," Anila said. "We need a big social event in Trinidad, to break all the tension that's in the air. It will be wonderful. I'll invite everybody who's anybody."

"That would be great, Mom," Kiran said. "I love big parties."

"It's not really necessary, Mother," Deviane said.

"Nonsense. I want to celebrate my little baby's engagement. It's a mother's right."

"Okay, whatever makes you happy."

As the conversation continued, the Prime Minister entered the room. He was dressed up and looked quite impressive. Anila ran over to him and gave him a big hug.

"Congratulations, honey. I heard the vote came out well."

"Yes, but it was a razor thin victory. Not the mandate I needed to push through the reforms this country needs."

"Well, I'm sure that, in time, you'll get the support you need, honey. Anyway, we were just discussing Kevin and Deviane's wedding. I want to have an engagement party for them in a couple of weeks."

"That would be nice, but I'm afraid I'm going to have to borrow Kevin for a few hours. We need him down at the courthouse."

"Oh no, not again. We need him here to help plan the wedding."

"Oh, I think you all will do just fine without me. I better go and help out, if I can."

"Don't keep him long, Daddy," Deviane said.

"I won't, you have my word on it."

The Prime Minister left the room with Kevin at his side. They left the hospital and got into a waiting automobile.

"So what's going on? You have some more suspects?"

"We've captured a high ranking NDC officer, one of Malcolm Mann's right hand men. We're sure you must have seen him."

"Why would I have seen him?"

"He must have been at the warehouse with Malcolm."

"Hmm."

"So you really love Deviane, huh?"

"Oh yes, I do..., more than anything."

"I've never seen her so happy. I guess you two were meant for each other, huh?"

"Yes, we're going to be very happy together."

"I suppose this means I'll have a dozen grandchildren running around destroying my house?"

Kevin laughed. "I don't know, we haven't talked about kids yet, but I'm sure some day we'll have one or two."

"That's okay, you've got plenty of time for that later. Live it up now, while you're young and can enjoy it!"

"We plan to."

"Kevin, you know that Malcolm Mann escaped, don't you?"

"Did he? Damn it!"

"Well, this man we have in custody is the highest ranking NDC official in Trinidad. It's imperative that we convict him. Otherwise, our government will look feeble and lose face. The leader of the UAR has warned me that he will withdraw his support of the government if I don't make some progress in arresting and convicting NDC officials. I was very disappointed that you were only able to identify one person out of the twenty-four we showed you last week. Why couldn't you have recognized eight or ten of them? What difference would it have made?"

"Sir, we've had this conversation before. You know how I feel."

"Yes, and it's too bad, because if you don't help with this problem today, you can leave Trinidad and forget about Deviane."

Ahmad's words hit Kevin like a jolt from an electrical socket. Incredulous, he turned and glared at Ahmad.

"What? You're joking, right?"

"I am sorry, Kevin, but I am completely serious. If you don't recognize our prisoner as being at the NDC headquarters on the day of the kidnaping, then I'm going to take you directly to the airport and send you back to America!"

"You can't do this! Deviane won't stand for it. Your wife won't stand for it."

"They will both do as I say! It's time for you to face reality, Kevin. Sometimes we have to do things we don't like to do, but we still do them if it's necessary to survive, or to get what we want."

"That's bullshit! I thought you believed in law and justice. You're no better than Malcolm Mann!"

"Ha! You've been here one week and you think you understand what's going on in this country? You know nothing about Trinidad! Nothing! You think you've got all the answers, but you don't even know the questions."

"You're absolutely right, I know nothing about Trinidad, but I know a lot about justice and democracy, because I live in America. What you're doing is wrong."

"I don't care what you think, Kevin. Let me make it as clear as a crystal goblet to you. If you don't identify this man as being one of the traitors who beat you up, then you'll never see Deviane again."

Kevin didn't reply. He just shook his head and turned away from the Prime Minister. When they arrived at the courthouse, Kevin reluctantly followed the Prime Minister inside. They went to the interrogation room and Kevin sat in front of the two-way mirror. The man being questioned had his face turned away so Kevin couldn't see it. He waited, praying he would recognize the face so he could put an end to this madness without having to make a choice between his integrity and Deviane. When the man finally turned his face toward the mirror, Kevin's heart sank. Suddenly feeling very dizzy, he nearly collapsed. The Prime Minister grabbed him, to keep him from falling over. Once he was stabilized, he looked in the very familiar face, the face of a saint, his protector, Obatala!

"Shit, you can't do this! That's the man who saved our lives. He's the man who saved us from the death squad."

"I don't think so. You thought he was saving you, but he was actually delivering you to a location where the NDC could find you and take you away."

"That's total bullshit! Obatala hates the NDC. He loves freedom and liberty. He's one of the kindest men I've ever known! I will not accuse him of having any association with the NDC. I can't believe you would do this to the man who saved your daughters' lives. I've totally misjudged you. You're just a ruthless tyrant!"

"All right, Kevin, if that's what you want! We'll go back to the hospital, pack your bags and you'll be on your way back to Texas! Don't even think about taking Deviane with you! She's already been taken home, where she'll be safe. Don't call her or write her, and don't even dream about coming back here to see her. You're not welcome in Trinidad. Do you understand?"

"She won't stand for this, you know. You'll have to make her a prisoner in her own house. She'll hate you for the rest of your life."

"Like I said, sometimes we have to do things we don't like to do. We have to do what's best for Trinidad."

Tears began to well in Kevin's eyes. He couldn't bear the thought of leaving Trinidad and never seeing Deviane again. *Oh, God. What am I going to do? This can't be happening. Just when I thought everything was going to work out– Damn it! What a evil bastard you are, Ahmad.*

"Come on, let's go," the Prime Minister said.

*No, I need time. I've got to stall. I need time to think. There has to be a way out of this.*

"Can I talk to Obatala before we leave?"

The Prime Minister considered the request and then nodded his assent. Kevin hurried over to the door to the interview room and knocked. The door opened and the guard poked his head outside.

"Let him see the prisoner for a moment," the Prime Minister commanded. The man opened the door and let Kevin in. He left them alone in the room.

"Obatala, are you all right?"

"Kevin, I wasn't expecting to see you."

"Nor I to see you. Are you okay?"

"More or less. If this is gratitude, I'd hate to have them mad at me."

"I know, this is so ridiculous," Kevin moaned.

"What are you doing here?"

"They wanted me to identify you as a high ranking NDC official. Since Ray and Malcolm got away they need a fall guy—someone they can parade in front of the people as an example, I guess. They said if I didn't identify you, I couldn't marry Deviane."

"You were going to marry Deviane?"

"Yes, we've already started to plan the wedding."

"Do you love her?"

"Of course. She's the woman I've been searching for all my life. We were meant for one another."

"So what are you going to do?"

"Do you have to ask? I couldn't betray you. I told him, no way. I wouldn't help send an innocent man to his death. I certainly wouldn't send a man who saved my life twice."

"But, you'll lose Deviane."

"Maybe not, but if so, then that's better than letting you die. I couldn't live with myself if I betrayed you. And I don't think Deviane would want me to either."

Obatala closed his eyes and thought for a moment. Kevin wondered what was going through his mind. *Do you know I killed your brother? Oh, God. Will you ever forgive me?* Obatala opened his eyes and smiled faintly.

"Go back and tell him you changed your mind."

"Huh?"

"Tell him you'll testify against me. Tell him I'm the number three man in the NDC. Living around Ray, I know everyone in the organization. I know how they operate and I can give the Prime Minister exactly what he wants."

"Obatala, no. They'll hang you."

"Tell him I'll do it on two conditions. First, he must swear to me, in front of his daughters, that I will not hang. Secondly, he must let my family leave Trinidad and provide them with fifty thousand dollars, to start a new life in America."

"Obatala, why would you do this?"

"Because, like I told you before, the NDC stole my brother from me, and turned him into a ruthless beast. The only way I can get revenge is to see to it that every last remnant of the NDC is destroyed!"

"There's something I need to tell you about your brother."

"What?"

"Oh God, Obatala. I'm so sorry!" Kevin said and then began to cry.

"What is it?"

"I'm afraid. . . I'm afraid he's dead."

Obatala closed his eyes and sighed.

"Oh God, I hoped somehow he would escape this nightmare. Damn it!"

"You haven't heard the worst of it."

"What could be worse than his death?"

"To be looking at his killer."

"What?"

"I killed him. He beat me up and raped Deviane. I had no choice. I'm sorry. I'm really sorry, not for him, but for you."

Obatala stood like a rock in a hurricane, his eyes fixed on Kevin. Then he lowered his head and took a deep breath. Breathing heavily, he walked a few steps away and stared at the two way mirror.

He mumbled, "Then he deserved to die. I'm ashamed he was my brother."

Kevin wiped away his tears and took a deep breath.

"Don't worry about Cetawayo and the children. Deviane and I will watch out for them. I think you should ask for a hundred thousand dollars. Fifty thousand won't last long."

"Okay, so be it."

"Are you sure you want to do this?"

"Yes, go tell the Prime Minister."

"Thank you, Obatala. You've saved my life again. I

couldn't have lived without Deviane."

"Go on, get out of here before I change my mind."

"Goodbye, I'll always remember you."

Kevin and Obatala embraced. Kevin left reluctantly. He went directly to the Prime Minister who had been waiting impatiently for him.

"Okay, I've changed my mind. In fact, I've talked the prisoner into making a full confession. He knows everything about the NDC, their plans, how they operate and he'll cooperate fully in bringing every last NDC member to justice. Of course, it's all a lie, but you don't care, do you?"

"Why would he do this?"

"Because he's a decent man. He truly despises the NDC and what they stand for. You know he's Ray Mohammed's brother, right?"

"Of course, that's why we suspected him."

"Well, he tried to get Ray out of the NDC, but couldn't do it. Now he wants to do whatever it takes to bring them down. He also wants to see Deviane and I married. He cares about us, but I guess you wouldn't understand that, would you?"

"I love Deviane, but sometimes we have to make sacrifices."

"Tell that to Obatala's wife and three kids. Oh, there are a couple of conditions."

"What conditions?"

"Obatala will not hang, you must swear to it in front of your daughters. And you'll arrange for Obatala's family to leave Trinidad and go to America. Of course, they will need cash to live on, two hundred thousand would be about right."

"Two hundred thousand dollars?"

"Yes, that's pocket change considering how much you're going to get from him. You'll save a million dollars in prosecution costs alone."

"Okay, it's a deal."

"Good, then take me back to Deviane. I miss her already."

"Kevin, I hope you will forgive me some day. Some-"

"I know, sometimes you have to do things you don't want to do. I don't know if I will ever be able to forgive you, as long as Obatala is rotting in some prison for something he didn't do. I'm sorry."

"Will you tell Deviane?"

"How can I keep it from her? She's going to be my wife. We will not have secrets from each other. She will know everything."

"I'm doing this for them, you know. It's for their benefit. Anila loves being the Prime Minister's wife. She would be devastated if I were thrown out of office."

"I don't think you give her enough credit. She loves being in the limelight, but she loves you more. She'll stand by you no matter what happens."

"I'll make this up to you Kevin, I promise."

"Sure, can we get back now? The girls are expecting us."

"You go ahead. I'll have the driver take you back to the hospital. I need to stay here and make sure Obatala does what he has promised to do."

"Oh, he will, he's a man of his word. I promise."

# Chapter 22

Kevin agonized over the situation as he was driven back to the hospital. He knew that if he told Deviane about the deal he had made with her father, she would be devastated. He considered keeping it a secret, but dismissed that idea. The one thing they both wanted was a totally honest relationship. There couldn't be secrets between them. He thought of ways he could phrase her father's treachery that might be easier for her to take, but Deviane was not stupid, she would quickly understand that her father was using her as a pawn in his political games. Finally, he decided there was nothing he could do but tell it exactly like it happened. If Deviane never spoke to her father again, it was his own fault. Kevin gathered his things together and went back to the car to be taken to the Prime Minister's home. When he arrived, Deviane was waiting for him. She rushed to him as he got out of the car. They embraced.

"Boy, am I going to get greeted like this every time I come home?"

"Of course, I missed you."

"I've only been gone three hours."

"It seemed like a week."

Kevin smiled and pulled Deviane's lips to his. Kissing her was like being plugged into a two hundred twenty volt socket. Kevin's knees weakened from the jolt.

"Hmmm. That was sweet," he said.

Deviane winked at him.

"Just wait, the best is yet to come."

"Why wait, I'm ready now."

"No, no. You can't have all the candy at once, you'll get sick."

"I'll chance it."

"Yeah, I bet. Come on inside. I want to show you the pictures of my mother's wedding. It will give us some ideas for ours."

"Okay."

Kevin followed Deviane inside to the parlor, where she had three large photo albums out on a table. She sat and started turning the pages. Kevin stood behind her, looking over her shoulder.

"Wasn't my mother a beautiful bride?"

"Oh God, yes. It's obvious where you got your beauty."

"Silly, I'm not as pretty as Mom."

"Bullshit! You're just as pretty, maybe prettier."

"Do you think so?"

"I know so."

"Hmm. Do you like the lavender dresses?"

"Yeah, they're okay."

"My mom was married in the Cathedral, do you think we should do that too?"

"I thought you wanted to be married in the Botanical Gardens?"

"I do, but do you think it would be bad luck not to be married in the church?"

"Not as long as a priest marries us. It shouldn't matter."

"Wasn't Daddy a handsome groom?"

"That he was," Kevin said and then sat in the chair next to Deviane.

"Speaking of your father, I need to talk to you about something. It's not a pleasant topic."

Deviane looked at Kevin

"What?"

"You know, sometimes honesty can be painful. I know

we've pledged to be totally honest with each other, but there are some things that I think would be better left a secret. I'm asking you to let me have one secret. It would be better if you didn't know it."

"Kevin, what are you talking about?"

"There is something that I should tell you, but if you want my opinion, you'd be better off not to know it. Please give me permission not to tell you."

Deviane gave Kevin a hard stare.

"I don't know, Kevin. I would always wonder what your deep dark secret was. I don't know if that would be good. I've got quite a vivid imagination, you know. I'd think of a hundred possibilities. I would always feel sick inside wondering which one it was."

"You would never imagine this one. But, it's okay, I knew I'd have to tell you. I just didn't want to have to do it."

"What is it? Tell me."

"Your father almost sent me home to America today."

"What?"

"There was a prisoner, who he believed was a high ranking NDC official. He told me, if I didn't identify him as being at the warehouse before the assault, that he would ship me back to America and I would never see you again."

"No, Kevin. It's not true! You misunderstood him."

"There was no mistake, sweetheart. I'm sorry."

"Daddy wouldn't do such a thing. He loves me and he knows how much I love you. He wouldn't do something like that."

"I told you it would be better kept a secret."

"Kevin, this is a joke, right?"

"No! This isn't a joke, Deviane. I wouldn't kid about something like this."

Deviane began to cry.

"Why would he do such a horrible thing?"

"He's desperate, I guess. He says his government might not survive if he can't find someone to punish for the NDC's crimes against Trinidad."

Deviane wiped the tears from her eyes with her sleeve.

"You're still here. If what you say is true, why aren't you on your way to America? You couldn't have agreed to this scheme."

"I did refuse, but something unbelievable happened."

"He changed his mind, he came to his senses, right? God! You scared the crap out of me."

"No, I'm sorry, honey. When they showed me the *so called* high ranking NDC official, it turned out to be Obatala."

Deviane's mouth dropped.

"Oh God, no! Oh, Kevin, I can't believe this."

"I nearly died right on the spot."

"Did you tell Daddy who he was?"

"Yes, but he didn't care. This was the man he wanted me to falsely accuse of treason."

"So what did you do?"

"I said no, I wouldn't do it. I told him you would never stand for it either. So I told him to take me away and do whatever he had to do."

"You were really going to let him take you away without even saying goodbye?"

"What choice did I have? Obatala's life was at stake. At least, that's what I initially thought."

"What do you mean?"

"Well, as we were leaving I thought I should say goodbye to Obatala. Your father was gracious enough to grant me that last request. When I told Obatala what had happened, he said I should do what the Prime Minster wanted."

"What? He consented to being hanged for treason?"

"No, not exactly. One of the conditions of the arrangement was that your father would have to promise that Obatala wouldn't be executed. He would also have to guarantee the safety of Obatala's family. He wanted them to be sent to America, and given money to live on."

"I can't believe Obatala would agree to that. How could he just leave his family?"

"He knew that, because he was Ray's brother, he would probably go to prison anyway, whether I testified or not. This way he could be sure his family would be safe and protected. I promised him you and I would keep an eye out for them in America."

"How can I ever look my father in the face again after this? I thought he loved me. Now I know I'm just a piece of property, a possession that he'll sell to the highest bidder. Take me home with you to America. We'll get married in Texas."

"I knew you would say that, but what about your mother? She'll die if you don't get married here in Trinidad."

"We can't have it here, the wedding will be nothing more than a political event. It will just be part of my father's games. I want our wedding to be about us, about truth and honesty, not deceit and treachery. My mother can come to our wedding in Texas."

"It won't be the same. She'll be humiliated. I love your mother and I hate for this to happen to her, just because of your father. Besides, if you disown your father, what would keep him from hanging Obatala? Once I testify, there would be nothing to stop him. Only his love for you will insure he honors his commitment."

"I'm not so sure he loves me anymore."

"I think he does. He's just under a lot of pressure and is not thinking clearly. In his mind, he's doing what's best for you and the family, as well as Trinidad."

"He's doing what's best for himself."

"Maybe, but I don't think we have a choice."

"Damn it! I hate when someone else controls my life!"

"Why don't we get away from here awhile? I'd like to go home before the trial. My parents have been worried sick, besides they haven't met you yet. I want you to meet all of my family and friends."

"Oh, that would be fun," Deviane replied. "We'd have three weeks before the trial."

"That's plenty of time. We can check out some colleges while we're in the United States too."

"That's a good idea."

"You know what?" Kevin said. "We should take Obatala's family with us. That way we can make sure they get out of Trinidad."

"That makes sense. We can help them get settled before we come back for the trial."

"Exactly. I'll go call Cetawayo and see if we can go over to her place and talk to her."

"Okay, I'll go change and put on some make-up."

"You don't need make-up. You're beautiful just the way you are."

"Yes, I do. I won't be long."

Kevin called the Prime Minister and told him he was going to see Cetawayo, to advise her of the deal. He agreed, but didn't like the idea of them going to her home, as it would be too dangerous. He suggested dinner that evening at Michael's, in their private dining room. He said he would make all the arrangements. Kevin agreed and advised Deviane when she came down from her room.

Kevin and Deviane were driven to Michael's that evening. When they arrived, they were taken to a table where Cetawayo was already seated. Although she tried to hide it, it was obvious she had been crying a lot. Her eyes were bloodshot and she looked like she hadn't slept in days. She got up when she saw Kevin and they embraced.

"Cetawayo, it's so good to see you again. This is Deviane, the Prime Minister's daughter, and soon to be my wife."

"Oh," Cetawayo said coolly.

"Deviane had no part in this, believe me."

"I'm so sorry about your husband, Cetawayo," Deviane

said. "He's a wonderful man who saved my life. I'll be forever indebted to him."

"Then why don't you get your father to let him go?"

Kevin took a deep breath.

"Okay, let's sit down and talk about this. I know this is difficult."

Cetawayo and Deviane didn't move.

"Come on. Sit down," Kevin said and gestured toward the table. "We'll talk about this while we eat."

Deviane walked over to the table and sat down. Cetawayo reluctantly followed her. Kevin sat down last.

"This is what Obatala wants, Cetawayo. He knows that there is no escape for him, because he is Ray's brother. He's made a deal with me and the Prime Minister. You and the kids are to go to America and live. The Prime Minister is going to give you two hundred thousand dollars so that you'll have plenty of money to live on until you can get settled."

"Is two hundred thousand dollars the price of his life?"

"No, the Prime Minister has promised he won't be executed. He'll just go to prison for awhile. A long while I'm afraid, but at least he won't die. This way, you and the kids will be safe. Deviane and I will be living in America, so we'll be there for you if you need us."

"But, if I'm in America, the children and I won't be able to visit Obatala."

"I know, but you won't be safe here. Obatala's going to take the NDC down. He's going to testify against everyone involved. It's going to get pretty ugly."

"Oh God, this isn't fair. Obatala had nothing to do with the NDC. He hated it!"

"Exactly, and now he has a chance to destroy it."

Tears flooded from Cetawayo's eyes. Deviane went to her and tried to console her.

"Your kids will like America. They'll be happy there. I

know they'll miss their father, but it would be more painful for them if they were here and had to read all the nasty lies about him in the newspaper, and hear them talk about him on television."

"This is our home. We love Trinidad."

"I know, but I hear America is a wonderful place," Deviane said. "Your children will be better off there."

"When we would we leave?"

"Soon. Kevin and I will be going to Texas to meet his family. We'll take you with us."

"What about school, and my job?"

"We'll find a job for you in America, and the schools there are good."

"I don't know if I can leave Obatala."

"He wants you to leave. He'll be worried sick about you if you stay," Kevin said.

"This is terrible. Why did this have to happen?"

"I don't know, but you've got to come with us," Deviane pleaded. "If not for yourself, think of your children."

"All right. If it's what Obatala wants me to do."

"It is. I'll arrange for you to see him before we leave," Kevin said.

"Yes, *please*. I need to see him. I'm so worried about him."

"You will, you'll see him soon," I promise."

# Chapter 23

The following day, Kevin arranged for Cetawayo to visit Obatala at the courthouse. The visit lasted about an hour. She seemed resigned to her fate by the time she left him. She went home to begin packing and making arrangements to leave. That night, Kevin and Deviane broke the news to Anila about their plans to go to Texas.

"Mom, Kevin wants to go home and see his family before the trial. His parents are really anxious to see him since the kidnaping and everything. I'm going to go with him, so I can meet them."

"Oh, when did you decide this?"

"Just in the last couple of days. We've been thinking about it and feel it's not fair to Kevin's family not to get a chance to meet me before the wedding."

"But we have so much to do."

"You don't need me. I want a wedding just like yours. Whatever you do will be fine. Anyway, I'll only be gone a couple of weeks. We've got months until the wedding."

"I guess we've been kind of selfish. Why don't you invite Kevin's parents here? They could be our guests."

"No, I need to meet all of his family. We're also going to look at some colleges while we're there."

"I guess I can get along without you for a couple of weeks, but promise me you won't stay any longer."

"I won't. Kiran will help you too. She likes planning social events."

"When will you leave?"

"Tomorrow. The trial is in three weeks and Kevin has to testify, so we need to leave right away."

"Have you told your father?"

"Yes, he understands."

"Well, I'll miss you two."

"I'll call you every few days to tell you how things are going."

"Good, I'll be worried about you."

"I'll take good care of her, don't worry, Anila."

"I know you will, Kevin."

"Well, we've got to go pack. We're leaving early in the morning."

"Do you need any help?"

"No, Kevin will help me."

"Alright, good night, dear."

"Good night, Mom."

The next morning, Kevin and Deviane were taken to a military air base. They were surprised to see a United States jet parked on the runway. They were escorted aboard and were delighted to see that Cetawayo and the children were already there. They gave Cetawayo a hug and said hello to the children. The captain came back and introduced himself.

He asked them to take their seats and buckle their seat belts until they were airborne. Just as everyone was set for the takeoff, the door to the plane opened and Ambassador Rawlins boarded carrying a black brief case and a raincoat.

"Hello, Kevin, Deviane."

"Mr. Ambassador, I didn't know you were going with us," Deviane said.

"Well, it was a last minute thing. You didn't give us much notice of this trip. We really had to scramble."

"I just thought we were going to take BWIA," Kevin said. "I didn't expect you to send a jet."

"The President didn't want anything more happening to

you two. Besides, he wants you to come to the White House for dinner tonight."

"Really?"

"You don't mind, do you?"

"No," Kevin laughed. "I've always wanted to see the inside of the White House. I can't believe this!"

"I didn't bring anything nice enough to wear to the White House." Deviane said.

"It's all right, we'll arrange for you to get a gown when we arrive."

"Wow! This is exciting," Deviane said. "What about Cetawayo and the children?"

"We've made arrangements for them. The President has agreed to grant them political asylum in the United States. It will take a few days to process them. We'll take good care of them, don't worry. In a few days they'll join you in Dallas."

"Oh, the Prime Minister wanted me to give you this briefcase, Kevin. I don't know what's in it, but he said you would know what to do with it."

"Oh, thanks," Kevin said as he took the briefcase from the Ambassador.

"I guess congratulations are in order."

"Oh, thank you." Deviane said.

"Have you set a date?"

"After the first of the year, during the dry season. We're getting married at the Royal Botanical Gardens."

"Oh, that should be beautiful. You know, this is going to be quite an event. An American hero marries the richest and prettiest girl in Trinidad."

"That's not true."

"Which part?"

"Kiran is prettier than me."

"I'm not so sure, my dear."

"I'm on your side, Ambassador," Kevin said smiling at Deviane.

She blushed and turned her head to look out the window. Kevin and the Ambassador laughed.

"Hey, with all this publicity you're getting, you ought to think about a career in politics."

"Really?"

"Yeah, you're damn near a household name. I bet you could be the youngest congressman on the Hill."

"Hmm."

"Well, I better go buckle up. The captain's ready to take off," the Ambassador said.

While Kevin and Deviane were excited about the prospect of going to the White House, they were more curious about the briefcase.

"Should I open it?" Kevin said.

"Wait until the Ambassador is gone. I don't know what's in it."

"Okay."

A little later, the Ambassador went to the back of the plane to use the restroom.

"Hurry," Deviane said. "Open it!"

Kevin opened the briefcase and exclaimed, "Oh shit! It's full of money."

"Really? How much?"

"Two hundred thousand I bet. This must be Cetawayo's money. I guess I get to take care of it for her."

"Yeah, because they've got to go through State Department processing, It might be difficult for Cetawayo to explain why she had two hundred thousand dollars."

"Good point."

Deviane noticed the door to the commode open.

"Put it away, the Ambassador is coming,"

Kevin closed the briefcase and put it under the seat.

He smiled at the Ambassador as he sat down.

"The attendant will serve us some lunch later on. If you want a Coke or anything, just push the button over your seat."

"Thanks. This is so cool, flying in our own private jet," Kevin said.

"Your daddy has a private jet, doesn't he, Deviane?" the Ambassador said.

"Yes, I've been in it a few times. We went to Caracas once."

"Well, you might want to relax and get some shut eye. You're going to have a long day."

"Good idea," Deviane said as she started fumbling with her seat. "Kevin, wake me up for lunch."

"Okay, sweet dreams."

Deviane closed her eyes and quickly fell asleep. Kevin looked out the window at the ocean beneath them. He was much too excited to sleep. All he could think about was eating dinner at the White House. He thought back to that moment of decision, when he knew he had to act if he was going save the Prime Minister. He was so glad he hadn't stopped to think and just let his instincts guide him. He thanked God for putting him in the right place at the right time.

At two-thirty, the plane landed in Washington, D.C.. The President's helicopter was waiting for them at the airport. Kevin, Deviane and the Ambassador were taken aboard immediately. Cetawayo and the kids were escorted to a State Department van that was waiting not far away. The helicopter ride took thirty minutes. When they landed at the White House, they were escorted to guest rooms, where they could rest and prepare for dinner and their meeting with the President. One of the First Lady's aides found Deviane a gown, and a hairdresser came in to do her hair and nails. Kevin found a tux hanging in his closet. One of the White House servants came by to ask him if he needed any alterations or help getting dressed. Kevin politely declined. At six, the guests were called to the Blue Room for cocktails.

As Kevin walked into the elegant room, he noticed the

magnificent candelabra and the picture of James Monroe on the wall. He admired the aqua upholstery on the chairs that matched the rich wallpaper. Then he saw the most beautiful thing in the room. It was Deviane, dressed in a magnificent, long, silver satin dress with a plunging neckline. It gave him goose bumps. He stared at her a moment, like she was a stranger. When she saw him, she waved and he quickly walked over to her.

"My God! You look stunning. I was mesmerized when I first saw you."

"Thank you. You look pretty handsome yourself. I was wondering what you'd look like in a tux."

"Is the President here yet?"

"I don't think so. I've already seen someone I know, though."

"Really, who was that?"

"The wife of the ambassador to Barbados. I had dinner with her one time, when we were on holiday."

"Well, that's good. I doubt I'll meet anybody I know."

Just then, Ambassador Rawlins spotted them and came over.

"Hey, let me take you two around and introduce you to everybody. My, you look fantastic, Deviane. You better keep a close eye on her tonight, Kevin. She might get kidnapped again!"

The Ambassador took Deviane by the arm and escorted her to a group of people. Kevin followed and the Ambassador introduced them. Thirty minutes later, the President made his entrance and immediately found Kevin and Deviane.

"Kevin, you did well in Trinidad I see," the President said.

"Yes, I'm very lucky."

"So, you two are going to take the plunge, huh?"

"Yes, in January," Kevin replied.

"Congratulations. I must say we had some very

concerned moments back here when you two were kidnapped. That must have been quite an experience."

"It definitely was *that*, sir."

"How are you both feeling? I heard you both were badly beaten."

"I'm okay, I just got hit a few times," Deviane said. "Kevin is the one they really hurt."

"I'm feeling a lot better. I had a couple of broken ribs, and you can still see the bruise on my forehead. It's still a little tender."

"How did it feel to kill that terrorist, Ray Mohammed?"

"It felt good, at the time."

"I bet it did. Are you going to be all right with it?"

"Yeah, I had to do it."

"It's never easy to kill someone, no matter how evil they are," the President said.

"No, it's not."

"So, Deviane, have you been to America before?"

"Yes, we went to Florida once, when I was pretty young."

"Well, I hope you enjoy your stay."

"I'm sure I will."

"Will you two be living in the United States?"

"We're not sure, but we'll definitely be going to college here."

"Great, do you know where you're going yet?"

"No, not yet. In fact, we're going to look at a few colleges while were here."

"Oh, you should go see Georgetown while you're in Washington. It's a fine school."

"Maybe we will."

"So, what do you think of the White House?"

"It's magnificent!" Kevin replied.

"Play your cards right and maybe you can live here some day."

Kevin raised his eyebrows. "Well, I don't know about

that, Sir."

"Kevin and I are thinking about going to medical school," Deviane said.

"Both of you? My word, you two are ambitious."

"We'd like to open up a free clinic for the poor," Deviane said.

"That sounds great. Well, we better get this dinner on the road, Pierre gets cranky if we're late for dinner. Come on everyone, let's go to the dining room. Dinner is served!"

Since Kevin and Deviane's arrival, the crowd had swelled to over a hundred. The gigantic horseshoe-shaped table was an incredible sight. Kevin was impressed by the gold silverware and fine china. Before they sat down, the First Lady came over and introduced herself. After they had talked a few minutes, she left and everyone was seated. Before dinner started, the President asked for everyone's attention.

"Ladies and gentlemen, I'd like to say a few words and then propose a toast to our guests, Kevin Wells and Deviane Shah. Several months ago, we all witnessed a most courageous act. Kevin Wells, without blinking an eye, jumped up to protect a head of state who was a guest here in America. He prevented a horrible tragedy from occurring and thwarted an attempt by terrorists to forcibly take over Trinidad. We thought that was as much heroism as anyone could expect from one individual in a lifetime.

"Well, as you know Kevin was called upon again to demonstrate extraordinary courage. This time, he and the two daughters of the Prime Minister of Trinidad were chased through the forest by enemy guerrillas, who had orders to kill them. One of the girls was shot. Kevin carried her, under fire, for several miles until they thought they had been rescued. Unfortunately, it was a trick. Kevin and Deviane were bound and gagged, thrown into a helicopter at gun point, and then dumped in a dark prison cell. By the grace of God, they were rescued and we welcome them here tonight!"

The crowd gave them a rousing round of applause. Kevin smiled and bowed slightly. Deviane wiped a tear from her eye.

The President continued, "Raise your glasses and toast this most extraordinary American, Kevin Wells. You're an inspiration to us all!"

Everyone took a drink and then gave them another round of applause.

"If you haven't already heard it, there is a fairy tale ending to this story. Kevin and Deviane are to be married in Trinidad, in January!"

Several women in the crowd signed, "Ohhh!"

"Here's to Kevin and Deviane! To many wonderful years together!"

After dinner, the President excused himself, as he had to attend to matters of state. He suggested Kevin and Deviane spend the night in the White House. He told them he'd see to it that someone gave them a tour of Georgetown in the morning. Then, they could take an afternoon flight to Dallas. They accepted, thanked the President and were taken to the Red Room for coffee with Ambassador Rawlins and other State Department officials.

"Kevin, I'd like you to meet Monty Crandall. He's my boss at the State Department. I promised him I'd introduce you both to him before you left town."

"Hi, it's a pleasure to meet you." Kevin said.

Deviane smiled and said, "Hello."

"I'm not going to bore you with more accolades. You've had enough of that tonight, I'm sure. What I wanted to tell you was that the President wants to provide you with some security while you're in the United States. We don't want anything happening to you. We'll provide a jet to take you anywhere you want to go. I'm assigning three men to watch out for you."

"Is that really necessary?" Deviane said.

"Yes, you're the daughter of a foreign head of state, so this is just diplomatic courtesy. We want your stay here in America to be pleasant and uneventful. Besides, the press could be a problem, so we'll help you manage that situation."

"The press?" Kevin said.

"Yes. You two are a hot item. They'll be stalking you wherever you go."

"Really?" Kevin said.

"Yes, we also want to be sure you get back to Trinidad to testify. This trial is very important to the United States. We want to be sure Deviane's father stays in power. He's been very friendly to the United States and we don't want anything to jeopardize that relationship, particularly since the Cocos Bay discovery."

"Okay, whatever you say," Kevin replied.

"If you two want to be alone before you go to bed, there's a sitting room on the third floor that you can use. Or, if you want to see a movie, just let one of the staff know."

"Thank you. That's very thoughtful," Deviane said as she smiled at Kevin.

"If you need anything at all, just let someone know."

"Thank you, sir," Kevin said.

"Well, the Ambassador and I must run. It was a pleasure meeting both of you."

"Yes, it was nice meeting you. Thank you for everything," Kevin replied.

After the Ambassador and Mr. Crandall left, Kevin and Deviane went up to the sitting room to talk for a while before bed. Someone from the kitchen staff brought them a snack and asked if they needed anything else. When they were alone, they kissed for a while, then held hands as they gazed out the window at the cars traveling down Pennsylvania Avenue.

"You know, this *is* a fairy tale," Kevin said. "Sometimes I think I'm dreaming and I'm afraid I'm going to wake up."

Deviane smiled. "I know what you mean. When I saw you for the first time on Jay Leno, I just knew we were meant to be together. I was so scared that I wouldn't be able to have you. Then, when you thought you loved Kiran, I wanted to jump off the roof."

Kevin laughed. "I'm glad you didn't."

"Now, I'm so scared something will happen and I'll lose you."

"No chance. You're stuck with me now."

"You promise?"

"Scout's honor."

Deviane put her arms around Kevin and squeezed him tightly. Kevin began to stroke her hair and caress her neck. Then he kissed the top of her head gently.

"I love you," he said.

# Chapter 24

The next morning, Kevin and Deviane met the men who would be their escorts for the duration of their stay in the United States. The three Secret Service agents briefed them on their security procedures and promised that they would stay out of their way as much as possible. A driver took them to Georgetown University, where they were given a tour by an assistant dean. When they had seen everything of interest, they were taken to a nearby military base, where their jet to Dallas was waiting. It was a warm, clear day, perfect for flying. Once airborne, Kevin and Deviane talked about their unique experience.

"I wouldn't mind living in the White House," Kevin said.

"It was rather nice, actually. I could get used to it."

"I don't know if I'd like having Secret Service agents crawling all over me though."

"I know, we're not going to have any privacy."

"Did you sleep well last night?" Kevin asked.

"Pretty good. It took me a while to fall asleep, though," Deviane replied.

"I didn't sleep well at all. Everything that's happened to us recently kept running through my mind. I don't know why. I should have been exhausted, but something was bothering me."

"Well, I'll shut up and you can take a nap."

"No, I want to talk while we've got a little privacy."

Deviane smiled, took Kevin's hand and squeezed it. "So what was bothering you?"

"Everything. It was like our life was an open book."

"What do you mean?"

"Like—How did the Ambassador know we were going to get married?"

"My father probably told him."

"Why would your father tell him that when it hasn't been officially announced yet? Your mother was going to have an engagement party and announce it then."

"He's not too good at keeping secrets, I guess."

"Do you think he called the President and told him?"

"No, obviously the Ambassador told him, or Mr. Crandall."

"That's what I mean. Everybody knows every move we're making."

"Hmm," Deviane sighed.

"And the briefcase full of money. It wasn't locked. You're going to tell me that the Ambassador didn't open it up to see what was in it?"

"What are you saying, Kevin?"

"The Ambassador knew exactly what was in the briefcase, so he must have known about the deal we struck with your father."

"Well, he had to know since my father had to arrange political asylum for Cetawayo and the children."

"True, but he could have made up an excuse. I can't imagine your father divulging his plans to commit bribery, extortion and obstruction of justice to the Ambassador, unless—"

"Unless what?"

"The Ambassador was in on it."

"No, I don't think that's likely. My father doesn't like foreigners trying to influence his decisions. I've heard him complain about that a lot."

"I don't know. Last night I kept thinking of what Malcolm Mann said, about how everyone was a slave of the Wall Street business cartel and they didn't even realize it."

"Yeah."

"Well, I'm beginning to understand what he meant."

"I don't understand."

"No one in Trinidad would ever dream that the United States was in control of its affairs, right?"

"No, that's ridiculous."

"Well, last night I got the impression that Mr. Crandall was calling the shots in the NDC prosecution. I'm beginning to wonder if he doesn't make a lot of decisions for the Trinidad government."

"I didn't like him much. He made me feel uncomfortable."

"I bet that two hundred thousand came from the Ambassador's safe."

"My father has always been pretty close to the Ambassador."

"Is your father really the richest man in Trinidad?"

"I guess, I don't know for sure."

"Has he always been rich?"

"No. Up until about six or seven years ago, we didn't have all that much money. We were comfortable, but I remember there were a lot of things we couldn't afford. Then my father's oil company went into partnership with another company. They were able to get some good leases. They've done very well ever since."

"Do you remember the name of the company?"

"Sure, Navet Exploration, Limited."

"Hmm. I wonder who owns Navet."

"I wouldn't know."

"We can check it out at the library or on the internet when we get to Dallas."

"So who do you think owns it?"

"Well, if it were a United States company, that would certainly be interesting."

"So, you think my father is working for the United States government?"

"The thought crossed my mind. That would explain why

he would use you and Kiran as bargaining chips. A father wouldn't do something like that on his own. The Ambassador probably suggested it rather strongly."

"I can't believe my father would do that."

"I know, I'm sorry, honey. I hope I'm wrong."

"You must be, he loves Trinidad. He would never betray his own people."

"Just like he didn't betray you and Kiran."

Deviane didn't respond.

"Did you notice how everyone suggested I start thinking about politics as a career? Even the President mentioned it indirectly."

"Yeah, what was that all about?"

"I think they're hoping to suck me into their game, now that I've got some notoriety."

"I don't know, Kevin. Do you think, maybe we're getting a little paranoid?"

"Maybe, but after what has happened to us, I don't think we can be too careful."

"I guess you're right. I'm just so sick of all this intrigue. Why can't everything be the way it appears?" Deviane asked.

"Because nobody gives a rat's ass about truth and honesty anymore. Everything today is about power and money."

"I hope we don't get caught up in that game."

"We're already caught up in it, but maybe after our wedding, we can change things and live an honest, decent life."

"I hope so."

Two hours later, the State Department jet landed at Love Field in Dallas. A car was waiting to take Kevin and Deviane to Plano. It was a hot, muggy day, so the air conditioner was going full blast. Although the sky was clear, visibility was bad. There was an ozone alert in effect.

The car left the airport and headed west on Mockingbird

to I35. It traveled north to LBJ Freeway, then east to the Dallas North Tollway. Ten minutes later, it pulled up in front of Kevin's house in Plano. Kevin's parents were waiting anxiously and came out to meet them. As soon as Kevin got out of the car, his mother embraced him. The secret service agents stepped out and scanned the neighborhood.

"Hi, Mom."

"Kevin! Hi, honey."

"Oh, I'm so glad to see you. I've been so worried about you."

Kevin put his arm around Deviane and smiled.

"Mom and Dad, this is Deviane."

"Hi, Deviane. It's so nice to meet you at last. How are you feeling? I read about how the terrorists beat you up."

"Oh, I'm okay now."

"Good, I can't believe what you two have been through."

"Who are these men with you, Kevin?" Mr. Wells asked.

"It's our Secret Service escort. Can you believe that?"

"Really? How come?"

"It's because Deviane is a diplomatic visitor and the President wants to be sure I get back safely to testify in Trinidad."

As Kevin was talking, a big television van pulled up. It was followed by several other press vehicles. A reporter leaped out and rushed up to Kevin. The Secret Service agents quickly went into action and started moving everyone inside.

"Mr. Wells, how was your visit with the President?" the reporter asked.

"Oh, it was great."

"Is it true you and Ms. Shah are engaged to be married?"

"Well, I haven't had a chance to buy her an engagement ring yet, but we plan to visit some jewelry stores in the next few days."

"So it's true you're going to get married?"

"Yes, in January."

"What is your reaction to Malcolm Mann's statement that you'll never live to testify against Obatala Mohammed?"

Kevin's jaw dropped. A cold chill radiated down his spine. "I don't know. This is the first I've heard of it."

"Okay, that will be all," one of the Secret Service agents said as he took Kevin by the arm and escorted him into the house. Once inside the agents began a security check of the house.

While Kevin's parents were distracted by the agents, Deviane took Kevin aside to talk.

"What did the reporter say about Malcolm Mann, Kevin?" Deviane asked.

"It sounded like he made some sort of threat to kill me."

"Oh my God! Where is he?"

"I don't know anything other than what the reporter said."

"Damn it!" Deviane said. "I wish you would have killed him, too. "

"It's just talk, honey. There's no way he could hurt us here."

"What's wrong, Kevin?" Mrs. Wells asked as she approached them.

Kevin turned and looked at his mother's worried face.

"Oh. Ah. . . nothing. I guess I may have let the cat out of the bag about our wedding."

Deviane forced a smile.

Kevin looked at Deviane. "I hope I didn't spoil it for your mother. I know she wanted to make the announcement."

"It's okay. I don't think it's much of a secret anymore."

"The wedding?" Mrs. Wells said.

"You haven't heard about it?" Kevin asked.

"No."

"Oh, good. We wanted to tell you before you heard it on the news. Deviane and I are getting married."

Mrs. Wells eyes widened. "Kevin, this is so sudden. You two haven't known each other very long."

"I know, but we fell in love. What can I say?"

"You haven't finished high school yet, and what about college?" Mr. Wells asked.

"I'll finish high school this summer and then we're going to go to college together. We looked at Georgetown while we were in Washington."

"Georgetown, you never mentioned being interested in Georgetown," Mr. Wells said.

"The President wanted us to see it," Deviane said. "I kind of liked it. It had a certain charm."

"Have you set a date, honey?" Mrs. Wells asked.

"Not exactly, it will be sometime in January. I hope everyone won't mind flying to Trinidad."

"Oh my word! You're getting married in Trinidad?"

"Of course, Mom. The bride's family always puts on the wedding. You'll love Trinidad. It's a beautiful country. We're getting married at the Royal Botanical Gardens. You won't believe it. It's absolutely incredible. It's probably the most beautiful place on earth. I can't wait for you and Dad to see it."

"My mother will see to it that it's a memorable wedding, believe me," Deviane said. "It will be the biggest social event Trinidad has had in years."

"Is that right? Well, this is all so exciting. I don't know what to say."

"Don't worry, Mom. I know all this is all pretty overwhelming but you'll get used to it. I'm starting to."

"I guess I could take my vacation time in January," Mr. Wells said.

"Yeah, Dad. It'll be forty or fifty degrees warmer in Trinidad than in Dallas. It'll be a good break from the cold winter weather."

"Where are you going to go on your honeymoon?" Mrs. Wells asked.

Kevin and Deviane looked at each other and started to laugh.

"We haven't even thought about that, Mom. Maybe we'll stop by a travel agency tomorrow, when we go shopping."

"I like Barbados. It's a beautiful island," Deviane said.

"That's too close to Trinidad, Deviane. We should go somewhere far away, like Hawaii."

"Oh, I've always wanted to go to Hawaii. I like that idea."

"Good, that was easy."

"Where are you going shopping tomorrow?"

"We thought we'd go to the Galleria and check out the jewelry stores. I need to buy Deviane an engagement ring. We might stop at Victoria's Secret while we're there too."

"Kevin!" Mrs. Wells said.

"For our wedding night, Mom. We've got to think ahead."

"Uh huh."

"I hate to bring up minor details, but how do you plan to finance all of this?" Mr. Wells asked.

"Oh, I was going to ask you if I could borrow your Visa card, Dad," Kevin replied.

Mr. Wells frowned.

"No, luckily I listened to you and I've been saving my pennies. I've got a few bucks in the bank. Fortunately, the government has been flying us everywhere, so we haven't spent a nickel since we left Trinidad."

"I haven't told Kevin this before, but I've got quite a lot of money in a trust fund," Deviane added. "Money shouldn't be a problem."

Kevin looked at Deviane. "You've got a trust fund?"

"Yes."

He smiled. "Aren't you full of surprises. How much?"

Deviane shook her head and replied, "We'll talk about it later."

"Hmm, well, I guess you don't have to worry about us having enough money, Dad."

"That's good. I just wanted to be sure everything would work out for you."

"I know. Hey, we're going to go watch television in the guest room, okay?"

"Oh, I forgot to tell you. Your friends are coming over to see you in a little bit. They've all been worried about you."

"Oh, great. I wanted Deviane to meet them. Who all's coming?"

"Paula, Alice and Brent."

Kevin smiled at Deviane. She gave him a distressed look and he laughed. "Don't worry. It will be all right."

Deviane took a deep breath and returned a half smile.

It wasn't long before the doorbell rang. Kevin got up quickly and went to the door. Deviane followed him, but only went far enough to see the front door. Kevin opened it and embraced Paula. Alice walked past them, went straight over to Deviane and extended her hand.

"You must be the princess," she said.

Deviane frowned as they shook hands.

"Come on, Alice," Kevin said, "Deviane's not a princess. They don't have royalty in Trinidad."

Brent came forward shaking his head. "I don't know, she may not be a princess, but there's no doubt she's a goddess."

Deviane blushed a little and then shook Brent's hand. Kevin laughed. "You noticed, huh...? Forgive my friends, Deviane, they're not—well actually they *are* usually this rude."

They all laughed. "Yes," Paula said. "Please forgive us. You've been through so much. I don't know how you two did it. I can't imagine being kidnaped by terrorists."

"Let's not talk about that," Kevin said. "That's one nightmare we're trying to forget."

"I can imagine," Paula said. "We've just been so worried about you two."

"Thank you," Deviane said. "Kevin has told me what

wonderful friends he had back in America. I'm so glad I finally got to meet all of you. I hope you all can come to Trinidad for the wedding."

Paula's face stiffened. She looked over at Kevin.

"Wedding?"

"Yes, it's going to be in the papers tomorrow so we best tell you now. Deviane and I are getting married in Trinidad in January."

Paula turned away as she struggled to keep her composure. Kevin watched her intently. Deviane watched them both.

"Wow! I can't believe you're getting married," Alice said. "Congratulations!"

"Thank you," Deviane replied. "My father will provide all of you transportation and you'll be our guests while you're in Trinidad."

"Are you serious?" Brent said.

"Yes, Kevin's friends are my friends . . . at least I hope so."

Paula turned and looked at Deviane.

Alice said, "Well, you must be some kind of woman to land this Texas lunker. I'd be proud to be your friend."

Kevin laughed. Alice and Deviane embraced.

Paula took a deep breath, wiped a tear from her eye and said, "Yes, of course, I'd be honored to be your friend. You're a very lucky woman."

Deviane smiled tenderly. "Yes, I know."

It was several hours later when the reunion broke up. As Kevin was walking them out to the car, Paula pulled him aside.

"Congratulations, you finally found your virgin," she said.

Kevin took a deep breath. "Listen, Paula, I'm sorry things didn't work out for us. I do love you, but as a friend."

"You know what really bothers me?"

"What's that?"

"When I had sex the first time I had no idea what I was giving up. If I had the slightest inkling that you were out there, I wouldn't have let anyone touch me. I just never-"

"Paula, even if you'd been a virgin, I'm not sure we'd have ever gotten together. I wasn't just looking for a virgin. That was just one of the qualities I wanted in my wife. Besides, you must know by now Deviane isn't a virgin. What happened to her was in all the papers."

"Well, that was speculation by reporters. I hoped it wasn't true."

"It is true. She was raped by Ray Mohammed. That's why I killed him."

"Oh, my God!" Paula said. "You must have been devastated."

"Well at the time I didn't realize I was in love with Deviane. She'd told me how she felt about me but I thought I was still in love with Kiran. Then, when Mohammed took her, I felt like taking that gun and blowing my own brains out. Just when I realized Deviane was the woman I had been searching for, she was snatched away from me. So what was the point of living? But I figured out pretty quick that nothing had really changed. She was still the same woman. All we had to do was erase a few hours from our memories.

"I wanted her back no matter what condition she was in. It didn't matter that she'd been raped. I couldn't live without her. If she hadn't come out of shock, then that's when I would have definitely taken a gun and blown my brains out."

Paula began to cry. They embraced.

"I'm so sorry, Kevin. I had no idea. I've been so selfish."

Kevin pulled away and looked Paula in the eye. "Bullshit. You've been a wonderful friend. One of these days I'll be coming to your wedding and you know what?"

"What?"

"I'm going to be a little jealous myself."

Paula smiled. "Really?. . . . I don't believe you, but it was nice of you to say it anyway."

Kevin took Paula's hand and squeezed it. She turned and walked to the car. She got in and they drove off. Kevin turned and saw Deviane standing at the door. He smiled and went to her.

"That was awkward," he said, "but I'm glad we got it over with."

"She really loves you," Deviane said.

"I know, but she'll get over it."

"But will you?"

Kevin put his arms around Deviane and replied, "I only have room in my heart for one woman. I've always known that and now that I have you, there's no room for anyone else."

They embraced before rejoining Kevin's parents in the den. "We're going to go watch TV in the guest room," he said.

"Why don't you watch it in the den?" Mrs. Wells asked.

"It's cozier in the guest room."

"You two be good," Mrs. Wells said.

"I think you know you don't have to worry about that."

"I know. It's been nice talking to you, Deviane," Mrs. Wells said. "Maybe if Kevin will let loose of you one afternoon, we could go to lunch."

"That would be fine," Kevin said. "As long as you promise not to tell her anything bad about me."

"I never make promises I can't keep."

"Don't believe everything Mom tells you, Deviane."

"Oh, I doubt your mother would lie to me."

"Hmm. Why is it you put two women together and a conspiracy always begins?"

"That's how we keep men under control," Mrs. Wells replied.

"I believe that. . . . Okay, so after we go shopping in the morning, why don't you two go to lunch? I've got an errand

I've got to run anyway."

"Oh, wonderful. Is that okay, Deviane?" Mrs. Wells said.

"Yes, I'd like that very much."

"Good, it's settled then," Kevin said. "Come on, Deviane. Let's go watch TV."

The next day, Kevin took Deviane to the Galleria. She was amazed by its size and loved the department stores, hundreds of shops and the ice rink inside. She made Kevin sit and watch the skaters for thirty minutes since she had never seen an ice rink before, except on TV. After doing their shopping, which included the purchase of an impressive one carat engagement ring, they drove around North Dallas. Deviane was impressed with the miles and miles of beautiful homes and busy shopping centers that adorned this part of town.

When they got back home, Mrs. Wells was patiently waiting to go to lunch.

"Hi, Mom," Kevin said as he walked into the kitchen.

"Oh, hi. How did your shopping go?"

"Well, look on Deviane's finger and you can judge for yourself."

Deviane extended her hand proudly exhibiting a beautiful diamond engagement ring. Mrs. Wells took her hand and lifted it up so she could get a good look at it.

"Oh my Lord, that *is* beautiful!" Mrs. Wells exclaimed. "I love it!"

"Isn't it exquisite?" Deviane said, twisting her hand so the diamond would sparkle.

"Oh, yes. I'm so jealous."

Kevin watched his mother and Deviane with great satisfaction. He was glad they liked each other. He thought maybe having Deviane around would help fill the void left after Diana's death. At least he hoped so.

"Okay, I've got to go on my errand, so I'm going to leave

you two. Have a good lunch."

"We will. I thought we'd go to Bennigan's and then do some more shopping at Stonebriar Mall."

"Have fun. Oh, I think two Secret Service agents are going with you. The other one is coming with me."

"All right, we'll see you later."

Kevin went outside and got in the State Department car. His thoughts immediately turned to Cetawayo, who was scheduled to arrive with her children at Love Field. He wondered how she had made out and whether the State Department had treated her well. He remembered how strange he felt when he landed in Trinidad, so he could appreciate what a traumatic experience this would be for her and the children.

The driver took them out to the private runway where the jet was just pulling into its parking slot. Several men pushed a portable stairway in front of the door. Then they climbed up the stairs and opened the main hatch. Cetawayo looked scared as she made her way off the plane with her children in hand. Kevin rushed over to her and gave her a hug. Then he picked up one of the kids and shook hands with the other two.

After collecting their luggage, they were driven to a motel, where Kevin checked them in and helped them unpack. Then he showed Cetawayo her money.

"My word, look at all that cash! I've never seen so much money before," Cetawayo said.

Kevin laughed.

"I haven't either. Isn't it beautiful?"

"It will be nice to know it's there, if we need it."

"Lets go put it in the bank where it will be safe. You can't afford to take any chances with it. I saw a Guaranty Bank and a Comerica Bank a few blocks away. You don't want to put more than one hundred thousand in one bank. That's the most that is insured. We'll put half in each bank."

"Okay, whatever you say."

They went back out to the car and were driven to Guaranty Bank. The Secret Service agent waited outside to give them a little privacy. They walked inside and took a seat at the new accounts desk. The kids sat quietly next to their mother. A middle-aged lady, dressed in a business suit, approached them and sat down at her desk.

"Hello, can I help you?" she said.

"Yes," Kevin replied. "Mrs. Mohammed needs to open a bank account."

"Okay, what kind of an account?"

"Just a regular, interest bearing checking account."

"How much will you be depositing?"

"Oh, just a hundred thousand."

The lady looked up and gave Kevin a stunned look. "Oh, is it cash or check?"

"Cash."

"Then I'll have to fill out a Cash Transaction Report."

"What's that?"

"Any cash deposits over ten thousand dollars must be reported to the government."

"Oh really. Well I don't have time to fill that out right now, so we'll just put nine thousand nine hundred ninety-nine dollars in the account. Will that work?"

"Certainly."

"Who will be the signatories?"

"Just Mrs. Mohammed."

"What about in the event of an emergency?"

"I don't know. What do you think, Cetawayo?"

"Why don't you sign, in case something happens to me? You're the only one I know in America, and you'd have to look after the kids if something happened to me."

"Hmm. Okay, if that's what you want."

The clerk filled out the necessary paperwork to open the account and Kevin gave her the money to deposit. When they were done, they went to the lobby and sat down on a sofa. Kevin thought for a moment.

"We don't want to report this money to anyone, particularly the government. They may know about it already, but just in case they don't, we can put it in a safety deposit box," Kevin said.

"Okay."

"Go back to the car with the kids. Tell the Secret Service agent you're not feeling well. Ask him to take you home and then come back for me. I'll go to the Comerica Bank down the street. I don't want the Secret Service knowing where you have the bulk of your money. I'll sneak down to that bank after you are gone and get a safety deposit box. I'll come back here when I'm done and wait to be picked up. That way, nobody will know where the other money is located, except you and I.

"Do you think that's really necessary?"

"It never hurts to be careful."

Kevin went out the back door. He returned twenty minutes later. The Secret Service Agent was just pulling up when he walked outside. When he got back to the motel he gave Cetawayo the safety deposit key. He had her sign the signature card and told her to mail it back to the bank. They both left Guaranty Bank and went out to the car, where the Secret Service agent was waiting.

After going to the store to buy some groceries and showing them around Dallas a little, he dropped them off at their motel.

"Okay, Cetawayo, I know it's got to be hard for you to be suddenly dumped in Dallas like this. I'm sorry I can't spend more time with you."

"It's okay, you've been very helpful."

"If you need anything, you've got my phone number. After Deviane and I leave, you can call my dad. He'll be happy to give you a hand. Before we leave, Deviane and I will help you find an apartment, okay?"

"Thank you, Kevin. You've been so nice to us. We'll be all right now. Don't you be worrying about us, okay?"

"Are you going to try to get a job?"

"After I get the kids in school and learn my way around a little bit, I'll see about getting a teaching certificate here in Dallas. Once I do that, then I can look for a job."

"Great, we'll see you next week then."

Kevin left the motel and asked his driver to drop by the Dallas Library on the way home. He had done a search on the internet on his home computer for ownership information on Navet Exploration, Ltd. but hadn't found what he wanted. There was a lot about the company, but no details on ownership. Once inside, he went directly to the reference section and asked the librarian on duty for assistance. She directed him to several international business directories. Kevin searched through the two volumes until he found what he wanted. He scanned the short paragraph on Navet Exploration. The last sentence provided the answer; Navet Exploration was owned and controlled by Sureguard Ventures, Inc. of Santa Barbara, California but had several other undisclosed partners.

Kevin closed the book and left the library. He felt like he had confirmed his suspicions about the Prime Minister; that he was on the United States payroll. Sure, it wasn't conclusive evidence and he didn't understand exactly how it worked, but to him it stunk, any way you smelled it.

Deviane and his mother were in the kitchen cooking supper when he came in. Deviane rushed over to him and they embraced and kissed excitedly. Mrs. Wells watched them a moment and then went back to her cooking.

"Okay, Kevin. If you want to eat, you'd better release Deviane. She's in the middle of making the salad."

Kevin and Deviane finally let each other go.

"Come on, Mom. We've been separated nearly four hours. Have a heart."

"You'll have plenty of time for kissing later."

"Okay," Kevin replied.

"Enjoy all this affection now, Deviane," Mrs. Wells said.

"When you get my age, you'll be lucky to get a little peck in the morning and swat on the ass at night."

Deviane laughed. "I don't know, Kevin's pretty passionate. I hope he doesn't change."

"He will, it comes with age."

"So, Kevin, how did your errand go?" Deviane asked.

"Very well, actually. I got Cetawayo and her kids settled, and the money put safely away."

"Good, how is Cetawayo?"

"She looked a little tired, but I think she'll be okay. Her kids are angels. They didn't give us any trouble at all. Oh, I went to the library on the way home."

"Oh. So were you right?" Deviane asked.

"I'm afraid so."

Deviane frowned and shook her head. Kevin shrugged and gave her a sympathetic look.

"So what are you kids going to do tomorrow?"

"I'm going to take Deviane to Six Flags."

"Oh. That will be fun."

"Do they have amusement parks in Trinidad, Deviane?"

"No, but I went to Disneyworld once with my family when I was about twelve or thirteen."

"This Saturday, we're going to go check out SMU and TCU. On Sunday, I've got tickets for a Cowboy game."

"You two are going to be busy."

"Well, we've got a lot to do. Next week we have to go back to Trinidad."

"Oh, there was a message for you from someone at NBC."

"What did they want?"

"I don't know, you'll have to call them and find out."

"They probably want an interview. What should I tell them, Deviane?"

"It's up to you, honey. If you want to give them an interview, it's okay with me."

"I guess I'll give them a call."

Kevin went to the telephone and dialed the number on the message. It was a long distance call to Burbank.

"Hello, Kevin. Thanks for returning my call."

"No, problem."

"Listen, Jay heard you were back in the states and wondered if you and Miss Shah wanted to come on the show?"

"Oh, really?"

"Yeah, we thought it would be a great follow up after your last appearance. You know, since you were kidnaped and now you've found a bride."

"Let me discuss it with Deviane and I'll get back with you, okay?"

"Sure, we were thinking about Tuesday night. We had a cancellation, so that would work out well."

"Okay, I'll get back with you. Thanks for calling."

Kevin hung up the phone and went back into the kitchen.

"Guess what?"

"What?" Deviane said."

"Jay Leno wants us on the Tonight Show."

"No way," Deviane said.

"Why?" Kevin asked showing obvious disappointment.

"Kiran said he made fun of you on his show the night we were kidnaped. He thought it was so funny, that you wanted to marry a virgin. If we go on the show, he'll probably humiliate us."

"He's a comedian. He's supposed to humiliate people. Nobody takes it seriously."

"I don't care. Our marriage should be private. I don't want our relationship debated on national television. We'll never have any privacy if we don't put a stop to all this publicity, right now."

"Good point. I'll call them back and decline the invitation. We don't have time for it anyway."

# Chapter 25

Before going back to Trinidad, Kevin and Deviane helped Cetawayo move into an apartment. It was late in the afternoon, all the new furniture had been delivered, and the girls were lining the shelves and putting away groceries. Kevin finished up the installation of a set of bunk beds while the three boys, Kimba, Taiwo and Atiba, watched.

Kimba was eight-years-old and would have his own room. Taiwo and Atiba were six-year-old identical twins and were destined to occupy the bunk beds, once Kevin was finished.

Finally, Kevin tightened the last bolt and stood up to admire his work. Taiwo and Atiba immediately climbed on the beds and started jumping up and down, laughing hysterically. Hearing the clamor, Deviane and Cetawayo, came in to see what was happening.

"Kevin, you're finished, huh?" Deviane said. "They look good."

"Putting those suckers together was a royal pain in the ass."

"Thank you, Kevin. I'm glad I didn't have to do it," Cetawayo said. "Obatala always did those kinds of things. He was the mechanical one in the family."

"When is Daddy coming home?" Kemba asked.

Kevin looked at Deviane and Cetawayo, not knowing how to respond. Cetawayo knelt down and spoke to Kemba.

"Like I told you before, sweetheart, your daddy had to

go on a trip. He won't be back for a long time."

"Why did he have to go?"

"To protect you and your brothers. If he didn't go, you might have been hurt. He loves you very much. Someday he'll come home."

"I want him to come home now, Mommy. Will you tell him to come home?"

"I wish I could, Kemba, but I have no way of talking to him."

"Can't you call him on the phone?"

"He doesn't have a telephone where he is."

"Is he mad at us? Were we bad?"

"No, no. You've been good kids. Like I said, someone was trying to hurt us. He had to go away to protect us."

Kemba finally gave up and ran off into the living room.

"He just doesn't understand," Cetawayo said to Kevin and Deviane.

"I don't either," Kevin replied.

"Well, thank you both for helping me. You've been wonderful. I know you need to leave and pack for your trip back to Trinidad."

"You're welcome," Kevin replied. "I'm glad we could help."

Cetawayo started walking toward the door. "You two be careful back in Trinidad, okay? I don't want to read about you in the newspaper again."

"We'll try to keep a low profile this trip," Deviane replied.

"Do you think you'll be able to visit Obatala?"

"Yes, I plan to visit him," Kevin said.

"Would you tell him I miss him terribly, and that I love him?"

"Of course," Kevin replied. He opened the front door and held it for Deviane.

"You take care now, Cetawayo," Deviane said. "We'll see you after the wedding."

"Oh I wish I could see it. I know it will be beautiful."

"We'll bring back pictures, okay?"

"Good, I'll look forward to seeing them. Go now, it's getting late."

"Goodbye, Cetawayo," Kevin said, pausing to give her a quick hug.

"Take good care of your mommy, you guys," Deviane said to the children who had huddled up next to their mother. She looked up and smiled at Cetawayo. "We'll pray for Obatala," she said.

"Thank you, goodbye."

The next morning, Kevin felt the first pangs of depression. From the expression on Deviane's face, she shared some of his sadness. They had enjoyed the visit to Plano so much, they hated to leave. The prospect of facing Obatala's trial in Trinidad was sobering to say the least.

The small jet finally landed after a long five hour flight from Los Angeles to Trinidad. Anila and Kiran greeted the weary travelers at the government airport. It was raining when they deplaned. Kevin held a large umbrella over their heads as they rushed to the awaiting car.

"Deviane!" Anila cried.

"Hi, Mother," she said as they embraced.

"Hi, Kevin," Kiran said.

"Hello, how are you?" Kevin asked.

"Fine. How was your trip?"

"Excellent."

"Oh my God! Look at that diamond!" Anila said. "Oh, Deviane, it's so beautiful."

"Kevin picked it out. He has good taste, don't you think?"

"Oh yes, I love it," Anila said.

Kiran looked at the ring carefully and smiled, but didn't say anything. Kevin watched her until their eyes met. Then he looked back at Deviane.

"Anything happen here, while we were gone?" Kevin asked.

"Not really. The trial is set to begin the day after tomorrow. The press has been all hyped up about it, as you would expect. Everyone is saying that if Obatala and the others aren't convicted, Father's going to be in serious trouble."

"Is there any chance they won't be convicted?"

"I'm afraid so. Sharad says that much of the evidence is circumstantial. If they get any NDC sympathizers on the jury, it could be difficult to get a conviction. Everything seems to depend on Obatala's testimony. If he isn't convincing, then we might have a problem."

"He knows a lot about the NDC. They had a lot of meetings with Ray at his house. I'd bet he'll be pretty persuasive."

"I hope you're right," Kiran said.

When they got back to the Prime Minister's residence, Kevin and Deviane went to their rooms to unpack. It was well past dinner time, so Anila had someone fix tea and a snack. While they were sipping their tea, the Prime Minister arrived home.

"Deviane! You're home."

"Hi," Deviane said.

"How was your trip?"

"It was wonderful," Anila said. "See what she got."

Anila held up Deviane's hand so Ahmad could see her ring.

"Oh, very nice."

Deviane turned away from her father. He frowned.

"Kevin's parents are great. I really like them."

"I heard you had dinner at the White House," Kiran said.

"Oh, and you should have seen Deviane," Kevin replied. "She wore a magnificent silver gown. She was the most beautiful woman there."

"I wish I could have seen it," Anila said. "Did you spend

much time with the President?"

"Fifteen or twenty minutes," Deviane said. "He arranged a tour of Georgetown for us."

"Really? How did you like it?"

The Prime Minister pulled on Kevin's arm. "Kevin, I need to have a word with you. Would you come to my office?"

"Sure." Kevin got up and followed the Prime Minister.

He poured a couple of glasses of Scotch, handed Kevin one and set the bottle on the table in front of him. "You will need the bloody bottle before we're done, I'm afraid."

Kevin looked at the drink. *Oh, God. What's happened now?*

The Prime Minister downed his drink and poured another. He sat down behind his desk and looked at Kevin and swallowed hard. "Listen, I'm afraid our preparation for the bloody trial has not gone well. Many of the witnesses have vanished into thin air. Others are refusing to cooperate. Obatala's testimony is going to be absolutely critical if we're going to convict the NDC leaders."

Kevin took a swig of his drink without taking his eyes off the Prime Minister. "That's what Kiran told me."

"Sharad would like you to meet him in the morning, to prepare you for the trial. He'd like you to take a look at some more of the bloody traitors, to see if you can identify them. We must have your help here, Kevin. There is a lot at stake."

Kevin sighed. *Oh God! Is there no end to this?* "I realize that, but I won't lie. I'll testify about Obatala's actions without defending him, since that's what we've all agreed. Hopefully, these men you have picked up will be ones that I recognize. Have you had any luck locating Malcolm Mann?"

"Yes, he and some others are in Cuba. The government there has granted them political asylum."

"Damn! I wish he hadn't got away."

"Yes, it was very unfortunate. If I'd gotten hold of him before he got away, I'd have kicked his bloody ass all the way to Cuba!"

"So, what did you want to tell me?"

The Prime Minister downed his second glass of Scotch and squirmed in his chair. "Oh, yes. . . . I spoke to the chief prosecutor and suggested rather strongly that Obatala be shown mercy for his cooperation in testifying against the other NDC leaders. He agreed to make that recommendation."

"Recommendation?"

"Yes. You see, it's not his decision, you know. The bloody judge must decide. Unfortunately, I have no control over the judge. I can't guarantee that he'll take the chief prosecutor's recommendation."

"You promised Obatala wouldn't be executed!" Kevin jumped to his feet.

"I said I would do all that I bloody could to prevent it."

"Damn it! We had a deal."

"Relax, the judge will probably go along with it. I'm just warning you that it's not really my decision. I've done all that I can to honor our arrangement."

Kevin shook his head hardly able to contain his anger. *You lying son of a bitch! You knew all along you couldn't guarantee Obatala's life.*

Kevin took his drink and the bottle and stormed out of the meeting to find Deviane and break the news to her. The thought that poor Obatala might die after all consumed him. *What will Cetawayo think when she finds out Obatala's been betrayed? Will she think I was a part of it? Oh, God. I hope not.*

He thought about calling the whole thing off and blowing the whistle on the Prime Minister. He knew it would be the end for he and Deviane, but at least he wouldn't be a part of this ruthless scheme to manipulate the judicial process.

He wondered how many of the so-called NDC leaders were actually innocent citizens, just like Obatala.

When he found Deviane, she was shocked to see him with a bottle of liquor in his hand. She realized by the smell of his breath, he'd consumed a fair amount of it already.

"What's wrong? Why are you drinking?"

"Your father's a bastard."

"Kevin! Someone might hear you."

"I don't give a shit!"

"Come into my room and tell me what's going on." Deviane took Kevin by the hand and escorted him into her room. Kevin sat on her bed and put the bottle of booze on her night stand. "Okay, I'm waiting. What's going on?"

"Your father lied to us. He knew all along that he couldn't keep them from executing Obatala."

Deviane stared at Kevin. "Oh no! You mean Obatala's going to die?"

"You got it. He's a dead man and I might as well have pulled the trigger!"

"Oh, God! Kevin, I'm so sorry."

"Tell that to little Kemba and the twins."

Deviane frowned. "Are you blaming this on me?"

Kevin sighed. "No, of course not. It's all my fault. I should have let your father ship me back to the United States rather than selling out to him."

"You didn't sell out. Obatala wanted you to do what you did. We all just trusted my father, that was our mistake. We should have known better after he tried to use Kiran and me to get what he wanted."

"So what are we going to do now?"

"I don't know, Kevin, but you better tell Obatala the truth. He has a right to know."

"When he refuses to testify, your dad will know I told him. He'll be pissed off. He may lock you up and refuse to let me see you."

"He'll have to kill me, because I won't be a prisoner!"

"Oh, God, Deviane, I couldn't live without you!"

"Nor could I. I'd die if I lost you!"

Kevin polished off another shot and then handed Deviane the bottle. She took a swig and grimaced from the bitter taste. Before long, the bottle was nearly empty and Kevin and Deviane fell asleep in each other's arms. They slept soundly until the next morning when light flooded into Deviane's bedroom.

Kevin opened his eyes and quickly stuck up his hand to shield himself from the glare. He looked down at Deviane, asleep in his lap, amazed that they'd been that way all night long. He yawned and stretched causing Deviane to wake up. She sat up and suddenly grabbed her head.

"Is this what a hangover feels like?" she said.

"You've never had a hangover before?"

"No. Thank God."

"Huh, well this may be the first of many."

"I hope not. My head feels like it's going to explode."

Kevin looked at his watch.

"Oh crap! It's already eight-thirty. I'm supposed to meet Sharad at nine."

"What about Obatala?"

"I'll ask Sharad if I can see him while I'm there. Are you sure you want me to tell him?"

"No, but it's the right thing to do, isn't it?"

"Yeah, I suppose," Kevin said. "How could we live with ourselves if we allowed this to continue?"

"We'd have to drink a lot."

"Two guilt-ridden alcoholics. Wouldn't we be a sweet couple? Okay, we'll have to do what's right and take our chances. While I'm gone, you better do a lot of praying."

"Believe me, I'm going to wear out my rosary beads!"

"What if I never see you again?" Kevin asked.

A tear rolled down Deviane's cheek. "That can't happen. I won't let it happen!"

Kevin and Deviane embraced and kissed each other

fervently. When they finally took a breath, they looked into each other's eyes, wondering if they would ever see each other again. Kevin lingered as long as he could. Finally he reluctantly left Deviane's room to get ready for Sharad.

He took a quick shower and brushed his teeth to rid himself of the stench of alcohol. After getting dressed, he ran downstairs and opened the front door. As he stepped outside, the car was just pulling up to take him to the capitol building. He got in, took a deep breath and tried to relax. *Maybe the judge will go along with the recommendation after all. It's possible. Ahmad may have exaggerated the risk.* As the car drove away, he looked back, praying that he would be returned safely to Deviane that evening.

The capitol building was crowded with spectators, government officials and the press. It was obvious from the activity that the government was in turmoil. Kevin felt a thousand eyes on him as he made his way to Sharad's office. He opened the door and stepped inside. A tall, slender Caucasian receptionist smiled at him.

"Mr. Wells?"

"Yes."

"Have a seat, I'll tell the Attorney General you're here."

"Thanks."

Kevin noticed a copy of the *Daily Express* on the end table. He picked it up. He saw his own picture and one of Obatala on the front page. The article was entitled–*Key Witnesses To Put Nail In NDC Coffin.* Kevin scanned the article, which summarized the testimony expected of him and Obatala. He cringed at the thought of the consequences if he and Obatala refused to testify. He was beginning to feel light headed when Sharad finally came out of his office to greet him.

"Kevin, how are you?"

"Fine."

"Thanks for coming by. I notice you've seen this morning's paper. What do you think of the article?"

"It looks interesting."

"I don't know how these things leak out, but somehow, they always do. I've got a dozen or so additional defendants I need you to take a look at. They're being held downstairs. Let's go ahead and get that out of the way. Afterward, the chief prosecutor wants to go over your testimony with you, all right?"

"Sure."

Kevin followed Sharad down the stairs to the basement. They took a long corridor to a small detention room. Inside, two detectives were having a cup of coffee and talking. They stood as Sharad entered the room.

"Okay, this is Kevin Wells. Bring in the men, one at a time."

Kevin sat down and watched through the two-way mirror as each suspect entered the room and was briefly interrogated by the detectives. Kevin didn't recognize the first or second suspects, but when the third one entered, he stood to get a good look.

"Yes, I remember that guy. He's one of the men who kidnaped us from Miss Victoria's place."

"Excellent," Sharad said. "Bring in the next one."

"Yeah, that guy was there, too. There were six or eight soldiers who captured us."

Sharad was delighted as Kevin identified seven of the twelve men as being involved in the kidnaping. Kevin hoped that this would take some of the pressure off Obatala if he decided to renege on his deal.

"Well, Kevin, this was a profitable meeting."

"I'm glad you found these guys. I was beginning to think everybody got away."

"Okay, I'm going to take you by the prosecutor's office and then you can go back home."

"Sir, do you think I could see Obatala before I go? I

have a message for him, from his wife."

Sharad considered the request for a moment.

"I guess it couldn't hurt. I'll arrange for you to see him right after you meet with the prosecutor."

"Thanks, I really appreciate it."

Kevin met with the prosecutor for several hours. When they were finished, he was escorted to the jail where Obatala was being held. Obatala smiled when he saw Kevin and they embraced.

"Kevin, what a surprise."

"Hi, Obatala. How are you holding up?"

"Not too well, actually. They're wearing me out."

"You do look tired. What are they doing to you?"

"Everyday they spend hours and hours with me, going over my testimony. I don't know what's truth or fiction anymore. I'm just so tired of it. I wish they would leave me alone."

"God, I'm so sorry, Obatala. I wish there was something I could do."

"I know. How's Cetawayo?"

"She's fine and she said to tell you that she loves you."

"Did everything go all right?"

"Yes, we got them all settled in an apartment in Dallas. It's very nice and I think they'll be happy there."

"How are my boys?"

"They're fine. Kemba really misses you. He doesn't understand why you can't be with them."

"He's a fine boy. I miss him so much," Obatala said as he tried to hold back the tears.

"I told my dad to check on them every once in a while, to make sure they're okay. They've got plenty of money. I put the two hundred grand in the bank for them."

"Two hundred thousand?"

"Yeah, I figured if you're going to be bought, you shouldn't go cheap."

They laughed.

"It's too bad I won't be able to spend it."

"I know, you finally get a few bucks and you can't even spend it. It's a pretty sad world we live in."

Obatala put his hand on Kevin's shoulder. "Thank you, Kevin, for doing this for me."

Kevin took his hand and squeezed it. "It was a pleasure. Cetawayo is such a nice woman. Deviane and I really love her so."

"So, how are you and Deviane?"

"We're okay. We had a good trip to Dallas. We even stayed overnight at the White House."

"The White House? Really?"

"Uh huh. It was a big shock to me too. It was quite an experience."

"I can imagine."

"So are you ready for the trial?"

"Yes, I just want to get it over with."

Kevin swallowed hard. "Listen, Obatala. There's something I have to tell you."

Obatala looked at Kevin anxiously. "What is it?"

"I'm really sorry. I know the Prime Minister promised that if you cooperated and testified against the NDC, that he would be sure you only got a prison sentence and didn't get the death penalty."

Obatala closed his eyes and exhaled slowly. "Oh, God."

Kevin struggled to maintain his composure. "I'm so sorry, Obatala, but he may not be able to keep that promise. He says it's totally out of his hands. Frankly, it looks like no matter how much help you are to them, they may still sentence you to hang."

Obatala shook his head and grimaced. "That bastard! So what's the point of my testifying? What will I accomplish, other than to insure Ahmad stays in power?"

"I wouldn't blame you if you told them to forget the deal. That's probably what I'd do."

"What about Cetawayo? Do you think she's out of

danger?"

"I don't know. There's some kind of a connection between Ahmad and the United States government. I don't know how safe Cetawayo would be if you suddenly lost your memory."

"What about you and Deviane?"

"It would make it tough for us obviously, but we don't want that to play a part in your decision. We'll figure something out either way."

Obatala got up and walked to the cell door. He grabbed the bars with his hand and hung his head dejectedly. Finally he turned and looked at Kevin.

"I'm prepared to die, if it must be. I will keep my bargain, even though Ahmad is a cheat and a liar."

"Are you sure?"

"Yes, Kevin. I will die for you and Deviane, for my wife and my children, and for Trinidad!"

Kevin began to cry. "I'm so sorry, Obatala. I wish there was something I could do! You're a fine man. You don't deserve this."

"Don't cry for me, Kevin. I'm tired and I just want to get this over with. Just promise me one thing. Don't let my children forget me!"

"I won't, I promise! Your children will know what a great man you are."

# Chapter 26

Tensions were high at the dinner table the night before Obatala's trial. Kevin and Deviane were silent and made no eye contact with the Prime Minister. Kiran and Anila felt the animosity in the air and made several attempts to strike up a conversation. Each time, it quickly ended in an uneasy silence. Ahmad looked at Deviane several times, but she did not respond to him. He picked up his wineglass and took a sip. Suddenly he slammed it hard on the table, startling everyone.

"You think I like doing this? Everything your mother and I have worked to achieve these last ten years is at stake!"

Deviane looked at her father. "Is being Prime Minister so important that you would betray your own children and send innocent people to their death?"

"You don't understand. It's not for me. It's for you and your mother and for Trinidad."

"Don't say you're doing this for me, because I don't want any part of it! And I seriously doubt that the people of Trinidad want some goon from the U.S. State Department running their country."

"That's ridiculous! Who told you that garbage?"

"We know about Navet Exploration and Safeguard Ventures." Kevin said.

"So what? It's just a business partnership."

"An American partnership that's made you very rich," Deviane replied.

"It's made all of us rich. You've enjoyed it as much as the rest of us."

"Yes, but I didn't know where it came from, nor did I know of the strings that were attached."

"So now you're telling me my money's no good! Then you won't mind if I revoke your trust fund."

Deviane stood up and threw down her napkin. "You can keep the bloody trust fund! I don't want it!"

"Fine, consider it done!"

"Good. And if you kill Obatala, you can forget I was ever your daughter. I can't forgive murder. Kevin and I will leave and you'll never see us again."

"Maybe I won't let you go."

"Then you'll have to kill us, because we won't be your prisoners."

Deviane left the dining room and went up to her room. Kevin looked at Anila sorrowfully.

"Why couldn't you leave our children out of your dirty politics?!" Anila said.

"It wasn't my choice. It was just meant to be. How could I have anticipated any of this?"

"Why does Obatala have to die? He saved your daughters' lives and you promised them you'd spare his life if he cooperated."

"It's out of my hands. I can't tell the bloody judge what sentence he should impose. It would be improper."

Anila stood up and glared at Ahmad. "So you'll stand by and watch your own family be destroyed, just as long as you retain your precious political power?"

"No, it's all of you who are deserting me, just when I need your support more than ever."

Anila shook her head. "What happened to the honest, idealistic man I married? I never thought I'd see you stoop to such depths."

"Don't worry, Anila. I'm still the same man you married. We're facing a very complex and delicate situation, but it will all work out. You know our family is of paramount importance to me. I've always pulled us through the bad times, haven't I? You, of all people, should trust me."

"I'd like to, but I'm not blind, Ahmad."

"No, you're not blind, but that doesn't mean you always see the bloody truth."

"All I know is, if you drive Deviane away, I'll never forgive you," Anila said and then stormed out of the dining room.

Kiran looked at her father nervously. She got up and excused herself. Ahmad stared for a moment at the empty table.

"Ungrateful bastards!" he screamed as he sent three place settings of fine china crashing to the floor. Two servants came rushing in to see what had happened. Ahmad glared at them and spoke.

"Get my car and then clean up this mess!"

# Chapter 27

The courtroom of the Port of Spain Third Criminal Court was packed with spectators and members of the press. The judge ordered the trial to commence and asked the prosecutor to read the indictment. Obatala listened without emotion as the prosecutor read the long list of charges against him. When he was done, the judge remarked that he understood the defendant intended to plead guilty. Obatala's defense counsel rose and responded.

"Yes, Your Honor, the defendant and the prosecution have made an arrangement, whereby Mr. Mohammed will fully cooperate with the Court in the trial of the thirty-three other defendants, in the hope that the Court will take this into account in passing its sentence."

"Very well," the judge said. "I will withhold sentencing until the conclusion of the trial so that I can determine the extent of the defendant's cooperation and the genuineness of his remorse. You may proceed with the other indictments."

The prosecutor read the indictments against all of the other defendants and then proceeded to give his opening statement. After the numerous members of the defense counsel had addressed the court, jury testimony began. Obatala was the first witness.

"Please state your name," the prosecutor said.

"Obatala Mohammed."

"Are you the brother of Ray Mohammed?"

"Yes."

"And was Ray Mohammed a member of the National Defense Coalition, sometimes known as the NDC?"

"Yes."

"How did you first become aware of this organization?"

"My brother held NDC meetings at my home."

"Who was the leader of this organization?"

"Malcolm Mann."

"Did you know Mr. Mann?"

"Yes, I saw him often."

"During the course of your involvement with the NDC, did you become aware of a conspiracy to assassinate the Prime Minister of Trinidad, Ahmad Shah?"

"Yes, I did."

"How did you acquire that knowledge?"

"My brother told me about it. I also overheard a member of the NDC talking about it."

"Would you explain how the operation was to be implemented?"

"A single assassin would travel to Dallas, Texas via Canada. He would be traveling on a counterfeit passport under the assumed name, Peter Gosne. A second person would go to Dallas separately, to assist in the escape."

"How was the escape to be handled?"

"A helicopter would be rented from a nearby airport. The pilot would meet the assassin on the roof of the convention center to take him to a secluded location north of Dallas. The helicopter would be abandoned and the two men would escape in a car, which they had left there. They would drive to Tulsa, Oklahoma. From there they would fly to Salt Lake City and then on to Vancouver. From Vancouver, they would return to Trinidad."

"Do you know the identity of the assassin?"

Obatala looked down and shifted in his seat.

"Can you tell us who was to be the assassin?" the prosecutor repeated.

"Yes. It was my brother, Ray Mohammed."

The audience suddenly came alive, buzzing with excited conversation. Members of the press scrambled in and out of the gallery. The judge banged his gavel to restore order.

"How do you know this?"

"He told me. I drove him to the airport and took care of his family while he was on the assignment."

"When did he come back?"

"About a week later."

"Did you pick him up from the airport?"

"Yes. He was very upset that the assassination attempt had failed. Apparently, the NDC had planned a coup during the chaos expected after the Prime Minister's death. He was afraid that the government would come down on he and the other NDC leaders once they figured out who was responsible for the attack."

"What was Ray's reaction when he heard Kevin Wells was coming to Trinidad?"

"He knew it would be the end of the NDC if Kevin ever identified him as the assassin."

"So how did he plan to deal with that problem?"

"He concocted a plan to get Kevin here a day early. I was to pick him up and take him to a predetermined location, where he would be murdered. The body would be dumped downtown, like he was the victim of an ordinary street crime."

"So, why wasn't this plan carried out?"

"It was, to a degree. We managed to get Kevin here a day early and picked him up, but as I drove him into Port of Spain, I realized I couldn't be part of his murder. So I took him to the Prime Minister's residence, as he requested."

"What was Ray's reaction to the disobedience of his directive?"

"I lied to him. I told him Kevin wasn't at the airport. He either didn't come or someone else picked him up. Ray was livid, but what could he do? I'm his brother."

Obatala was on the stand the rest of the day; explaining the inner workings of the NDC, identifying many of the thirty-three defendants as members and outlining the NDC's second plan to take over the government of Trinidad. Toward the end of the day, the prosecution passed the witness. Because it was so late, the judge decided to reserve cross-examination for Tuesday.

Cross-examination took several days due to the size of the team of counsel assigned to defend the NDC members. It wasn't until late Thursday that Kevin took the stand.

"Please state your name for the Court."

"Kevin Wells."

"Mr. Wells, you're an American citizen, is that correct?"

"Yes."

"And where do you reside?"

"In Plano, Texas, U.S.A."

"And did you have an occasion to be at the Caribbean Free Trade Conference in Dallas?"

"Yes, I was part of the ROTC color guard."

"It's well known that you were shot trying to save the Prime Minister."

"Yes."

"Did you have an opportunity to see the person who shot you?"

"Yes, I saw him when he first came into the building and then, just before he pulled the trigger."

"Do you know the identity of the man who shot you?"

"Yes, it was Ray Mohammed."

"How do you know that?"

"I identified a picture of him from some mug shots the FBI showed me. Later on, while I was being held hostage, he and Malcolm Mann visited us in our prison cell."

"Did you immediately recognize Mr. Mohammed as your assailant?"

"Yes, there was no doubt. He later admitted to me that he was the one."

A murmur went up in the gallery. Kevin looked out at the hundreds of spectators who had been anxiously listening to testimony all week long. The judge banged his gavel and the prosecution resumed. Kevin continued to testify about everything that had happened to him after he arrived in Trinidad. At five, the Judge recessed the trial until the next morning. On Friday morning the prosecution asked about Obatala's rescue.

"Now, when you reached the road, you say there was no one there?"

"Yes, we were very upset, because we expected government troops to be patrolling the road. Then we saw headlights. It turned out to be Mr. Mohammed. We jumped in his cab and took off just in time to avoid being captured by the NDC."

"Later on though, you were apprehended by the NDC."

"Yes."

"And it was Mr. Obatala Mohammed's idea to take you to the midwife, Victoria's place?"

"Yes, he said she could provide Kiran medical attention."

"And shortly after you arrived, the NDC showed up?"

Kevin looked over at Obatala, took a deep breath and then replied.

"Correct."

The team of defense counselors cross-examined Kevin all afternoon. At six, the judge recessed the trial until the following Monday. Kevin watched sadly as Obatala was led away. *I wonder what you really think about all this, my friend. Do you hate me? I wouldn't blame you if you did. It must be horrible to know your life will soon be over. What a painful way to have to face death. I hope when it's my time, death will be quick and without warning.*

That night, Kevin and Deviane had dinner at Cafe Savannah. It was the first time they'd left the Prime Minister's residence in several weeks. Since Kevin's involvement in the trial was over, there was no reason to think his life was still in danger.

It was a warm, rainy night and the pair had to use their umbrella to avoid getting soaked. The headwaiter, having been warned of their arrival, took them to a secluded part of the restaurant, where they would be less likely to be noticed.

"You've got to try the Callaloo soup," Deviane said.

"Oh really? What in the hell is that?"

"It's made with taro leaf, okra, pumpkin and crab meat. It's wonderful."

Kevin laughed. "That's all right. I think I'll pass on that one. What else do they have?"

"The Lobster Soucouyant is good."

"Lobster. That sounds safe. I'll have that."

The waiter came over and took their orders. Deviane ordered the Callaloo soup and pork steak. Kevin got the lobster and asked for a bottle of white wine. While they were waiting for the wine, Kevin gazed thoughtfully upon Deviane.

*You are so beautiful. I can't believe you'll soon be my wife. Everything has happened so fast. In just a few short months, our lives have taken such a drastic turn. Never in my most delirious moment would I have seen myself in Trinidad, opposite the most beautiful woman my mind could have ever concocted. I am such a lucky man, having truly found my soul mate. But why, instead of feeling joy, am I afraid? Petrified, to be more exact, that something will happen to prevent the fulfillment of our union.*

Deviane smiled sympathetically, seeming to understand the agony and torment he was feeling. Under the table she extended her foot and began massaging his inner thigh. Kevin's anxiety suddenly evaporated as he became greatly aroused. He squirmed in his seat.

"I'm sorry," she said giggling. "I shouldn't do that to you, but it's so much fun. Soon this will all be over and we'll be married. Then you can ravish my body at will."

"God, I hope so. Waiting is such torture," Kevin replied.

"I know, but nothing can keep us apart now. We'll always be together. I'm certain of it."

"So, how do you think the trial is going?"

"It seems to be going well. Daddy is elated. I heard Sharad tell him a conviction of all of the NDC thirty-three is a certainty."

"I hope so. Do you think your father will be able to keep them from hanging Obatala?"

"Yes, he told Mother not to worry about it. He said she should trust him. Mother is convinced he's figured out a way to be sure Obatala is not sentenced to death."

"Well, he shouldn't be. He certainly served up the NDC on a silver platter for your father. I just hope, while he's in prison, one of them doesn't put a knife in his gut."

"Do you think that could happen?"

"Unfortunately, it could."

"Why can't they keep him away from the other inmates? That seems like the least they could do."

"We should discuss it with your father."

"Yes, we should."

"What are we going to do if Obatala is sentenced to die? Are you really going to leave the country immediately?"

"We won't have a choice. I won't be escorted down the aisle by a murderer!"

"We'll have to live frugally, since you gave away your trust fund."

Deviane half smiled. "Did that upset you?"

"No. You did the right thing, but you've got to admit it's a little unsettling to throw away that kind of money."

"I don't want the money, Kevin. I want you and I to earn our own living. I want to sleep soundly at night knowing that we've always been honest and forthright with the people we encounter in life. You and I can accomplish so much good together if we can just divorce ourselves from the evil around us. If we can do that, we'll be happy. The reason I know this is that I've already felt it. In fact, I'm feeling it now, just being near you."

Kevin shook his head. "You're something else, Deviane. God, was I lucky to find you! I know what you mean. I feel the same way right now. I just wish we could leave Trinidad right this minute, before something happens to spoil our future together."

"It won't be long, now. We just have to be patient and trust God."

"I know."

"I love you, Kevin. I will always love you. You know that." Deviane laid her hand on the center of the table and smiled.

Kevin took it and squeezed it gently. "I love you, too. Always and forever, until death do us part."

"No, no. We'll be together even after death too," Deviane protested. "I just know it!"

"I pray to God you're right."

# Chapter 28

Several weeks passed before the trial of the NDC thirty-three was over. At the conclusion of the trial, the jury found seventeen of the defendants guilty of high treason, conspiracy to overthrow the government and murder of the soldiers killed in the assault on NDC headquarters. Sixteen defendants were acquitted and sent home to their very relieved families. The courthouse was packed as the judge was scheduled to pass sentence on the seventeen defendants and Obatala. Kevin and Deviane were seated in the front row of the courtroom, next to the Attorney General. The Prime Minister and Anila were at home in the study, waiting for the judge's decision.

"Ladies and gentlemen, it is now my duty to pass sentence on the defendants standing before me. The defendants will please rise."

All the defendants came to their feet. Kevin's eyes were fixed on Obatala.

"Treason is the greatest offense a man can commit against his country and his people. Our young republic is dependent on loyalty and allegiance to the Constitution. When citizens conspire to gain power by force, in contravention of the will of the people, they must be punished quickly and severely, so that others will be deterred from committing such a grievous crime. Accordingly, I have little choice but to sentence the seventeen remaining defendants to death by public hanging."

Screams and wails emanated from the families of the condemned. A buzz of excitement radiated throughout the court from those supporting the government and the constitution.

"The sentence of the last defendant, Obatala Mohammed, I must say, has been the most difficult of my life. Here is a man in the thick of the conspiracy to overthrow the government, but who has remorse and tries to stop what has been started. Although he is powerless to arrest the plot himself, he cooperates and helps bring justice to Trinidad. It is a tribute to this man that he came to his senses and had the decency to try to stop the evil he had helped conceive.

"But is that enough to cleanse him of his crime? Many, even the chief prosecutor, believe his life should be spared, but I think not. One cannot undo what has been done. Obatala is not an evil man, but he made a grievous mistake. An example must be made of him, so that others will know of the certainty and severity of punishment for any act of treason. This is necessary for the very self-preservation of our Republic. Therefore, I sentence Obatala to death by lethal injection. For his remorse and aid in bringing justice to the Republic, I will let him die without pain and with a measure of dignity."

Kevin rose to his feet and screamed.

"No! No, you can't kill him!"

Deviane's head fell as tears poured out of her eyes. The Attorney General grabbed Kevin's arm.

"Kevin, the press will see you!"

"Why?! Why does he have to die? It isn't necessary. Aren't seventeen lives enough?"

"Kevin, we did everything we could."

"You obviously didn't do enough!"

Deviane took Kevin's arm. "Come on, Kevin. We need to go home and pack. I want to leave as soon as possible," she said.

When Kevin and Deviane arrived home Anila was waiting.

"Sweetheart, you can't leave. Your father did everything he could to save Obatala. He loves you very much. If you leave like this, it will kill both of us."

"I can't live in a country where traitors rule and good men are murdered in the name of justice. If I see my father again, I will spit in his face!"

Deviane ran upstairs and slammed the door.

"Kevin, you've got to talk some sense into her! Running out on her family won't accomplish anything."

"You know there's nothing I can do to stop her, even if I wanted to. She has a mind of her own. We know politics sometimes require certain moral sacrifices, but Deviane and I don't want to be a part of that."

"I was so looking forward to your wedding. This is such a tragedy. Please try to change her mind."

"You've been very good to me, Anila. You and Kiran will be welcome at our home anytime. I'll write to you often, even if Deviane doesn't."

Kevin took Anila's hand and squeezed it lovingly. Then he gave her a hug and ran upstairs to pack. Thirty minutes later, Kevin and Deviane were at the door, ready to leave. As they were deciding how to get to the airport, the Prime Minister's limo drove into the driveway. Ahmad got out and walked over to them.

"Do you think I'm just going to let you pack up and leave my house, Deviane?"

"I'm eighteen years old. You can't stop me. This is still a free country, isn't it?"

"Deviane, you're upset and confused. Don't do anything rash. Stay here a few days and think this through. If you don't want to stay here at the house, I'll put you up at the Hilton."

"I'm sorry, nothing will change in a few days. Now, are you going to have someone take us to the airport or do I have to call a cab?"

"Don't think you can come running back here when you run out of money, or your infatuation with Kevin wears off."

"You bastard! I hate you!" Deviane screamed. "Kevin, lets go!"

Deviane picked up her bag and started down the driveway. Kevin picked up the other suitcase and started to follow her.

"Wait!" the Prime Minister said as he motioned to his driver. "Take them to the airport and make sure they leave the country." The driver nodded and took Deviane's bag from her hand. As she and Kevin got in the big limo, Ahmad glared at her and said, "You're no longer my daughter! . . . Don't ever come back."

Deviane looked back at her father and replied sadly, "Don't worry, father. You'll never see me again."

Ahmad swallowed hard as the limo pulled away.

The ride to the airport was quiet. Kevin held Deviane's hand and caressed it gently. After a while, Deviane laid her head on Kevin's shoulder and closed her eyes. Kevin watched her sleep. *God I hope we're doing the right thing. How will I take care of you, Deviane? You have always had everything and I have nothing to give you. I can't believe you left your family for me. Am I worthy of your trust? God, I hope so. It feels so strange to be responsible for you now. If I screw up your life I'll never forgive myself. But I won't screw it up, I promise. I'll figure out a way to take care of you and bring you happiness. I am so glad you will always be at my side. I am truly a lucky man.*

Kevin looked down at Deviane's dark, shiny hair. He leaned down and took a deep breath, breathing the sweet fragrance of her body. He felt a rush of excitement so exhilarating, he nearly cried out with joy. Tears began to flow from his eyes.

Deviane looked up at him, smiled. "You're all I've got

left, Kevin. Don't ever leave me."

The flight to Miami went quickly, but there was a long layover before the connecting flight to Dallas. Kevin called home to let his parents know he was coming. They were happy, but surprised by the call. It was mid-afternoon, so the two travelers went to the Starbucks in Concourse C to kill time.

"How are we going to tell Cetawayo about this?" Deviane asked.

"I don't know, but we've got to tell her before she reads about it in the newspaper."

"I hope it's not on the television news."

"Maybe we should call her."

"Oh God, she'll be devastated. We should be there in case she reacts badly."

"Yeah, you're right. We'll be home before the evening news comes on."

Deviane sipped her coffee and then frowned. "I'm sorry we won't be able to get married in the Botanical Gardens. It would have been magnificent."

"That's all right. We have a beautiful church in Plano. We'll have a nice wedding there."

"Do you think my mother and Kiran will come?"

"If your father lets them."

"If Mother wants to come, he couldn't stop her."

"Then she'll be there. She still loves you."

"Was I foolish to give away my inheritance?"

"No, I don't want it. All I want is you. If you had a million dollars, you might wonder if I really loved you. Now you'll never feel that way. We've got what we always wanted, right?"

"Yes, we do."

"So drink your coffee, it's about time we left for the gate."

It was nearly eight o'clock when the big Boeing jet

landed at Dallas-Fort Worth Airport. Kevin's parents met them at the airport and took them directly to Cetawayo's apartment. When Cetawayo answered the door, her eyes were red and swollen. She had already heard the news.

"I'm so sorry, Cetawayo," Deviane said as she embraced her. "I left immediately, when it was apparent my father had betrayed us."

"Come in. I'm so glad to see you. I know you did all you could. I'm sorry this affair has driven you from your family."

Kevin and his parents followed Deviane and Cetawayo into the apartment and took a seat.

"This is my mom and dad, Pat and Glen Wells."

"Hi, it's nice to meet you."

"Do you want to come stay at our house tonight?" Kevin asked. "We'd love to have all of you."

"No, thank you. Frankly, it isn't a shock to me that this happened. I've been mentally preparing myself for weeks. I knew it was unlikely they would spare his life."

"When I saw him last, I warned him this was a possibility," Kevin said. "He seemed to have resigned himself to his fate. He made me promise that his children wouldn't forget him."

"I won't let them forget him. He was their father and he was a great man," Cetawayo replied.

As they were talking, Kemba ran into the room.

"Kevin! It's Kevin and Deviane!"

Soon the twins had joined Kemba, who had made himself comfortable in Kevin's lap.

"I'm afraid you're the only man they know in America."

"He looks pretty good with kids in his lap, don't you think?" Deviane asked.

"Oh yes," Mrs. Wells said. "He'll definitely make a good father."

"All right, that's enough, girls. Why don't you take one of these guys? I only have two knees."

Cetawayo got up and took one of the twins from Kevin.

"Thank you for stopping by. I'll be fine. You don't have to worry about me."

"Have you got a job yet?"

"Not yet, but I took the test for my teaching certificate. I should get the results in a couple of weeks."

"Good," Deviane said.

"The kids have been going to school and they seem to be adjusting well. I've found a day care that will take them home after school, when I go back to work."

"Excellent," Kevin said. "Well, be sure and call us if you need anything."

"I will."

"I guess we better go, we're kind of tired from our trip."

"I can imagine. Thanks for stopping by. I'm so glad I finally got to meet your parents, Kevin."

Everyone stood up and started towards the door.

"If you need anything, call us," Mrs. Wells said.

"I will."

It was late when Deviane and the Wells' got home. Mrs. Wells made coffee and they talked for several hours, discussing what had happened and making plans for the upcoming weeks.

When Kevin's parents finally went to bed, Kevin and Deviane were still too keyed up to sleep, so they went into the den and turned on the TV. As they sat on the sofa, in each other's arms, they wondered what the future would hold for them. Finally, they succumbed to their exhaustion and fell into a peaceful sleep.

# Chapter 29

Several weeks passed with no communication between Deviane and her parents. Due to his escapades in Trinidad during the last two months of the school year, Kevin had to attend the last session of summer school in order to graduate from Plano High School. Realizing that Kevin's savings wouldn't be sufficient to sustain them long, Kevin and Deviane decided to go to junior college for their first year. With only a one-week break, he and Deviane began classes at Collin County Community College in late August.

It was a Saturday morning in early September. Kevin and Deviane were about to eat breakfast. Kevin went outside to get the *Dallas Morning News*, which was delivered to their door each morning. On the way in, he looked at the front page briefly and then pulled out the sports section. Once inside, he threw the rest of the paper on the table and went to pour himself some coffee. Deviane picked up the front page and began reading it. After finishing it, she started leafing through the rest of the section for articles that might interest her. Suddenly she froze.

"Kevin, look! It's an article about the NDC executions."
"What does it say?"

**"*Confessed NDC Leader Executed in Trinidad*.** The National Defense Coalition member whose testimony was instrumental in the conviction of seventeen NDC members in August was executed today in Port of Spain. Obatala Mohammed was the brother of Ray Mohammed, who was suspected of being the gunman in the attempted assassination of Prime Minister Ahmad Shah last April. Mohammed's execution came very quickly after his conviction and sentencing, since he refused to appeal the decision of Port of Spain's Third Criminal Court. The execution by lethal injection was carried out in private, in accordance with the Court's ruling. The ruling provided that Mohammed would not be publicly hanged like the other seventeen NDC members due to his cooperation with authorities. Since no one has claimed his body, prison officials announced that Mohammed's remains would be cremated. The remaining seventeen NDC members have appealed their convictions. Those appeals are expected to take up to a year before they are finally resolved and the public executions can take place."

"I can't believe he's dead," Deviane said. "I kept thinking something would happen. Somehow, he would be allowed to live. My mother said not to worry, trust my father."

"At least it's over. Maybe now we can bury the past and focus on the future. I'm just sorry you lost your family over all of this."

"At least I found you, Kevin. If you hadn't showed up, I would have been forced to sell out, just like my father."

"Maybe not, I'm not sure your mother knows what's going on. Surely, Kiran isn't a party to your father's treachery."

"My mother knows. Maybe not every detail, but she knows my father better than anyone. He couldn't keep this kind of secret from her."

"Then why would she tolerate it? She seems like such a good person, so full of love."

"I don't know," Deviane said as she wiped the tears from her eyes. "I wish I could understand it."

"We should go to Cetawayo, she'll be needing us."

"You're right. We'll stop by the florist and bring her some flowers. Maybe she'd like to go to the church and light a candle for him."

"Good idea, come on."

It was a beautiful morning and traffic was light. It didn't take long to get to Cetawayo's apartment. They stopped at a florist along the way and bought a dozen white daisies. Cetawayo was surprised when she opened the door and saw them.

"Kevin, Deviane. What are you two doing here?"

"I guess you haven't seen the paper this morning."

"No. The kids. . . . Oh no! Oh God! Did they kill him?"

"I'm afraid so."

Cetawayo burst into tears. She struggled to the sofa and collapsed. Deviane went into the bathroom, found a box of tissues and brought them to her. She sat down next to her and put her arm around her. They both cried for some time as Kevin watched wishing he could do something to comfort them.

"You know," Cetawayo finally said. "I'm glad it's over. We've been living with this so long. I think it will be easier for Kemba if he knows his father is dead. Now, he thinks he was deserted. His teachers have been having a hard time with him. They say he's bitter and hostile to everyone. I've been at a loss. You'd think, as a teacher, I would know what to do."

"I think you're right," Deviane said. "Now maybe he can bury his father and the healing process can begin."

"Hey, why don't we go to the church and light a candle for him," Kevin said.

"I'd like that. I better go tell the children. They have a right to know."

"Sure. Do you want us to wait outside?"

"No, just have a seat. It will take me a few minutes to get them ready to go."

Kevin and Deviane spent the rest of the day with Cetawayo and her children. They went to a Catholic church near Cetawayo's apartment and lit a candle for Obatala. Then they took the kids to the zoo and the Omni Theater so they wouldn't have time to think about their father. When they finally arrived back at Cetawayo's apartment, it was late and kids went right to bed. Kevin and Deviane hugged Cetawayo one last time and then left her alone to grieve.

Several more weeks passed. Kevin and Deviane began making plans for their wedding. It would be simple and inexpensive, but they didn't care as long as they finally made it down the aisle. Late one Thursday afternoon they had planned to go to Collin Creek Mall to look at wedding invitations. As they were leaving they got a frantic call from Cetawayo. She was hysterical, something about someone packing up her things and taking her away.

Kevin and Deviane left immediately and raced down Central Expressway towards Cetawayo's apartment. They couldn't imagine what was going on. When they arrived, the apartment was empty. Cetawayo and the boys were gone.

Kevin and Deviane stared at the empty apartment in shock. They ran to the manager's office. A young lady was sitting at her desk.

"Miss, what happened to Cetawayo Mohammed? Where did she go?"

"I have no idea," she replied, "but at least she had the decency to pay off her lease."

"Who packed up her stuff?"

"A whole moving crew came, packed her up and then left with everything. Two men took her and the kids. They were driving a blue Buick."

"They didn't say who they were?"

"No."

"Did Cetawayo go voluntarily or did they force her to leave."

"I don't know, I just try to mind my own business."

Kevin and Deviane left the manager's office and went back to the apartment to search for clues as to where the men had taken Cetawayo and the children.

"Do you think it was Malcolm Mann?" Kevin said.

"Oh my God! If it was, there's no telling what he'll do to them."

"What about the money? I wonder if they got the money?"

"Let's go to the bank. They may be there now!"

"Okay, come on. It's almost five, we don't have much time."

As they turned to leave the apartment, they saw a short, black man in the doorway. They strained to make out his face in the darkness. They inched closer and closer.

"Hi. Did you know Cetawayo?" Kevin said.

"Yes, I did."

"Do you know what happened to her?"

He laughed. "Don't you recognize me?"

"No, should I?" Kevin replied.

The man took a few steps out of the shadow.

"Oh my God! Obatala? Is that you?"

"Yes, Kevin. It's me!"

"But–"

"You mustn't tell anyone you saw me. I'm officially dead."

Deviane grabbed Kevin's arm to keep from fainting.

"Oh my God! Obatala, you're alive!"

"No, Obatala is dead. I'm Haywood Alexander. My family and I are moving. Somewhere, I don't know exactly where. The FBI is rather secretive about it."

"But we read about your death in the newspaper."

"I know, they had me fooled too. When they strapped me in the chair and gave me the lethal injection, I was prepared to die. When I woke up two days later in Florida, you can imagine how shocked I was."

Kevin rushed over to Obatala and embraced him.

"You *are* alive. For a moment I thought you were a ghost."

"Come here, Deviane. Feel me so you too will know that I'm alive."

Deviane walked over to Obatala slowly. When she saw him clearly, she ran into his arms.

"Oh, God! Obatala, I'm so glad you're alive!"

"The feeling is mutual, believe me."

Kevin stood back and shook his head.

"I just can't believe it."

"Nor can I. I just wanted you two to know that everything worked out. . . . I've got to go now, they've only given me two minutes to talk to you and our time is up."

Obatala pulled an envelope out of his pocket.

"I almost forgot. I'm supposed to deliver this letter to you."

Deviane took the letter and held it gingerly.

"Thanks for taking care of Cetawayo and the children. Maybe someday we'll be able to get together and talk about everything. I've got to run now. Goodbye."

Obatala disappeared just as quickly as he had come, leaving Kevin and Deviane shaken and confused. For a moment they just stared at the empty doorway. Deviane, with tears streaming from her eyes, turned to Kevin and they embraced.

"I'm so happy, Kevin! You don't know how happy I am."

"It's a miracle! I can't believe it. Obatala is alive!"

Deviane wiped the tears from her eyes and looked at the envelope. "I guess I should read the letter."

"Yes, open it! What does it say?"

Deviane ripped open the letter and began to read it;

*Dear Deviane,*

*As you know by now, I did keep my promise. Please forgive me for the pain I've caused you and Kevin. Maybe someday you'll understand why it had to be this way. Please come home. Your mother has been sick with grief since you left us. We all love you, and Kevin too.*

*Love,*
*Ahmad*

*P. S. No one knows of any of this, not even Kiran and your mother. So please destroy this letter and keep everything you've learned to yourselves.*

Deviane looked at Kevin and smiled.

"What do you think?"

"I think we should make plane reservations."

"Oh, Kevin. I can't believe it. It's like I woke up from a terrible dream. I'm so relieved!"

"Me too. Let's get out of here. We've got packing to do."

# Chapter 30

Twenty thousand spectators jammed Queen's Park Savannah to watch the wedding procession as it made its way from the Royal Botanical Gardens, through the streets of Port of Spain to the Hilton Inn, where the reception was scheduled to take place. It was a warm January day. White, billowy clouds danced across the tropical sky, providing an intermittent reprieve from the hot sun. Hundreds of snow white cranes, resting on the lawn along Queen Elizabeth Avenue suddenly ascended in unison, forming the image of an angel ascending into the heavens. Five ivory limousines carried the bride and groom, the Prime Minister, family and honored guests to the reception at the Hilton's famous Flamingo Room.

It was to be the most spectacular wedding in Trinidad's history. Not only had the marriage of Kevin Wells to Deviane Shah captured the imagination of the citizens of Trinidad, but it was carried live via satellite to the United States, where millions of Americans watched with tearful joy as America's newest hero wedded a West Indies goddess. It was, without doubt, the wedding of the decade, comparable to the best of the royal weddings of Great Britain.

The Prime Minister and Anila stood in the long reception line, soaking up the compliments and accolades of the elite of Trinidad as well as the many foreign dignitaries and representatives from nations all over the world. In just a short six months, the government of Prime Minister Ahmad Shah had come from the brink of collapse to being the most stable government in the West Indies.

The Wells Accord, now firmly in place, was creating a flurry of economic activity between the United States and Trinidad in anticipation of huge oil exports in the near future. As a result, the Trinidad stock market surged ahead eighteen percent in the final quarter of the year. Economists were predicting a banner year for exports, a huge influx of cash into the poor nation and a significant reduction in Trinidad's traditionally high unemployment rate.

Kevin and Deviane Wells took to the dance floor, much to the delight of their guests. To many, they were a blissful aberration in a decadent society. Hopefully, they were a sign that the pendulum of social morality had reached its zenith on the side of iniquity and was destined to swing back, towards honesty and decency. As the orchestra played, Kevin and Deviane glided across the floor, gazing into each other's love-filled eyes, together emitting an enchanting radiance that brought tears of joy to nearly every spectator's eyes.

When the time had come for the reception to conclude, Kevin and Deviane bid their farewell and took the elevator to the seventh floor. They held hands as they rushed down the hall to the honeymoon suite. Kevin unlocked the door and pushed it open. Then he turned, lifted Deviane up and carried her over the threshold, all the way to the magnificent canopy bed. He dropped her gently onto the mattress and then fell upon her, smothering her with joyful kisses. She laughed and then pushed him away.

"Kevin, let me change before you ravish my body."

"But I can't wait!"

"You've waited this long, you can wait five more minutes, you crazy boy."

"Okay, but hurry. I'm in utter agony."

"I'm going to change in the bathroom. Your suitcase is in the closet. Wear the silk pajamas my mother gave you as a wedding present. I picked them out especially for tonight."

"Okay, hurry up."

Kevin went to the closet and found the pajamas. He ripped off his tuxedo and threw it on a chair. He looked in the mirror at his naked body, wondering if it would excite Deviane. Then he pulled on the silk pajama bottoms and climbed onto the bed. He listened intently to Deviane in the bathroom, working diligently to prepare herself for their lovemaking. Curiosity overcame him, so he slid off the bed and moved quietly to the bathroom door. It was cracked slightly. He peered inside at Deviane sitting naked before the mirror. Mesmerized by Deviane's inviolate body, Kevin held his breath to avoid detection. Finally, he retreated to the bed and collapsed on the mattress, hardly able to restrain himself from rushing in after her. Deviane finally appeared in a long, white, sheer gown.

Kevin's eyes widened as she got closer and he saw the silhouette of her body beneath her gown . His heart began to beat like the rhythm of a pan band. As she inched closer and closer, he became so aroused, he cringed in carnal pain.

Deviane gazed upon Kevin's naked torso as she crept toward him. Her eyes moved from his handsome face, down his muscular chest to his flat stomach. She smiled as she noticed the large bulge in his silk pajamas.

When they first touched, an electric charge jolted them. Kevin pulled Deviane down on the bed and began to caress her breasts while they kissed with a passion and fury as powerful a tropical hurricane. Their long suppressed lust for one another propelled them into a sexual frenzy neither could contain. For hours, they explored every inch of each other's body, reveling in feelings and joys they had never before experienced.

When they finally surrendered to exhaustion, it was well past midnight. Their naked bodies inextricably intertwined, they slept in peaceful silence until dawn. As the first ray of sunlight shone through the thick hotel drapes, Kevin

became conscious of the hot body snuggled up next to him.
He smiled as the memory of the previous evening danced
through his mind. He waited impatiently for his bride to
awake for another round of carnal delight. Finally, Deviane
began to stir. She picked her head up from his chest,
opened her eyes and looked up at him.

"Oh, it's you! I couldn't remember who I was sleeping
with," Deviane said and then laid her head back on his
chest.

"Ah!" Kevin replied and then ran his hand along her
buttocks and gave her good pinch.

"Ouch!" she screeched as she sat up and began to
laugh.

Kevin grabbed her hand and pulled her towards him.

"Come here, show me number11 again."

Deviane struggled briefly and then began to crawl on
top of Kevin like a lioness preparing to devour her prey.
Kevin eyed her warily as she dipped her head down next to
his ear and sunk her teeth gently into his neck."

"Oh, God! Jesus! No! . . . Oh! Oh! Yeah. Don't stop."